SATAN'S LAMBS

SATAN'S LAMBS

A Novel

Lynn S. Hightower

Walker and Company
New York

First published in the United States of America in 1993 by Walker Publishing Company, Inc.

Published simultaneously in Canada by Thomas Allen & Son Canada, Limited, Markham, Ontario.

ISBN 0-8027-1229-0

Printed in the United States of America

*This book is dedicated
to my sister, Rebecca.*

Acknowledgments

I am always grateful and surprised by the generosity of people who will share their time and expertise with writers.

My thanks to the multitalented Matt Bialer, a gifted photographer, as well as the world's best agent and my particular friend.

And to my friend and editor, Peter Rubie, whose insight and flashes of brilliance helped make this a stronger book. I'm glad we didn't kill each other.

To my good friends Jim and Becky Lyon, who answered my endless questions on criminal law, the legal system, and various matters of plot—usually while cooking me dinner and entertaining me with bagpipes. And most especially to Jim, who prepares me for the real world by disagreeing with everything I say.

Also to attorneys Jeff Darling and Sharon Hilborn of the legal firm Lyon Golibersuch & Darling, and to Lexington attorney C. Wayne Shepherd.

My thanks to Ron Balcom, of Balcom Investigative Services, for generously inviting me to his office and letting me bombard him with questions.

To Captain Dick Owen for advice and answered questions, and to Officer T. Jay Wilson, for letting me ride along, answering my questions, and sharing insights, even though I fell asleep during a suspected B&E.

SATAN'S LAMBS

1

We're poor little lambs
Who've lost our way. . . .
We're little black sheep
Who've gone astray.

—"Gentlemen Rankers," *Ballads and Barrack Room Ballads,*
Rudyard Kipling

Lambs could not forgive . . . nor
worms forget.

—*Martin Chuzzlewit,* Charles Dickens

Lena knew the doorbell was going to ring. Mendez would come. He would tell her in person. She said "Thanks" softly to the woman on the other end of the phone, then hung up and waited.

She sat sideways, legs hanging over the arm of the chair, eating potato chips. Reddish brown crumbs had settled in the fur of the cat who slept in her lap when the doorbell rang.

Lena switched on the porch light and looked through the peephole.

The man on the steps wore a dark suit and tie, his shirt white and spotless despite the lateness of the hour. His hands were clasped in front of him in a steady formality that Lena secretly found endearing. He wore the ring—black stone, gold filigree markings. She had focused on that ring many times when she could not bear to see what was at hand—her sister, sprawled in the driveway, blood pooling across her belly.

The man was dark complected, his eyes brown and gentle.

There was a scar on his left temple that disappeared under thick black hair. His face was drawn and tired.

"Sergeant Mendez—Joel, come in."

He touched his mustache, smiled at the use of his first name. Sometimes she thought he liked her.

She was a striking woman, hair dark, coarse, and curly. Her eyes were brown and intense, almost feverish, the lines at the edges small and barely noticeable. She was pale enough that old ladies pinched her cheeks and told her to get a little sun.

Mendez scanned the living room—a roving, questing scrutiny. He had not been in the house for seven years, had not seen it without the ropes of yellow tape warning that the enclosed area was a crime scene.

Lena followed his gaze to the floor. The beige carpet, sporting a trail of bloody footprints, had been pulled up and lodged in a police warehouse. There was a new rug now, slate blue, pleasantly framed by the dark wood floors.

She spent a lot of time in this room now, and she kept it nice. If the rest of the house amounted to closed-off doors and rooms full of dust and memories, if outside the grass was weed choked and high, if chains flapped in the wind where a porch swing had once hung . . . at least there was one room that was pleasant.

Mendez walked past the rocking chair and settled on the edge of the couch.

"Get you something to drink?" She said it because it was the thing to say, and because it would irritate him. Polite chitchat was something he endured.

"No. Thanks." Mendez picked up Lena's book and read the back cover.

Lena passed him the bag of chips, knowing full well he didn't like them. Her movements were slow and languid, and she gave the impression of one who does not lift a finger unless absolutely necessary. Mendez took a potato chip and crunched it solemnly, then wiped his hands on his knees.

"He got it, Lena."

"I figured that much when I saw you at the door." Her voice was husky at the best of times. Right now she sounded hoarse. "Good news and you'd have called."

"I'm sorry."

"How'd you find out so fast?"

2

"Called in a favor."

"A shame it didn't extend to keeping him in jail."

Mendez was silent, and Lena sat down in the chair.

"Six years don't seem like much." She stared at the ceiling. "The baby would be in kindergarten now. And Kevin—he'd be eight. Third grade."

A white paw slid out from under the couch and patted softly at the side of Mendez's black leather shoe.

"I take it my statement didn't make any difference," Lena said.

"He had no priors, Lena. He has character references. He had the head sales manager of Finard's Chevrolet promise him a job as a salesman. He wears a suit and tie like he was born in them. He professes to have a renewed faith in God, and his prison record is exemplary."

"Six years. He gets two twenty-year sentences, and serves six years." She shut her eyes tight, then opened them. "That judge was an ass. That judge should have given him the death penalty."

"You can't get the death penalty for first-degree manslaughter."

"*Manslaughter*. It wasn't manslaughter. It was womanslaughter. Childslaughter. It was *murder*, premeditated. He came with a gun. That Prozac business was bullshit. The Prozac made me do it, the devil made me do it—"

"Diminished capacity, Lena. The precedent is solid. The DA did what he could."

"Saved the state some money with a guilty plea."

Mendez leaned back in his chair and closed his eyes. "Don't do this, Lena."

"Okay, you don't like that subject, how about this? Jeff's not the only one getting out. Archie Valetta is due out of Eddyville sometime in the next couple of months."

Mendez opened his eyes. "Valetta? How did you find this out?"

"Mice behind the walls, Mendez."

"One of your many informants?"

"They're not informants, Mendez. Not in the sense you mean. We're talking about a woman who's raising her grandchildren and working twelve-hour days doing scrub work at the prison, so let's not class her with the junkies you talk to, okay?"

Mendez sat forward. "Good to see you taking this so well."

Lena rarely smiled, but when she did it made her seem hugely vulnerable. "Quit. Don't make me laugh when I don't want to."

3

"Don't you ever want to?"

She would not meet his eyes.

"Lena, I don't think you need to worry about Valetta. He was in Eddyville before Jeff killed your sister. He was never part of that."

"He was Jeff's partner."

The white paw shot sideways and batted the cuff of Mendez's pants.

"They're convicted felons, both on parole. Any association, and the parole will be revoked."

"So *you* say."

Mendez dropped a potato chip in front of the couch. The white paw shot out, cupped the chip, and dragged it out of sight.

Mendez frowned. "Hayes is another matter. He made a lot of threats. He was white hot about the insurance settlement." Mendez met her eyes steadily. "I want to know if he calls, comes around, *anything*."

"Worrying won't keep Jeff from killing me, Joel. He told Whitney he'd kill her; he did it. He'll come after me if he wants to."

"Take steps."

"You think a restraining order will stop the bullets?"

"It's foolish not to accept help."

"What's foolish is depending on it."

He glanced at her left hand. "Are you living alone?"

"I'm not married anymore. Rick didn't want to come live here. He thought it would be bad for me."

"He was right."

"Funny, I don't remember asking him or you for an opinion."

"You shouldn't stay here wallowing in memories."

"God, Mendez, you make me sound like some kind of mournful pig."

"What's your interest in Valetta?" Mendez waited. She was capable of great stillness.

Lena swung her legs over the side of the chair. "They made me look stupid, didn't they? They dug into all that old stuff."

"Who?"

"The parole board. They got into the case files and made me look dumb."

"The subject matter makes anybody look bad, until the consequences become overwhelming. I told you that when you and your sister were in my office, that first day."

4

Lena closed her eyes, and she was back in Mendez's office, smelling stale cigarettes and scorched coffee. She could see the sun slanting in through white venetian blinds, making precise horizontal rows of light on the tile floor. Mendez had met her eyes steadily, hands flat on his desk. It was the image she remembered most, except for the bad ones.

"I told Whitney not to go in telling all that Satan stuff. She wouldn't listen, she said somebody better know what's going on. And it was all true. She never said he had power, or he sicced the devil on her. She just said he—"

"I know, Lena."

She nodded. She had always wondered what would have happened if Mendez hadn't been there—the only cop with any experience of occult crime, the only cop who had heard the ring of truth in Whitney's complaints.

My husband is a Satan worshiper, officer, and he supplies drugs and dirty pictures to other Satan worshipers, and I think he maybe had something to do with a child that was missing. And he hits me, and my son, and claims the boy isn't even his, which I assure you is patently untrue. I'm divorcing him, but he's sending me seashells, and that means he's going to kill me.

Maybe, the cop had said, he just wants to take you to the beach.

You don't understand.

Lady, we can't put a guy in jail for sending you a seashell.

And then Mendez was there, standing silently by the officer's elbow, casting a shadow across the desk. Let me talk to them, he'd said. And Whitney had been so grateful. Grateful, though the restraining order didn't keep Jeff from breaking in during the middle of the night. Didn't keep him from nearly running her down with his new Chevrolet, dealer tags on the back. Didn't keep the new puppy from winding up dead on the doorstep.

Lena looked at Joel.

"You told me you were involved in a lot of this stuff down in Miami. Occult crime. Some of the guys called you the ghostbuster."

Mendez nodded.

Lena reached into the drawer of the side table. It was crammed full of small tools, pencils, pads of paper, sales flyers. She took out a white cardboard box. Inside, on a square of cotton, was a gray seashell, white on the belly. The shell was rough, unpolished, crumbs of sand spilling out.

5

"I got this in the mail. Remember? Jeff used to send these to Whitney. It always upset her when she got them."

Mendez looked at the shell. He put the box in his jacket pocket and leaned forward, pressing his hands on Lena's knees. "Jeffrey Hayes has no special power. No magic, no forces of evil, other than what comes from within. You understand that, don't you?"

"Yeah."

"I'm talking about in the middle of the night, when you hear a funny noise. When you hear that noise, do you believe that Hayes has the powers of Satan?"

"Hell, no."

Mendez pulled back and smiled at her. "Good."

"Joel, why did you leave Miami?"

"Personal reasons."

"Such as?"

"What's your interest in Archie Valetta? Are you representing a client?"

"You never heard of client confidentiality?"

"You're a private investigator, not a priest."

They stared at each other.

"I'll let myself out." Mendez tapped her shoulder. "Be sure to lock up behind me."

"Leaving already? I haven't finished giving you a hard time."

He gave her one of his sad smiles, but she wasn't buying. No sympathy.

"Joel?"

"Yes, Lena?"

"Don't go buying any cars down at Finard's."

Mendez looked at her. "Cops can't afford new cars."

2

Eloise Valetta nudged the worn down nap of the carpet with the toe of her terry-cloth house shoe. The warm, sweet smell of baking was strong.

"I 'preciate you coming over—I got a cake going. I take orders, you know, weddings and all."

She was growing out a perm, and thick black hair fell in limp wiggles to her shoulders. She wore navy blue polyester pants, snagged and frayed across her wide, loose backside. Her nose was big and crooked. Lena wondered how many times it had been broken. There were wide white scars on the inside of her right arm and across both wrists. Large red weals spotted her arms, neck, and face.

"I heard, at the shelter I think, how you quit school and some job you had, and started taking these cases, you know, where women need help. Some of the girls down there call you the equalizer. Like the TV show."

Lena smiled. Ph.D. candidate to woman's equalizer. It would make for an interesting résumé.

Eloise chewed her lip. "I wasn't sure if you'd help me. Because of how I used to be married to Archie, and him working with Hayes. But then I figured, you more than anybody would know how serious it is to cross these boys."

"I know."

"And I didn't figure you had any love lost on Archie. You might not mind getting back at him some."

"Might not."

"At least Hayes is locked up."

7

"Not anymore. He just got parole."

"But how can that be? He got forty years!"

"He got two twenty-year terms, to run concurrently."

"Concurrently?"

"That's both at the same time. He's served twenty percent of his sentence. He's out."

"After what he did to your sister and her little boy, that was so awful. And her being pregnant." Eloise shook her head. "I remember reading about it. He ought to have got the death penalty."

"Wasn't possible," Lena said. "He had a solid out on diminished capacity. He was taking Prozac—that's an antidepressant. Prescription drug with known side effects."

"Like making a man kill his wife and little boy?"

Lena shrugged. "Says so in the warning on the side of the bottle."

"Oh, now. Are you kidding me?"

"Some."

"Maybe what I need is some Prozac. Seems like you can get away with anything in Kentucky except killing a white *man* or stealing his money."

"That's two of the big three."

"What's the other one?"

"Marijuana. Grow it or smoke it and they throw away the key."

Eloise grinned.

Lena felt an ache in the small of her back. "Do you mind if I sit down?"

"Gosh, no. I got to check my cake and see if Charlie's okay. I'll be right back."

The couch was dark green vinyl. Three Matchbox cars—a tiny dump truck, a police cycle, and a Thunderbird—were on the far right cushion. A *TV Guide* was open beside them. The television was going in the apartment next door.

"Now, Aint *Bea*," a male voice said in an irritated tone. A woman's voice rose and fell, followed by a ripple of laughter.

Lena heard the oven door open and close, and she went to the edge of the kitchen. A portable black radio was turned low, a male voice sputtering in barely audible tones. It was small room, warm and humid, the table and counters covered with bowls, spoons, cake pans. Batter dripped from a mixing bowl onto the edge of the sink.

8

Two pans of sheet cake had been set on the table to cool, cushioned by worn plaid dishrags.

A small boy sat up on his knees at the table.

"Charlie, you watch them pans."

The boy nodded and stared at Lena. Eloise turned around.

"Sorry, I didn't mean to leave you in there so long. Just let me—"

"Go on and finish," Lena said. "I'll sit down and talk to you while you work. I'd like to see *somebody* make a cake that isn't lopsided."

"You want some coffee?"

"Wait till you get a free hand."

"That's my boy there, that's Charlie. Charlie, say hi."

Charlie ducked his head.

"Charlie, *say hi.*"

"Hi."

He was tearing strips off magazines and gluing them to a sheet of newspaper. Lena watched for a while and saw the hint of a pattern. Charlie looked up at her.

"Looks good," Lena said.

Charlie smiled briefly. He wore a Batman T-shirt and a thick diaper. He looked too old for the diaper, and too young for the precision of his work.

"How old are you?"

Charlie held up four fingers.

"Almost five," Eloise said, not turning around.

"Do you want to talk in front of Charlie?" Lena asked.

"He always stays with me in the kitchen when I bake. It's sort of our routine—since he was a baby. It'll be okay."

Charlie sucked his bottom lip and tried to reposition a strip of paper. He peeled it back up, but a layer stuck to the glue. He scraped at it with his fingernail.

"On the phone you said Archie was going to—"

"K-I-L-L me. I meant it, too."

"What makes you so sure?"

"You know why he went to prison?"

Lena nodded. The year before Jeff had killed Whitney, Archie had robbed a savings and loan. He'd gotten away with three hundred thousand, give or take some change.

"He gave the m-o-n-e-y to me to h-i-d-e."

"But I thought—isn't that how he got plea-bargained down? He turned in his share, pleaded guilty, and testified against the guy with him. The security guard was killed, wasn't she?"

Eloise nodded. "The money Archie turned in was the other guy's. He had his stashed away with me."

"How come he had you hide it?" Lena said. That much cash, and the woman hadn't spent it? Lena looked around. It didn't look like she'd spent it. Lena cocked her head sideways and looked at Eloise. "Why didn't he hide it himself?"

"Thought he'd make bail, but he didn't."

"Why didn't the other guy—what was his name, Nesbit?"

"Yeah. George Nesbit. The shooter. He *did* tell, but nobody believed him. And he couldn't say where Archie's money was. So." Eloise shrugged. "I hid it. Back then, when Archie said do something, I did it." She turned around and pressed her back to the sink. "I'm not like that anymore. I used to drink, and I was snockered most of the time. But when I got caught with Charlie here . . ." The boy looked up and she smiled at him. "I don't know, it was like getting religion or something. I quit drinking—haven't had *anything* in almost six years. Maybe seeing what happened to your sister, or having a baby on the way. I don't know. But I got my GED"—Eloise smiled broadly—"and next fall I'll be taking classes at the community *college*."

"Give Archie his money, then, and get rid of him."

"That's the trouble. I went to check on it—I started worrying, you know how you do? And it was gone."

"Shi—" Lena glanced at Charlie. "Shoot." She rubbed her eyes. "When was the last time, before now, that you checked it?"

"Not since I put it there. Seven, eight years, I guess."

"You sure you looked in the right place?"

"God, yes. You think I wasn't careful, knowing Archie'd be back? It's in a special place I knew when I was a kid. In the woods. I can go straight to it."

"Who else knew?"

"Nobody, I swear. That's what's driving me nuts."

"Maybe somebody just found it."

"Not where I hid it. And Archie is going to be on my doorstep in about two months, wanting it back. I could disappear, run away. But he'd find me. And I got things going okay now, it would be a problem for me to move."

Charlie squirmed in his seat.

"Honey, you got to pee?"

The boy tore a corner off the cover of a *Reader's Digest.*

Eloise sighed. "Four and a half and still won't potty train. I'm ready to teach him to change himself. The last doctor I took him to said it may be physical, it may be allergies. She wants to run tests. But I got to be on a waiting list for those, and we're still waiting. None of the kids around here will play with him. They call him diaper boy, the space piddler. Seems to me the last thing he needs is to move. Be all unsettled again." She scratched her arms. "Hives. I get them every time I think about Archie getting out of jail."

"I'll say one thing for you, you do got a problem."

Eloise leaned back against the stove and folded her arms.

Lena chewed her bottom lip. "I suppose the cops are out of the question?"

"Won't they be mad about me hiding that money? It's one of the big three, remember?"

"You might cut a deal. Possible jail term for accessory."

"That's no good." She scratched the tops of her legs, her nails making scritching noises on the polyester. "I better tell you the even worse news. What I make from the cakes just barely keeps us. I do my best in June on the weddings, and I got more orders this year than I know what to do with. Could you wait till then for your money?"

"We'll work something out."

Lena frowned. If Eloise Valetta had taken the robbery money, she wouldn't still be here, worrying about Archie. Unless she'd spent it all?

Eloise was chewing her lip. "I was thinking one way we could do it. Like with Janette Swan. You helped her out, so she makes you chili every week. And you helped that guy's daughter, you know, the one that delivers Coke. And I bet you always have plenty of Coke. I was thinking that—you know I make these cakes? I could make you one once a week. They're good, people come down from Louisville to get them. And they have good bakeries there."

"Do me a favor and *don't* bake me a cake every week."

"You don't like cake? I bet you're allergic to eggs or something."

"No, I love cake. That's the problem. Look, when I need a favor you can help me with, I'll call you."

"Got to be something." Eloise scratched the back of her neck. "Your oven self-cleaning?"

"No. It's an old one."

"You're not one of those odd women likes to do housework? You hate to clean your oven, don't you?"

"Usually I don't bother."

"Goodness, you shouldn't let it go, you'll get mice up under the burners. How about I clean your oven every six months? You help me get out of this trouble, and I'll do it two times a year for the rest of your life."

"That's a long time to be grateful. How about just for the next two years?"

"Three years."

"You haven't seen my oven."

"Three years." Eloise shook her head. "Lord only knows how you make ends meet. And that's just in return for waiting till June when I'll pay you cash money. No, now look. I'm going to need your full attention here. Archie is pretty darn scary, and I got a baby to protect."

Lena smiled at Charlie and thought, just for a moment, of her nephew. "*We* got a baby to protect."

Eloise put a hand on Charlie's shoulder, and nodded.

3

That night Lena had the dream again.

It started with her parking the Cutlass by the curb out front. It was Friday and Rick was out of town. She and Whitney were going to eat chocolate cheesecake and talk.

The front of the house was dark, except for the glow of a nightlight in Kevin's window. Whitney had said she'd be out on the swing, so come around to the back.

It was full dark. A lightning bug glowed, then faded. A grass-hopper leapt from a forsythia bush and landed on Lena's shoulder. She brushed it off and went to the back of the house. Warm wind rippled the blades of grass, and made the wind chimes sing.

"It's me, Whitney."

The chains on the porch swing creaked. Lena wondered why the back porch light wasn't on—there was only a sliver of moon. She went up the porch steps slowly, feet thumping the wooden slats.

"Whitney?"

The swing creaked again; the wind had moved it. Whitney wasn't out on the deck.

The sliding screen door stood open. A black moth flew in the house. Lena went to close the door, then stopped.

A line of thick black dots had soaked into the boards of the porch. Lena followed the drips to the swing—the top slat was stained and splintered. Lena put her finger out, then jerked it back, feeling the silky stickiness of a spider web across her wrist.

She stuck her head in the doorway and flicked on the porch light. The drops of blood led down the porch stairs to the yard, but she didn't follow them. The back door was standing open. Little Kevin was inside.

A low-watt bulb burned over the sink in the kitchen. The counters were clear; the dishwasher hummed. The room was hot and smelled like baked potatos. A bottle of Flintstones Chewable Vitamins sat on the counter next to a child's yellow plastic mug.

Lena ran her tongue across her bottom lip. Her mouth was dry.

The hallway was dark, except for the faint glow of the night-light. Lena paused in the doorway of Kevin's bedroom, listening for his childish exhalation of breath.

The room was quiet.

She went in, squinting in the dim light. He was in his big-boy bed now—she had forgotten, expecting the crib. She could see his hair on the pillow.

She turned on the light.

There was a hole in the blanket over the small chest—a hole too big for this baby. The face was unmarked, sweet, tears still glistening in the thick black lashes. In his fist, he clutched the tail of a battered blue bunny, its whiskers dotted with blood.

There was blood on Lena's hands, so she must have touched him. Her footsteps were heavy now, slow. She turned lights on all over the house. She went to the kitchen and looked at the phone. A note was taped on the wall. Detective Mendez, it said, by a number. Lena had to dial it twice.

Mendez answered on the second ring; sane, safe, alert. Her own voice was low and sleepy, oddly slurred. She told him about the boy, the blood, the bunny. He told her what to do. She said no, and hung up the phone. She couldn't stay put until she found Whitney.

Lena went back on the porch and followed the blood trail down the steps.

The light from the kitchen and the back bedroom helped, but it was too dark to see if there was blood in the grass. Lena walked along the back of the house, then around to the side.

Whitney sprawled at the top of the driveway, her ankle touching the left front tire of her car.

The smooth sensitive flesh above the inside of her right elbow flapped open and bloody. A heavy-caliber bullet had torn her belly and killed the child within. Her left eye socket was a congealed mass of blood and tissue. The exiting bullet had ripped the back of her head in half. Blood pooled and ran under the car, soaking into the asphalt drive.

The next part, Lena knew, was the sirens. Tonight, in this dream, the phone rang instead.

Lena opened her eyes and rolled sideways, pushing hair out of her eyes and wiping sweat off her face. The phone rang again.

"Hello?"

"Caught you." The voice was male and pleasant—no particular accent. A voice you might hear on the radio. "Lena?"

She took a breath.

"Lena?" the man said. "You know who this is?"

"What do you want, Jeff?"

"Unfinished business, my sister-by-law. Just want to let you know, I'll be around again soon, to see you."

Lena hung the phone up gently. Her wrist grazed something cool, and there seemed to be grit on the sheet. She sat up and fumbled with the switch on the lamp. Light pooled over the top of the bed.

There was a seashell on the pillow—a yellow one, with swirls of pink, and grains of sand inside.

4

Calling Mendez went against the grain.

These days she called him when she needed cop favors—running an NCIC records check, the occasional peek at a file, a piece of backdoor information. No PI could function without access to a cop.

She liked calling him—a jab to her favorite target. Mendez never turned her down. Whitney was long buried, but between them the corpse was fresh.

This time felt different. This time was like asking for real help. The kind of help Whitney had needed, before Hayes shot her down. The kind of help a woman couldn't get.

There was a time in her life, long past now, when Mendez would have been the first and most natural step, but she was way beyond that now. Policemen, husbands, sisters—they always let you down. If Hayes wanted to start something, she would handle it.

Still, there was Eloise Valetta to think about, and Charlie. She pictured the boy, bent over the newspaper, arranging scraps of paper. He reminded her of her nephew. Both had that same air of knowing what they were about. She remembered Kevin sitting in front of the TV with a bowl of dry Cheerios, ignoring the cartoons and watching the commercials. She could see his chubby fingers lining up the Cheerios across the coffee table before he ate them one by one.

Maynard squirmed out from under the couch and sat at her feet.

"Yes?" Lena said.

The cat strolled into the kitchen and Lena followed. Maynard looked up at her, his tail high. He miaowed.

"Okay," Lena said. "I'm doing it."

She set a plate of food on the floor. Maynard hunkered forward and purred. Lena stroked the silky back, feeling the skin ripple under her hand.

"Did you see Hayes last night, Maynard?" She looked down at the cat. "If you see him again, you hide."

Lena realized, when she got to the outer office, that she ought to have called and made sure Mendez was there. It was just on 8:15. He might not even be in yet.

The woman behind the front desk was pudgy in her uniform, the style unflattering to the female figure. Lena wondered how many decades it would be before women cops got their own uniform.

"Is Sergeant Mendez in?"

Lena smelled coffee, cigarette smoke, floor wax. A tired-looking woman in blue jeans was cleaning the bathroom. The door was propped open with a big metal mop bucket. Lena heard water running and smelled the acrid odor of cleaning fluid.

The woman behind the desk was eyeing Lena's earrings. Lena pushed her hair back off her shoulders. The woman chewed the eraser on the back of her pencil.

"Those what they call shoulder dusters?"

Lena fingered the left earring. "No. Shoulder dusters come all the way down to here."

"I been thinking about getting my ears pierced. Everybody says you don't even feel it. Tell me now, *does* it hurt?"

"Bravest thing I ever did was get the second ear pierced."

"I knew it." The woman nodded her head and jerked a thumb over her shoulder toward the elevator. "Mendez is up there. I think I saw him come in about an hour ago."

"Thanks."

The elevator was slow. Lena slipped into the bullpen through a side door, avoiding the secretaries behind the fortresslike counter out front. Rows of desks were butted side by side like a schoolroom for adults. It was cold in the room and she shivered. She smelled overheated coffee.

Mendez had taken off his jacket and hung it over the back of the chair. His shirt was white, cuff links gleamed at the sleeves, and his thin dark tie was neatly knotted. He was making notes on a yellow legal pad and he wrote quickly, never lifting the pen from the paper. He stopped for a minute and took a sip from a Styrofoam cup. Lena crossed the room, ignoring the stares from other cops behind other desks. Twice she nodded at familiar faces.

"Hello, Mendez."

He looked surprised. He pulled a chair from behind an empty desk and set it beside his.

"Coffee?"

"No, I'm swimming in it."

He raised an eyebrow but didn't comment. He sat in his chair and looked at her. His lack of polite patter used to unnerve Whitney.

Lena fished the seashell out of her shirt pocket.

"Found this on my pillow last night."

Mendez leaned forward and took the shell. He looked it over and frowned, lips tight, then set it on the legal pad in the center of his desk.

"When do you think he got in?" Mendez sat very still in the chair. His voice was harsh.

"It wasn't there when I went to bed." Lena frowned. "The phone rang, around three this morning. It was Jeff. After I hung up, I turned on the light and found the shell."

Mendez picked up his pen, and put it down again.

Lena made a conscious effort not to grind her teeth. "He came in while I was asleep. Came up to my bedroom, and left that on the pillow. I never knew he was there."

"What did he say?"

"I *told* you, I didn't know he was there."

"On the phone."

"Oh. Something like he'd see me soon."

"Did he threaten you?"

Lena shrugged. "He said we had unfinished business."

Mendez picked the seashell back up.

"Which you think is worse, Mendez? Sand and shells in the sheets, or cracker crumbs?"

"How did he get in?"

"I think he came in through the basement. There's a ground-level window there, and it was unlocked this morning when I checked it."

"Did you lock it before you went to bed?"

"Usually I keep it locked. But I don't check it every night."

Mendez eased back in his chair and closed his eyes.

Lena smiled. "This is the part where you pat my back and tell me he just wants to take me to the seashore."

Mendez glared at her. Not, she decided, the best way to go about asking for favors. "I need your help."

He nodded. "We'll tap your phone. I want a look at the window. They won't assign protection. They'll send a patrol car up and down your street now and then, but it would be best—"

"That's not the favor. You asked me before about Archie Valetta. How I knew he was due to be out of prison."

Mendez cocked his head sideways.

"You probably already figured out that Eloise Valetta came to me for help."

"What does she need help with?"

Lena shrugged. "It's not police business. She's got a little boy, and she's having trouble arranging tests and stuff at the free clinic. Anyway, Archie getting out of prison is one of the things that's got her worried."

"Is Hayes bothering her?"

"Hayes? No."

"Does this connect to Hayes in any way?"

"Not that I know of. But they're partners, Mendez, so who knows? They may get back together."

"What's the favor?"

"I want to see the file. Valetta's file. Particularly concerning the last arrest, known companions, that kind of thing."

She wished she knew what he was thinking while he looked at her so steadily.

"Why?" he asked.

"Why? How about *because*."

"What's the robbery got to do with anything?"

"I study my adversaries from every angle, Joel. I like to know all the players."

He narrowed his eyes. He always paid attention when she called him Joel.

"How does this connect to the free clinic?"

"You said yourself, Archie is dangerous. Eloise is uneasy. I'm just keeping an eye out."

Mendez touched his mustache and frowned. Lena tapped her foot. Words never seemed to hurry or prod this man. She fingered the hem of her jacket, then looked up. "Help me or don't, Mendez. I was up most the night, and I'm tired."

"Okay." He picked up a folder from a neat stack on the right-hand corner of his desk.

"You got it right there? What's *your* interest, Mendez?"

"Hayes is out. Valetta's on his way. That's my interest." He studied her for a long moment. "The robbery money wasn't recovered."

"I thought it was."

"Not all of it." Mendez picked up his pen, tapping it lightly on the metal desk top. "Lena. How much do you know about Archie Valetta?"

She shrugged.

"He used to ride with the Grits," Mendez said. "You know them?"

"Southern fried motorcycle gang."

"Very low profile, and fairly new, but they've dug in all across the South—Kentucky, Tennessee, the Carolinas. They're moving very cautiously now, in Florida and Texas."

"You said *used* to ride?"

"Kicked out, we don't know why. We got a hint from an informant that it was some kind of blackmail scam—but we don't really know any details. Don't know why they didn't kill him, either. Happened before he hooked up with Hayes. This isn't your usual perp, Lena. Valetta plays rough and dirty. He's a hardcore case, and an opportunist like everybody else these days. If something dirty comes up, he'll go for it." He leaned back in his chair and narrowed his eyes. "Did you ever stop to think that Eloise Valetta may be using you? That she may not be leveling with you?"

"About the medical clinic?"

He frowned. "The little boy looks a bit like your nephew. Don't let that cloud your judgment. Don't get sentimental about the Valettas."

"Are you telling me to turn my back on the kid, Mendez?"

Mendez sighed and handed her the file. "You have a way of putting things. Come to me, Lena, when it gets to be police business."

5

Maynard was curled up peacefully in the rocking chair.

Lena took a breath. She hadn't realized she was worried till she saw the cat, safe and sound and asleep.

Hayes had a definite track record with animals.

There were two messages on the answering machine. Lena hit the Play button and picked up the cat. Maynard purred and Lena scratched him behind the ears. The machine whirred as the tape rewound.

"Ms. Padgett? This is Elwin Newcomb, from Paris Road Cemetery? Need you to give me a call, if you will. Extension 232. Um, thanks."

Lena pulled Maynard's tail. The cat miaowed.

The answering machine beeped, and a piano played. " 'We're poor little lambs, who've lost our way. . . .' " Lena frowned and sat down, and the familiar words poured from the tape.

> We're little black sheep who've gone astray. . . .
> Gentlemen rankers out on the spree,
> Damned from here to Eternity,
> God ha' mercy on such as we. . . .

Maynard squirmed out of Lena's arms, hind claws catching her left wrist and leaving a livid, bleeding scratch. Lena did not notice.

She saw Whitney, as clearly as if she'd been on the couch beside her, standing on the darkened stage, hair soft and silky on her shoulders. Lena had sat in the audience, fists clenched, nervous.

Whitney had hated auditions. She'd thrown up twice the night before. The play she'd been auditioning for was a musical; Lena could not remember what. Whitney had wanted to do something different, had wanted to stand out from the rows of pretty girls doing a number from *South Pacific*. She was going to put Kipling to music, and she'd sung a medley of Kipling ballads, starting with the little lost lambs. Lena had cut her Econ class to be there so she'd be able to answer Whitney's endless round of questions afterward— the tedious postmortem that made theater majors such a pain in the ass.

Did you notice I flubbed that second line? Could you tell my knees were shaking? I was sweating like a pig—could you see that?

It was the first time Lena had met Whitney's pal, the effervescent Rick Savese—a tap-dancing, piano-playing aspiring actor. He'd played piano for Whitney—his hair slicked back, a Camel cigarette dangling from his lips. He swore afterward it was his back-up that had made the difference, and gotten Whitney the part.

Whitney had introduced him to her little sister Lena, the up-and-coming economics major. He'd immediately asked Lena to lunch, and then dinner.

Jeffrey Hayes had been there too, hanging out with one of the backstage girls, the one who spent an inordinate amount of time at the student center playing Dungeons & Dragons. They'd been dating for more than a year, but it was over as soon as he heard Whitney sing. Jeff Hayes had fallen in love.

Or so it seemed.

Lena pushed the Save button, and played the message back.

He was getting to her, definitely getting to her. Lena walked through every room in the house. Her bedroom was as she'd left it, bed unmade, T-shirt thrown across the pillow. In the bathroom a wet towel was slung over the towel bar, a dripping washrag wadded over the soap dish in the tub, a bottle of shampoo open on the counter. No one had been in Kevin's old room. A mobile with a stuffed giraffe, a hippo, and a lion hung forlorn and dusty in the corner. The red-and-yellow wallpaper was still bright.

Lena closed the door and went to the basement.

Daylight streamed through the small ground-floor window, giving the room a murky illumination. Lena dodged the boxes and Kevin's old crib, and pulled the cord that hung from the light bulb in the middle of the ceiling.

Shadows, spiders, dust.

She sat on the bottom step of the rough wooden staircase. The basement was cool and humid, like a cave with a sour smell. She ought to have gotten rid of it all—the old clothes, the storybooks, the fuzzy brown pony on yellow rollers. She opened the box that was lodged near the bottom stair and found a pair of worn blue Osh-Kosh overalls. She remembered how Kevin had stashed toys down the front of the overalls till he could barely walk. She glanced at the third row of boxes, in particular the second box from the top. Hayes's stuff. Undisturbed. He'd hardly know what box to look in, if he even remembered that Whitney had those old things.

Lena stood on her tiptoes and stretched. No sooner did she have hold of the box than it slipped out of her hands and landed hard. She peeled back the cardboard flaps, and a cloud of fine-grained dust made her sneeze.

From the looks of things, Whitney had upended drawers and dumped them straight in the box. Lena burrowed through old bank statements, a ripped pair of Jockey shorts—size 34—and a copy of *The Nightmare Years*, by William L. Shirer. There were candle stubs, black and white, a thin dusty book with a black cover titled *Miniatore's Grimoire*, and a few wrinkled sheets of parchment.

And that was all. Except for a small tan spider.

Lena picked up the copy of *Miniatore's Grimoire*. It had an ancient, musty smell, and the cover was warped, as if it had been left in the rain. The words were in Italian, the print tiny and ornate.

She picked up the Shirer. It felt oddly light and lumpy. She flipped the book open, and smiled thinly.

Hayes had hollowed it out, cutting the pages away with jagged, laborious trouble, leaving an inch of margin all the way around. Inside was a hardbound notebook. Across the black cover, *Book of Shadows* had been written in calligraphy with blood red ink.

Jeffrey Hayes had been lettered on the inside cover. *1971.* Lena did a quick calculation. In 1971, Jeffrey Hayes would have been about fifteen years old.

Hail Satan was the opening salutation. The writing was spiky and slanted, the *t* crossed so hard the pen had scarred the paper. A goat's head had been sketched in the margin.

In only three days it will be Lammas Day. I can't sleep now because I think about it a lot. When I was little I did not like the altar. I did not like taking my clothes off, and that M saw everthing I had because I was naked. I liked seeing her though.

23

When we were little it was just watch and learn this and KEEP YOUR MOUTH SHUT. We were lambs then. But then they saw I was special.

That altar is heavy, it takes four fat men to get it out of the pickup. And the side by the fire is warm. Almost HOT. But that first time, boy did it feel cold on my back. And I didn't like drinking all that stuff. I love it now!!! Give me more!!!!

I close my eyes and think what it will be like. The smoke and all. That sweet stuff we burn up in bowls. It used to kind of make me sick. But I like it now.

Use to be HE would chant and put that oily stuff on me. And EVERWHERE on me. Thats what I do now to M. I like that so much, no wonder I can't sleep. The other kids are always scared of me because HE says I'm special. I never get cut. I DO the cut. In thee days I will pore oil on M. And then talk about kissing cousinas! And then the cuts. They give her lots of stuff so she won't scream. I wonder if they didn't give it??? We could hold her down.

666   666

         666

Lena closed the book. Maybe later she would read the rest of it. Maybe never.

6

The gloom of early morning had thickened, and the skies were muddy. The smell of rain wafted in through the open car window, and the wind blew Lena's hair in her eyes. Maynard huddled in the cat carrier, emitting a full throaty cry at regular intervals.

Lena poked a finger through the mesh of the carrier, feeling the downlike softness of the cat's fur.

Burial space in the Paris Road Cemetery had been expensive. The grounds were circled by an eight-foot wall of gray fieldstone, every inch in excellent condition. The black wrought-iron gate, spiked at the top, was freshly painted and hung open across the blacktop drive. Lena parked in front of the office next to a hunter green Volvo. She glanced back at the two cars. Hers was green too, around the rust spots.

The woman behind the desk huddled over a typewriter as if she were cold and the typewriter might warm her.

"Is Elwin Newcomb in?" Lena asked.

The woman frowned and looked up. Black cat glasses hung from a chain around her neck. She wore thick Pan-Cake makeup over her fragile wrinkled skin, red rouge on her cheekbones. Her hair was white, teased and sprayed in place, and it sat like meringue on the top of her head.

"Are you Lena Padgett?"

Lena nodded.

"Go on in, honey." The woman buzzed the intercom. "Elwin, it's Miz Padgett."

The office door opened before Lena got to it. Newcomb was a big man, tall and broad, with gray-flecked brown hair that was

25

clipped short, and a complexion ravaged by acne scars. He was frowning, his movements jerky and restless, unlike the smooth calm Lena remembered from their past associations.

"Please." He pointed to a chair upholstered in blue plaid. "Have a seat."

Lena sat. She crossed her legs. "What's up, Mr. Newcomb?"

He rubbed a finger across the blotter on his desk. "As I mentioned when you called, we, uh, had some trouble last night."

Lena pulled her left earring. It was loose, and she tightened it. "What kind of trouble?" she said finally.

"Well. Vandalism, I guess."

"My sister's grave?"

He nodded.

Lena bit her lip.

"Your nephew, too. I'm sorry."

"A child's grave? What kind of vandalism we talking about?"

"Spray paint, that kind of thing."

"Are the graves . . . disturbed in any way?"

"Oh, no, no, no. I'm sorry, I should have told you that off the bat. We don't . . . This kind of thing is unusual on our grounds. We're very careful, very security conscious. I can't tell you how sorry I am this has happened. We'll get it fixed up for you, no charge, of course. But I did want to let you know, in case you were to come out here, and see the gravestones missing."

"Missing?"

"We'll be sending them off for cleaning—sanding, actually."

Lena nodded. "Let's go take a look."

Newcomb grimaced. "Naturally, you're curious. It's not necessary, though, if you don't want to go see. Might be best not to. We'll get it fixed up for you, just like it was."

"I want to see it."

"Sure." Newcomb stood up. "I guess I don't blame you. Probably feel the same way myself." He opened the door. "We'll be back, Carol. Going out to take a look."

The white-haired woman nodded and stared at Lena's face.

"I'll drive you out," Newcomb said. He opened the passenger door of the green Volvo.

He drove slowly along the narrow blacktop lane that wound through the cemetery. Whitney and Kevin were way out, in the newer section. There weren't as many trees in that area, and the

26

grass was not as lush. But it was well kept, and nearly full. Newcomb pulled the Volvo to the side of the road, and Lena followed him up a small hill, past the deep, green-scummed pond, past the cottonwood tree.

Whitney's small headstone had been turned over on its side, the lamb over Kevin's grave turned upside down. Rough crosses made from sticks banded together had been inverted and thrust deep in the ground. There were letters painted in red in the grass over the graves.

SIH CINATAS YTSEJAM

Lena looked at the letters, then back at Newcomb. "You know what it means?"

He shook his head. "It's just nonsense, Ms. Padgett. Nonsense. Idle hands make the devil's work."

Lena looked at him. He blushed.

"I didn't mean—"

"Any other grave sites disturbed?"

He shook his head. "No."

Lena looked at Whitney's headstone. *Live* had been painted across the side.

"Live?" she said.

Newcomb shrugged.

"You ever had any kind of problem like this before?"

He hesitated. "No."

"You reported this to the police?"

"Yeah, I called this morning. They haven't been out yet."

Lena chewed her bottom lip. She didn't like it, didn't like thinking about unfriendly hands on the little marble lamb she had selected so carefully.

Lena looked at Newcomb. "There's somebody I'd like to have see this. He's a cop. Will you leave it be till I can get him out here?"

Newcomb put a hand on her shoulder. "Ms. Padgett, I know you're upset. But there's no need jumping on this with both feet. What I mean is, of course it is disturbing, the inverted crosses. It's offensive to a Christian, and I'm a Christian, I tell you that. But don't take this personal. What I mean by that is, I been in this business a long time. I was telling you the truth there, when you asked if we'd had this kind of trouble before; we haven't. But it does

27

happen, I'm afraid a lot more often than people have any idea. I'm very careful here, and I can't tell you how upset I am about it. But what I'm trying to say is, a cemetery can attract this sort of nonsense without it meaning anything specific to the grave that's . . . vandalized. It's got nothing to do with your poor sister, or your little nephew. The best thing you can do is forget it ever happened, and let me fix this up. I'll make it pretty here for you, as soon as I can. It'll be a nice place again, peaceful and pretty like I know you want."

"Just make sure nothing is messed with till my friend gets here. His name is Mendez."

7

The Schneider Collection Agency was on the ground level of a rundown office building at the intersection of Rey and Nold streets. There was a White Castle hamburger place next door, apartments across the street, and a mall down the road. Lena parked the Cutlass and left the windows open halfway. Maynard sniffed thoughtfully, smelling french fries.

Lena peered through the mesh of the cage. "How'd you like to visit your old daddy, huh? How'd you like to see Ricky?"

Maynard sniffed thoughtfully.

"Keep your paws crossed."

The outside doors of the building were painted in primary colors. The door of the Schneider Agency had been red, but it faced west, into the sun, and the paint and the wood were chipping. It was more pink now than red. Lena went in.

The girl in the front office was new. Lena decided she couldn't be more than eighteen. The girl typed delicately at a keyboard with the tips of long pinkish silver fingernails. Her hair was brunette, permed, and pulled up on top of her head in a ponytail held by a pink velvet bow. She looked at Lena and frowned.

"Rick in?" Lena said.

"Mr. Savese is on the phone."

"Go back and get him when he's off, will you?"

The girl wrinkled her nose. "I'll see if he can be disturbed. Who shall I say is here to see him?"

"*Mrs.* Savese."

The brunette's eyes widened. She got up slowly, glanced over her shoulder at Lena, then went through a door on the left. Lena

29

caught a glimpse of two women and three men at phone stations. The girl left the door ajar, and Lena pushed it open gently and stood in the doorway.

"Well, screw you." A woman in blue jeans and a Coors T-shirt grimaced. She caught sight of Lena and waved. The room was hot and stuffy. It looked like a student lounge, with posters on the wall, half-filled coffee cups, Coke cans, and an open box of doughnuts on a desk.

Rich was slumped at his station, a bored look in his eyes. The oh-honey routine, Lena decided. He had on the glasses, clear lenses, that helped establish the character. Somehow he always knew which approach to use.

"Oh, honey," Rick said, and Lena smiled. A boom box played a Phil Collins song. Too loud.

"You don't know *what* she'll do to me, my boss would freeze hell with a look." Rick leaned forward. "Oh, yeah, I got the social security number, it's the policy number I need." He paused. "Don't you know it? She would, too."

The brunette in the pink bow shifted her weight from one foot to the other.

Rick tapped his keyboard. "Yeah, it's coming up. Crap, we're losing it again. New software is a bitch, let me tell you. How much was that coverage for? One hundred thousand? Honey, you saved my life. I wish Memphis was closer to Wisconsin, I might tool down and see you. Oh, Lord, here she comes. See you, and thanks again, babe."

"Rick!" The girl in the pink bow spoke in an urgent stage whisper. "There's some woman here wants to see you. I think it's your *ex-wife*."

Rick looked up and smiled at Lena. It was a thousand-watt charmer, that smile, despite the wariness behind it. Rick's hair was dark blond and thick. It looked mussed and windblown, though Lena knew the time, effort, and hair gel it took to achieve the look. Rick folded the glasses and put them in his shirt pocket. The shirt was loose, white cotton, probably about eighty dollars new. His jeans were tight, a faded cornflower blue, and he wore black leather cowboy boots.

"Lena!" He stood up. "Hey, the earrings are great. Turquoise, I like it." He smiled at the brunette. "Ellen, I'm taking a break. Where's Arlan?"

"In his office talking to the repo guy."

"If he wants me, say I'm in the john."

He winked, and she blushed.

"Okay, Rick."

She watched him take Lena's arm and lead her out of the office.

"I'm *hungry*," he said as they passed the front desk. "I haven't had breakfast."

"You had a doughnut."

"I don't eat sweets anymore, Lena. I'm very healthy now."

"There's sugar at the corner of your mouth. But you look great, Rick. The extra weight looks good on you."

He looked down at his stomach. "I *like* wearing this shirt out, Lena. I could tuck it in if I wanted to." He put his arm around her shoulders. Counting the heels of the cowboy boots, he came in just under five feet seven.

The office door shut behind them. Rick looked up and squinted.

"Look at that sky. We're going to get it. Let's go in your . . . Lena. You still driving the Cutlass?"

She shrugged. "If it embarrasses you, we'll take your car."

"I'm, um, having a small problem with the payments. It's in hiding right now."

"What are you driving?"

"Miata."

"*Rick*. You can't afford a car like that."

"That's why it's hidden." He opened the passenger door on the Cutlass. "Who is this, now, who is this? John Maynard Kitty, how are you, sweetie?" He stuck a finger in the cage. Maynard purred. "You remember me, don't you?" He smiled up at Lena. "*He* still loves me. I should have got visiting rights." He looked down at the cat. "What a name she gave you, *Maynard*. Should have called you Olivier, yes we should. He misses me, Lena, I can tell."

"I think you're right, Rick. He does seem to miss you."

"You just don't like to admit he . . ." Rick looked at Lena across the seat of the car.

"Get in," she said. "I'll buy you breakfast."

They sat in the front seat of the Cutlass, parked discreetly in the corner of the White Castle parking lot, just out of view of the Schneider Agency. A rain-scented breeze swept through the open windows and ruffled the white bags of food.

Rick snapped on the radio and took a sip from a steaming

31

Styrofoam cup. "Why don't they have beer here?" He fooled with the knob, conjuring irritating bursts of static. "Hey, the Beatles. Remember that song?"

"No, I'm too young."

Rick grinned. "Sure you are." He took a large bite, consuming half of a small square hamburger. Maynard purred loudly and climbed into his lap. "Watch, Lena, see if he'll still do it."

He stuck a french fry in his mouth. The cat put his paws on Rick's chest and delicately took the french fry from his lips.

"There, see, he remembered!"

Rick peeled the plastic cap off his coffee and poured some into the lid. He blew on it and stuck his tongue in.

"Okay. It's not hot. Here, Maynard, here boy."

"Rick, he doesn't want that."

The cat sniffed the coffee lid, then lapped the brown liquid.

"There, see, he likes it."

"He'll eat anything you give him, Rick. So watch what you feed him."

"It's just a little coffee."

"No *beer*. No alcohol of any kind."

"What, you see beer anywhere?"

"Because I think you're right, Rick." Lena opened a bun and pried the pickle loose. She handed the hamburger to Rick. "Maynard misses you."

"Did I *say* you could have my pickle?"

"You always let me have your pickle."

"That's what I love about Judith. She doesn't eat my pickle."

"How's she doing?"

"Wonderful."

"Good."

"Don't be jealous. She likes you. *She's* not jealous."

"I like her, too. And I'm not jealous."

Rick frowned. "*Why* aren't you jealous? It's unnatural. The two of you should be at each other's throats. I should have to referee." He chewed thoughtfully. "Why do I always get involved with such abnormal women?"

Lena ate a french fry.

"So," Rick said. "How long do you want me to keep your cat? I assume that's what this has been leading up to?"

"Not sure."

"That you want me to keep him?"

"Not sure how long." Lena took a drink of Orange Crush. "Did you know Hayes got parole?"

"*No.*"

"It was in the paper. I forgot, you only read *Variety.*"

"Lena. God. I'm sorry." He put an arm around her shoulders. "They should have fried that sucker. Down in Florida, they would have."

"I'm worried about leaving Maynard alone."

"What? He has big parties while you're gone?"

Lena told him about Hayes.

"My God, he came into your house? Your *bedroom?*" Rick ate a handful of french fries. "And he left that song on your machine?" He took a sip of cold coffee. "God, I remember that so well. Whitney up on the stage . . . 'We're little black sheep, who've gone astray.' . . . Remember how she leered when she sang that part? Too campy, I thought, but the guys ate it up. 'Gentlemen rankers out on a spree, Damned from here to Eternity!' "

Rick was a baritone, his voice resonant and rich. One of his better features.

"You should be in pictures," Lena said.

Rick grinned. "Remember I slicked back my hair—"

"And had a cigarette dangling between your lips."

"A Camel. God, I can't believe we ever smoked those. So bad for the voice."

"Wasn't the worst thing you ever smoked."

"Lena, you were so cute then. So exuberant and happy and . . . energetic. Just enough of a bitchy streak to make you interesting, but not scary."

"Don't speak ill of the dead. Will you do it?"

"Do what?"

"Keep Maynard."

"Anything," he sang. "For my *baby* . . ."

"Good. I have another favor."

"Don't tell me you have a dog now, because a dog will make me sneeze."

"It's about a case I'm working on."

"Now, a goldfish is a possibility—"

"Pay attention, Rick. This was a robbery, and I need you to do

33

one of your telephone routines, and worm some information out of an insurance clerk."

"Prime meat, my sweet, what would you like to know?"

She told him about Eloise Valetta. "My main problem," she said, "is I can't get hold of the insurance investigator, and I need to talk to him. Should be no trouble for you to find him?"

"Naw. I can tell you anything about anybody, ain't no privacy no mo', babe. And hey, I see you've been off the pill awhile. You just saying no?"

"How'd you find that out?"

"If you charge it or write a check, I know what and when you buy it. I also peeked at your medical records. Dusty, girl, dusty. You ain't been sick in years."

"You won't get in trouble with Arlan for doing this for me?"

"Naw, it's just the odd tidbit here and there. Besides, Arlan treats me with care. Good skip tracers are hard to come by. Particularly artistes like myself. Though there's no telling how much longer I'll be *available*."

"Something up?"

He smiled, blue eyes bright and animated. "Going to Louisville next week for an audition."

"A good one?"

"You bet. By invitation. ATL."

"Actors Theatre? Rick, Rick, Rick."

"Yes, yes, yes."

She looked at his face and she was lost, suddenly, in another time and place, seeing the preaudition shine of hope and terror in his face. How many times had she heard the lines, heard the fears, massaged the knots out of tense shoulders?

Back then she had been that other person, the one with a career plan, a life, all that trust and energy. Hayes had put an end to everything. Sorry, but true, no going back, the old Lena had died, and Rick never liked the new one.

"What you thinking, Lena? You got that look."

"Just maybe I shouldn't eat your pickles anymore."

He lunged across the seat, scattering cardboard hamburger boxes and french fries.

"Eat 'em." He put his arms around her. "Come stay with me till this stuff with Jeff blows over."

"Wouldn't be room with Judith there."

"Hmmm. Hell, Lena, she probably won't care. God, you smell so good."

"I smell like hamburgers."

"No, it's you, the way I remember."

"My natural musk."

"Don't talk dirty, Lena, my pants are tight enough already."

8

Mendez met her at the black iron cemetery gate, right at closing time. Newcomb had told the custodian to stay and wait. Lena recognized the navy blue Mazda before it turned in the drive. Mendez had his lights on. It was just on five o'clock, but the sky was dark and heavy.

Lena was sitting on the hood of the Cutlass, and she saw Mendez smile, as if the sight of her, cross-legged on the car, amused him. He rolled down a window.

"Car trouble?"

Lena shook her head, though car trouble was something of a constant with the Cutlass. "I'm waiting for you."

"How far is it?"

"Couple miles."

"Hop in."

She dusted off her jeans and got in.

"Getting cold again," she said, closing the window. She reached for the seat belt, then didn't use it, on the off chance that Mendez might be annoyed. "Bear left here, then take the first right. It'll meander awhile, then I'll tell you when to stop."

She glanced at Mendez. His tie was neatly knotted still, here at the end of the day. Though for Joel, it probably wasn't the end of the day.

Lena had the urge to say something irritating.

The inside of the car was immaculate, unlike her own. There was a tape player, and a handful of tapes stacked in a compartment behind the emergency brake. Lena sorted through them. Classical. She curled her lip.

"We getting close?" Mendez asked.

"Hmm? Whoa. Passed it, sorry. Back up to that cottonwood tree."

The reverse gear made a whirring noise as Mendez backed the car down the narrow lane. He parked by the side of the road. Lena got out, slammed the door shut, then hesitated.

The wind was picking up and the cottonwood swayed, limbs creaking. Mendez moved quickly, and Lena lengthened her stride to keep up.

The headstones still lay on their sides, but the inverted crosses had blown over. The wind whipped the grass and made the painted letters hard to read.

Lena held her hair back with one hand, trying to keep it out of her face. She watched Mendez take it all in. His black hair streamed backward, his pants and sport coat billowed. He didn't frown or smile.

"The king of stoic," Lena muttered.

"Pardon?"

"I said did you ever see anything like this before?"

"Many times."

Lena let her hair go and jammed her hands in her pockets. "He knocked over the lamb."

Mendez looked at her, then put a hand on her shoulder. She almost pulled away—reflex—but this time she didn't. Turning the lamb over on a baby's grave was a violation. For once, they agreed.

"These are the only graves that were messed with," Lena said. "Whitney's and Kevin's."

"It's Hayes, Lena. You don't have to convince me. Anything else?"

"Just the song on the answering machine. I've got the tape."

"This is the one your sister sang?"

Lena nodded.

"I want to hear it," Mendez said.

"It's at the house."

"Let's eat first." He looked at her. "Can I take you to dinner?"

Lena looked at him, thinking the hand on the shoulder might be going to his head. "You like barbecue?"

"Yes."

"I'll take you. There's a place still owes me free dinners."

37

Mendez turned toward the car, but Lena grabbed his arm. She pointed to Whitney's headstone.

"What does that mean? 'L-i-v-e'?"

"Not 'live.' Read it backwards."

"Backwards? E-v . . . evil?"

He nodded.

She studied the letters on the grass. "S-i-h. His."

Mendez stood beside her. "His Satanic Majesty."

"You're good at reading backwards, Joel." A raindrop spattered her shoulder, making a dark spot on the red material. "He's really gearing up again, isn't he?"

Mendez took her arm and pointed her toward the car. "We'll talk about it after we eat."

The custodian was glad to see them go. The rain came down as they turned from the blacktop drive onto Fourth Street. Fat raindrops smacked the pavement and beat against the car, and the wind rocked the Mazda to the left. The windshield wipers slashed back and forth, but visibility was negligible. The windows fogged and Mendez turned the defroster on full blast. They forded a deep puddle, the sides of the car cutting into the water with a coarse, grating sound. A Chevy pickup passed in the left lane, throwing muddy splats of water onto the windshield.

Mendez glanced at Lena.

Probably checking to see if my seat belt's on, she thought.

Deke's Piggy Palace was on North Lime. By the time they found a parking place, three blocks away, the rain had eased.

It was good to leave the flow of traffic. The sidewalks were wet and muddy, cracked and ill-kept. The glassed-in storefronts were cloudy with condensation.

The restaurant was almost empty. A green sign that said Piggy Palace was nailed over the doorway. The front window had been coated with black paint. Tired yellow light glinted through the cracks. The door was propped open with a chipped concrete block, and a swatch of warped brown linoleum lay across the entrance like a welcome mat.

A tired-looking waitress sighed when they walked in. Lena guided Mendez to a booth upholstered in blood-red vinyl. There was a rip across the back that had been repaired with masking tape.

Mendez sat across from Lena. He took off his suit coat and folded it neatly, laying it on the seat beside him.

"Nice place."

Lena grinned. "Honest, Mendez. The food's fantastic."

"Which client?"

"Which client? Oh, the one got me the free dinners? The owner's sister. Her daughter was involved in one of those relationships, you know. One of those guys who are pathological liars that young girls can't seem to resist."

The waitress brought them two dog-eared paper menus.

"Owen here?" Lena asked.

The waitress narrowed her eyes. "In back."

"Tell him Lena's out front, okay? And bring us two beers and two orders of fried banana peppers." Lena glanced at Mendez. "You drink Coronas?"

He nodded.

"Good," Lena said. "Don't cut the lime so big it won't go down in the bottle."

The corner of Mendez's mouth lifted in a half smile. "I'm almost afraid to ask how you handled the boyfriend. Don't incriminate yourself."

"I rustled up a substitute. Boy who's the son of a woman I know. Nice kid, good-looking, rides a Suzuki. Girls that age are usually impressed with the bike."

"It didn't work?" Mendez said.

Lena shook her head. "The pathological liar creep was older, and this kid was really hooked on him."

"Like an addiction."

"Yeah, exactly like that."

The waitress came back smiling. She laid out two thick white napkins and two spotted forks, then unloaded the banana peppers and the beers. Thin slices of lime rested on the tops of the beer bottles.

"Owen says to give you this and say hi." She pulled a whole lime from her apron pocket and laid it down on the table.

Lena grinned. They ordered large pork barbecue sandwiches and a double order of onion rings.

Mendez picked up the lime and squeezed it gently. "So what did you do, Lena? How'd you get rid of the boyfriend?"

"Did some checking down at the courthouse, and found out he had a wife and two kids in Tennessee. I just wrote the wife and gave her the jerk's address—plus where he was working. All of a sudden he packs up and disappears."

Mendez dipped a banana pepper in the red cocktail sauce that came in a small plastic cup.

"Hard on the kid."

Lena squeezed lime into her beer bottle, then licked the juice off the glass rim. She studied the boar's head that was nailed over the cash register. Mendez ate another banana pepper. Lena looked out the window.

They'd had dinner together once before, after Whitney died. Lena tried to remember why they'd wound up eating together, but those memories, so soon after Whitney's death, ran together in her mind.

"You ever going to finish grad school?" Mendez asked her.

"I'm a PI, Mendez."

"You should have stuck with economics. Why don't you go back?"

"Too late, and I don't want to. That's a whole other world."

The sandwiches arrived, hot and soggy. Lena picked hers up, letting the sauce drip between her fingers. Mendez ate his with a fork.

"What did you get your degree in, Mendez?"

He cut a neat square off his sandwich. "Law enforcement."

Lena ate the edge off her pickle. "Figures."

"Do you always eat the pickle first?"

"*What?*"

"Do you always eat the pickle first?"

"You know what, Mendez? I know you said we'd talk *after* we ate, but we're down to pickles here. I want to know what you think, and what you know."

He chewed thoughtfully.

"I'm listening here."

"When I was a cop down in Florida, I was married. My wife was—"

"Mendez."

"Patience, Lena. My wife was Cuban."

Lena leaned back in her seat. "I didn't know you were divorced."

"I'm not."

Lena felt a flutter of disappointment. She checked his left hand.

40

No wedding ring. As far as she knew, there'd never been a wedding ring.

Mendez wiped his fingers on his napkin and took a sip of beer. "My wife spent most of her childhood in Grappa—it's a small Florida town. Very small. She was . . . unsophisticated. Religious. A practicing Santera."

"Santera?"

"You know much about Santeria?"

"I thought it was . . . I guess not."

"You thought what?"

"Voodoo stuff."

He nodded. "A common misconception in this part of the country."

"The redneck South."

"There *are* strong ties to Haiti, and to Africa. What you call voodoo stuff. It's also strongly influenced by Catholicism. Saints and the Ten Commandments. And it has its dark side—as does any religion."

"I could tell you things about Southern Baptists."

The corner of his mouth lifted in a half smile.

"The thing about being a cop in Florida . . . Religion is very mixed up in the drug trade. The dark side of Santeria—Palo Mayombe—can accommodate any profession. It's a good religion for criminals. You take a player who *believes*—who prays to his god for the latest drug deal to go down smoothly—that's dangerous. Gives him a sense of safety, invincibility, that makes him lethal to deal with. He won't put his knife away if he feels divinely protected from your bullets."

"You think Hayes feels invincible?"

"That's my guess."

"So where's your wife?"

"I was tracking down one of the Marielitos. A hard-core piece of trash from the bottom of Castro's prisons. He called himself a brujo. A witch. He threatened me. My wife. I made arrangements to see she was safe. Physically. What I didn't understand, at the time, was how much *she* believed. You understand? I didn't realize that believing she would die, could make her die. But this man, this Marielito, he knew this. And he sent her things—little tokens I didn't understand, but that had great meaning for her. I told her he could not get to her. I was wrong."

41

"What did he do?"

"She got a doll in the mail, a mutilated doll. There were five little black stones around it representing five gods, and a white candle on its head. From what we pieced together, the doll showed up that afternoon, sometime before lunch. She didn't tell anybody. She didn't call me, or anyone. She went straight upstairs and took a bottle of tranquilizers. Then she drank a bottle of brandy we'd gotten as a gift one Christmas."

"And she was dead when you found her?"

"One of my colleagues, one of the ones protecting her, got worried and found her."

"Did you catch him? The Marielito?"

"Yes."

"You feel guilty."

"Sad. It was why I left Miami. You can't get away from it down there, it's always hand in hand with the drug trade. So I came here."

"A fat lot of good that did you."

9

"It's in here somewhere."

Lena stood on a wooden chair, rummaging through the top shelf of the kitchen pantry. A small brown moth with black markings on its wings landed on the doorjamb.

"Don't worry about it, Lena," Mendez said.

"No, it's in here, unless Beth forgot to get it."

"Beth?"

"She's doing my grocery shopping for the next six months. I hate going to the grocery."

"Why?"

Two more moths flew from the bottom of the pantry, and soared out into the kitchen. Mendez waved them away.

"Because," Lena said. "It's always crowded. The stupid wheels on the baskets get bent and get stuck or veer sideways when you're trying to go straight. There's always a long line at the deli, people are grumpy, and I always *spend* more than—"

"I mean why is this woman doing your grocery shopping?"

"Umm. You told me not to incriminate myself. What did you think of the tape?"

Mendez shrugged. "I'd like to know what it means to Hayes."

"I don't know how much *significance* it has. He only heard her sing it that once, far as I know. An odd thing for him to remember. Well, maybe not. The first time ever he saw her face, and all that, plus . . . here it is. Clos DuBois, Cabernet Sauvignon. I wish she'd put it in the refrigerator."

"You're not supposed to refrigerate it."

"I don't care what the wine rules are, Mendez, I like it better cold."

"We'll put an ice cube in yours. Where are these moths coming from?"

"I guess the pantry. I been having all kinds of trouble lately."

"Where in the pantry?"

"I don't know, I'd have to clean everything out."

"Please?" Mendez said.

Lena stepped out of his way. She went to the cabinet for wine-glasses. Mendez started unloading food on the table.

"Joel, what are you doing?"

"Trying to figure out where . . . Lena." He pulled out a box of Cheerios, peered inside, and wrinkled his nose. "This looks like the problem. There must be a thousand of them right here, cocoons and everything." He turned the box over. "This cereal expired six years ago. How long did you say you've had these moths?"

"I don't know, Mendez, it's not the kind of thing you mark on your calendar."

"Where's your trash can?"

"Under the sink. You aren't going to throw them away?"

He stopped and looked at her. "Were you planning to keep them?"

"Mendez, I didn't invite you here to clean out my pantry."

He nodded and continued unloading boxes, stopping to look in a package of rice. "They're in here, too."

"You going to go through everything in there?" Lena took a corkscrew and eased the bottle of wine open.

"I want you to talk to me about Hayes."

Lena felt her stomach muscles tense. Images rose in her mind—bloody footprints, her sister—nothing she wanted to think about, not now, not tonight.

"You know everything I know," Lena said.

"Your sister told me Hayes was an abused child."

"Bullshit. That was all stuff he made up." Lena glanced at Mendez. He was scrutinizing a box of crackers.

"Why do you say that?"

"If you knew the kind of nasty stuff he told her, you'd know too."

"Why would he make things like that up?"

"As a turn-on. He has a disgusting and perverted libido." Lena handed Mendez a glass of wine, then reached over and loosened his tie. He smiled at her.

Lena stepped back and blinked. God, she thought. Must be feeling the beer. She tried to remember how many Coronas she'd had. What the hell. For one night, she could relax.

"Let's curl up on the couch and talk about something else." She frowned. "We've known each other a long time. Haven't we, Joel?"

Mendez smiled at her, the sweet smile she didn't see very often. He pressed a hand against the small of her back, then his smile faded. He turned back to the pantry.

"Potato chips," he said. "I have never seen so many half-eaten packages of . . ."

Lena drained her glass of wine. Mendez carried an armful of potato chip bags to the trash can. He picked the wine up and refilled Lena's glass.

"What's Jeff after now?" he said. "Why is he focusing on you?"

"Who knows?"

"Jeff gets out of prison, and comes straight after you. Valetta's on his way out, and you think he'll go after your client. This interests me." He glanced at her over his shoulder. "You think it's revenge?"

Lena shifted sideways in her chair. Valetta, at least, was after money. And Mendez was too damn smart.

"I don't know what's in Jeff's head. He's a nut case, Joel. I don't even try."

"I do." Mendez stacked canned goods on the table next to the wine. "So anything you can tell me about him helps me."

Lena put her chin in her hands. She felt dizzy. She closed her eyes and thought about Jeff Hayes. She didn't want to think about Jeff Hayes.

She was aware, suddenly, that Mendez was leaning over her, his face so close she could feel his breath.

"Talk to me, Lena." His eyes were very brown, very steady. She couldn't seem to look away.

"Okay." She swallowed. "Okay, one thing is." She took a breath. "Like Whitney always kept saying how he was two people. I mean that he felt like two people, like he had two sides. The good boy, and the bad boy. And that no matter how much he wanted to be the good boy, he couldn't. Because of what he'd already seen and done. He was marked by Satan, one of Satan's lambs. That's how he put

45

it." Lena put her chin in one hand and blinked at Mendez. She was starting to feel a little sick.

Mendez patted her shoulder, then turned back to the pantry. "Go on, I'm listening."

"She said he wouldn't go into a church because he'd been told, when he was little, that if he did, it would kill him. Eat him up inside with fire, is what he said. And how he joked about it, and said of course it wasn't *really* true, but still she never saw him go into a church."

Mendez unloaded six cans of Green Giant Blunt Cut Unsalted Green Beans on the table. "There are eight more cans of green beans in here."

"That's Beth," Lena said. "She's into coupons."

Mendez refilled her wineglass. "What else did your sister tell you?"

Lena took another sip of wine. She smiled, though she wasn't sure what she was smiling at.

"Go on," Mendez said.

"Trust me, Joel, you don't want to hear this."

"Yes I do."

"Okay, then, *I* don't want to talk about it." Lena's lower lip quivered. "Please, Joel—"

He was close again, bending over her, and she could smell his cologne. He pushed hair out of her eyes, his hands gentle.

"Did Hayes talk about being taken to ceremonies?" His voice was low and insistent. "About men and women and children, standing around a naked woman? Did he say he saw animals butchered, and drained of blood—that he had to taste the blood?"

Lena put her hands over her ears. She was breathing fast—too much wine, too many beers. Mendez pulled a chair up in front of her. He sat down and pulled her hands away from her ears, his fingers pressing against hers.

"Look at me, Lena."

"No."

"Look at me."

She tried pulling away but he kept hold of her, his hands warm, his grip tight.

"Let me tell you what else he said," Mendez told her. "He said he was forced to drink urine. Eat excrement. Hold a knife and use it. He saw a woman murdered, heard a baby scream."

"How do you know?" Lena took a harsh breath. "How do you know what he said?"

"Who took him? Who made him go to the ceremonies?"

Lena shook her head.

"*Who?*"

He was close to her, too close. Lena pulled back and glared at him.

"His *mother*. And his grandparents. There was an uncle and some cousins." Lena snatched her hands away. "You see what I mean? No mother would do something like that. You're telling me his family—"

"There are hard-core groups, Lena. Family groups. They brutalize their children from generation to generation."

"Here? In the kind of little town where Hayes grew up?"

Mendez nodded. "Hayes comes from a classic hard-core situation."

Lena stood up and walked across the room. She backed up against the kitchen counter. "So why didn't he tell anybody? Why didn't he get away?"

"Who would he tell? You didn't believe him; you didn't want to. What happened when Whitney tried to tell? What happened when you told the parole board that Hayes was a Satan worshiper who committed crimes in the name of his religion? Didn't buy it, did they?"

Lena shook her head.

"These people are not stupid. They are good at sleight of hand. They can impress a child, make them believe incredible things. Make them think they see a man killed, then come back to life. Remember, they're drugged. What happens when you drug a child, and tell him he's bad, he belongs to Satan, that Satan will always watch and know? There's a Santa Claus and an Easter bunny. Why not the devil? And when the child reports the things he *thinks* he sees, as well as the things he really saw—"

Lena sighed deeply. "No one believes. If one thing can't be true, the other probably isn't either." She sagged against the sink and folded her arms. "So how do you know what really happened?"

"You don't. But some groups are . . . extremists."

"Extremists. *Why?* What's the point of this?"

Mendez shrugged. "Power, acceptance, and always, always, drugs. The people in the group may be looking to fit in, to get high,

47

easy sex. But the leaders usually have a good, old-fashioned reason. Money and power. Pornography, sex—young women, boys, children to exploit."

Lena picked her wineglass up, then put it down. "I don't want to talk about this anymore. I don't want to talk to *you* anymore. This was supposed to be a nice evening."

"Was it?"

"I'm going upstairs and go to bed. You do whatever you want down here, Joel. When you're done with the pantry, the basement could use some work." Lena kicked her chair sideways. "And don't throw away my Cheerios."

10

Lena wondered what Mendez had done with the coffee.

The kitchen was spotless, the pantry neat and organized, the old box of Cheerios gone. When she opened the pantry door, nothing happened in the way of moths flying out.

The phone rang.

"Lena? Rick. Maynard is peeing on the rug in my bathroom."

"I wonder if he's sick or something."

"I think he just likes the rug."

"Keep the door closed."

"Keep the door closed, keep the lid down, we might as well still be married."

"Rick, if you just called to complain, I wish you would—"

"I *called* to tell you I found your man. Or didn't find him, more like. He quit right after the Valetta robbery. Advised paying the claim to the savings and loan, and turned in his resignation."

"Did he say why?"

"Now, how would I know?"

"Did he?"

"Resigned due to medical reasons. That's all I got."

"Where did he go after that?"

"Nada. Can't find a record of him anywhere."

"So access his medical records."

"I did. Nothing there. He had a case of the clap right before he resigned. No other problems I could see."

"That's funny."

"If you think the clap is funny, you ain't never had it, girl."

"No, it's odd. That he quit right then. It was Bennelton Insurance Company, wasn't it?"

"Um hmmm."

"Their home office in Cleveland?"

"Louisville."

"I thought that was a district office. Because I know somebody down there."

"Small world. Want me to keep looking for him?"

"Please. And wash the rug with white vinegar."

"Honey, I'm going to burn it." He was silent a moment. "Speaking of Louisville . . ."

"You always ace the audition, Rick."

"Yeah, I do."

"It's the performance you . . . I'm kidding, don't squawk. Break a leg."

Lena curled up on the couch with a pencil, a pad, and the telephone. "Bennelton Property and Casualty. May I help you?"

"I'd like to speak to Christy Neil, please."

"One moment."

"Bennelton Property and Casualty, how may I assist you?"

"Christy? It's Lena. Lena Padgett."

"How you been, girlfriend?"

"Surviving. You?"

"I be bad, I, hang on . . . *Bennelton Property and Casualty, how may I help you? I see. You would need to speak with Ms. Deener in our personnel office, please hold.* You there, girlfriend? How's Rick? He still got that ponytail?"

"No, he got rid of that."

"Umm, too bad. He fine, though. Any way you look."

"I don't look."

"He fine and you stupid."

"How's Marty? You still letting him sponge?"

"Marty know how to give a girl what she like, uh-huh, and that's all I need right now."

"What I need's to ask you a question. About a claims investigator who worked for Bennelton eight years ago. His name is Harry Straczynski. He quit after handling a robbery of a savings and loan."

"Straczynski, Straczynski. Lord, girlfriend, you mean Harry

50

Zyn. He bad, honey, but nice if you don't be hanging on. He probably dead now."

"*Dead?*"

"That why he . . . *Bennelton Property and Casualty, how may I assist you? Yes, ma'am. You would need to fill out a form for that and mail it to our office here in Louisville. I'll be happy to send it, just give me your address. Yes? Uh-huh. And the zip? Oh-eight. Yes. Thank you.* You there, girlfriend? Ole Harry, he real sick, he have the cancer or something real bad. Got a few months left, what he say. Tell all the girls good-bye, and quit the company. Going to travel, he say, for his last few weeks. He sad, he bad, everybody mad."

"What did you really think of this guy?"

"He one those boys you can have the good time with, uh-huh, but don't let it go no further, uh-unh, he break your heart and take you money."

"Like Marty."

"Marty, he fine. Nice thing, Marty, he scared of Christy. So long I keep him happy, he behave. But Harry Zyn, no ma'am, he got one my girls pregnant, she got his chile. Nice chile. Harry Zyn, he real smooth with the talking and drinking. How he get information for a case. Take you witness to a bar, and smile his big teeth, and order lots of drinks, and you tell old Harry anything he want to know."

"Good old Harry. Thanks, Christy."

"Anytime, girlfriend. When you coming up and we go out?"

"When you coming down?"

"One of us got to budge sometime."

"I may actually be up there in a few months."

"You call me, girlfriend, and tell me when."

"I will. 'Bye, Christy."

"Tell Rick hi from Christy girl."

"You trying to make Marty jealous?"

11

The Cutlass was low on gas and running rough.

Lena parked in the small lot in front of Eloise Valetta's apartment building. Weeds were sprouting through cracks in the asphalt.

"Ah, spring," Lena said.

The front door of the apartment building was warped and stuck in the mostly closed position. Lena had to brace one foot on the door frame and pull hard. She wondered how people did that with bags of groceries or babies in their arms.

The hallway was carpeted in worn lime green shag, and smelled of cigarette smoke and sour dishrags. Lena ran up the stairs to the second floor and knocked at Eloise Valetta's door. The television in the next apartment was turned way up. A man invited a shrieking woman to *"Come on down!"*

Lena heard little feet pounding a threadbare carpet, and the door swung open. Charlie put his hands behind his back and stared up at her.

"No, Charlie, how many times I told you, *don't—*"

"Hi, Charlie," Lena said.

He stuck a finger in his mouth. "Hi."

"Charlie!"

Eloise appeared behind him, scowling and out of breath. She looked scared for a moment, then her face cleared.

"Hi, Lena." She put a hand to her chest and took a deep breath. "Come on in."

There were newspapers and magazines on the living room floor. A cardboard box that said Del Monte Freestone Sliced Peaches was brimming over with clean laundry.

"Can I get you some—"

"No, thank you." Lena sat down on the couch.

The radio was playing in the kitchen. A coffee can full of broken crayons had been dumped out next to a thin pastel coloring book with the Easter bunny on the cover. The book was untouched. Charlie sat in front of the crayons and began arranging the pieces.

Eloise sat on a stool and went back to the laundry she was folding. "Tell Miss Lena what you got on."

Charlie ignored her.

Eloise leaned toward Lena.

"Batman underpants." She spoke in a whisper and grinned. "Second day, and *no* accidents." Eloise folded her arms tightly. "Been in his drawer for more'n a year, and yesterday, he points and says *no* to the diaper, wanting those underpants. I swear, I'm ready to jump up and down. Been so excited I coulda had an accident myself."

Lena tried to smile.

"Something's wrong." Eloise unfolded her arms and rested her hands on her knees. "Charlie. Take those crayons in your room."

Charlie peered at an orange crayon, hesitated, and set it down. He picked up a piece of yellow crayon.

"Charlie." Eloise scooped the crayons into the coffee can and handed them to her son. "Go on back in the bedroom. Right now."

Charlie took the coffee can and trudged down the hall. Eloise reached into the box of laundry and pulled out a pair of navy polyester pants. She folded them and set them on the chair in front of the stool.

"Tell me about Harry Zyn," Lena said.

Eloise rubbed a finger across a pulled thread on the pants. "Who?"

"Harry Zyn. Harry Straczynski. The Bennelton agent who covered the savings and loan Archie robbed."

Eloise pulled a tiny red-and-blue striped shirt from the box and smoothed it on her knees. She shrugged. "What's to tell?"

"I did happen to have it in the back of my mind," Lena said, "to find out what really happened to the robbery money. I thought if we knew what happened, maybe we could get Archie off your back." Lena shrugged. "Not much of a play under the best of circumstances. I don't see Archie as all that reasonable. Particularly as you did take that money." Lena frowned and looked at her feet. "What I don't understand is why you're still in his reach. The reason I'm here's to advise you not to be."

Eloise took a quick breath, and her chest heaved up and down. "I don't know why you got it in your head I took that money. If I can't change your mind I guess there's no more to say."

Lena nodded. "Probably not, if you take that attitude." She stood up and walked to the door.

"I have *dreams* about Archie coming here."

Lena reached for the doorknob. Hayes was problem enough to keep her busy for now.

"Worst thing is what'll happen to Charlie. There's nobody to take care of him but me."

Lena sighed. "I can give you some ideas on how and where to disappear."

"You going to give me the money, too?"

"I'm not the one who *has* a hundred and fifty thousand dollars."

"It was a hundred and thirty-eight thousand. And I ain't got it now."

"Must have been a great day for the malls."

"I never had it."

Lena leaned against the doorjamb. "See, I can't help you when you tell me lies. There's nothing to work with, besides being offensive."

"You honestly think I'd live in this dump if I had that kind of money? You think I'd put my clean laundry in a box, and my boy got no more toys than you see on this floor?"

"I think you're a pretty poor budgeter."

Eloise pointed to the couch. "You sit down there and I'll tell you what happened."

"I'm listening." Lena folded her arms.

"Harry Zyn is one of those men who looks at you like there's nobody else for miles, and listens to everything you say. Everybody likes him. And when a guy like that focuses on you . . . I told you I drank a lot. I didn't even know I told him about the money, until when I woke up one morning, we was in bed at the Red Badge Motel. He said we'd go off together, to Rio, but I guess you know the rest of that story. All I got from Harry was a night or two feeling pretty, and a whole lot of words."

"And the clap."

"How'd you know?"

"I checked your medical records."

"Now, how can you do that when I can't even look at them?"

Lena sat back down on the couch. "Eloise, the patient is about the only person who doesn't have access. That's beside the point. What are you going—"

The phone rang.

"Look," Eloise said. "I got to answer that. It may be a cake order. Please, don't go yet."

She went to the kitchen. Lena heard her say hello twice, mutter something about wrong numbers that hung up without even saying they were sorry, then put down the receiver.

Eloise came back into the living room and sat down on the stool. She leaned forward.

"I got no people I can go back to. Nobody that wouldn't be worse than Archie."

"They might protect your son."

"Yeah, but he'd be better dead. I won't have him grow up like I did. Them days is over, and I ain't going back. You don't want to help me, okay. But did you really expect me to say, yeah, I had the money, but *sorry*, now it's gone?"

"I expected the truth. If I'm wasting my time looking for something that isn't there, I can't help you."

Eloise lifted a small pair of boy's jeans and folded them. "I'm not sure what you can do to help me, anyhow."

Lena shrugged. "It comes down to inconvenience. If it is more inconvenient for Archie to bother you than to go away, he'll go away."

"He'll kill me first."

"There's that. He know about Charlie?"

"No."

"Then we can keep him out of it. I need to know more about Archie. What he's scared of—"

Eloise laughed. "Archie ain't scared of nothing."

"Got to be something."

"You don't get it. Archie hung around too much with your sister's husband. He thinks he got the devil on his side. That's why he didn't take care of that money like he should. He was sure Satan would get him off. He's nutty on it. He was shocked all to pieces when he went to jail."

Lena sighed. She unlaced her tennis shoes. "You mind?" she asked Eloise. "I think better when I'm barefooted."

"Go on and get comfortable."

Lena slipped her tennis shoes off and sat cross-legged on the couch. "Give me a pile of those clothes and I'll help you fold. And while we do it, we're going to talk about Archie. You were married to him once, you ought to know the soft spots."

Eloise grabbed an armful of clothes and deposited them on the couch. "He's allergic to peanuts."

"I guess that's a start. We could corner him and force-feed him Jif."

Charlie picked the cheese and pepperoni off a slice of pizza.

"Eat the crust, too," Eloise said absently. She leaned over and wiped sauce off his ear. "I can't think of nothing else. I told you everything except he wears boxer shorts."

"*Does* he?"

"Yeah."

"Doesn't seem the type."

"What is the type?"

"With men, you never can tell."

Lena leaned back on the couch, careful not to scatter the neatly folded laundry. She had suggested sending out for pizza without thinking and felt guilty because Eloise had insisted on paying half. But she knew a lot more about Archie now, including his preference for undershorts. He was a fanatical photographer, thought crickets were lucky, and didn't like spiders. He was allergic to peanuts, would not drink beer from a glass, worked, when he did work, as a roofer, loved basketball games, thought soccer was for sissies, and was happiest on his Harley.

"Tell me more about the motorcycle gang he used to ride with."

"The Grits? Don't know much. He'd quit them before we got married. He got a scar on his arm from when they burned off his tattoo."

"Burned it off? Nice. Why did he quit?"

"Got *kicked* out. Their tattoo was one of those, you know, like they have in those desert places. A scorpion. Black one, on his arm. When he got kicked out they took hot spoons and just made it into this awful red scar. Archie says he was lucky they didn't kill him."

"Why didn't they?"

56

"Stickboy. The . . . now, what he call him? The sergeant-at-arms. That was Stickboy Madison. He and Archie was real tight, and when Archie got kicked out, Stickboy burned the tattoo off and beat him up real bad. But he didn't kill him, and to hear Archie talk, it was some kind of big favor. I guess that's the one thing Archie *is* afraid of. Them Grits, and mainly Stickboy. He was always real careful to make sure he didn't do nothing to step on their toes."

"And you don't know why they kicked him out?"

"Archie never would say. But he hinted some. I think it was on account of some pictures he took? See, he used to have this little plastic camera, and he could hold it like at his waist? It was like them old-fashioned kind, with the little window in the top, so he didn't have to hold it up to his face. He called it something—oh, hip shooting, that was it. Most the time, nobody would notice that he was taking pictures."

"Camera of choice for blackmailers," Lena said. "You think he tried to blackmail somebody in the gang?"

"He wouldn't tell me if he did. But that'd be Archie all over."

"What do you know about the Grits?"

Eloise shrugged. "Not much."

"This may be the way to the ticklish spot. I'll have to research this gang, see what I can come up with. If Stickboy Madison told Archie to leave you alone, would he?"

"Oh, you bet."

"That leaves one really hard part."

"Which be?"

"Getting something on Stickboy to make him call Archie off for us."

"Be easier to convince the devil."

"That's an idea, too."

12

Lena saw him at the stoplight. The Cutlass was still running rough and she had the window down, so she could listen to the engine. The guttural sputter of a Harley caught her attention.

The man straddled his bike, one booted heel resting on the pavement. He wore a black tank top and blue jeans, his hair reddish gold and frizzy beneath a Greek fisherman's cap. It was hard to tell where the hair stopped and the beard began. But what really got her thinking was the scar on his bicep. A ragged red scar, where you might expect a tattoo.

The light turned green, and the bike roared through the intersection. Lena checked her mirror for cops, then did an illegal U-turn.

Definitely headed in the right direction. He pulled into the right lane, bike canting from side to side with grace and precision. If he turned right . . . but no, he was headed into Cutler's Food Mart.

Lena sighed.

The bike zigzagged through the grocery's parking lot and exited onto Kearney Street, avoiding the red light and the intersection. Lena pulled in after him. Whoever he was, he was less than two miles from Eloise's apartment.

The biker turned left at the stop sign, and Lena accelerated. The car jerked and did not respond. Lena checked the gas gauge. The needle was well to the left of empty. She coasted down the hill.

The car quit a half mile too soon. Lena pulled to the side of the road, and a man in a navy blue Lynx honked and roared around her. She looked for a pay phone, but the area was downtrodden residential, with nothing likely in sight.

She went to the trunk, got her baseball bat, wished for a gun. She took off running down the street.

The bike sat in the apartment parking lot, and the door to the building stood open. Lena steadied herself against the doorjamb, chest heaving, while she caught her breath. She knocked at the first ground-floor apartment. There was movement behind the peephole, but the door did not open. She knocked at the door across the hall. Nothing.

A child screamed, staccato and shrill.

"Call the cops!" Lena yelled, kicking the first door she'd tried.

She could hear Charlie wail as she ran up the stairs. Her hands grew slippery on the bat. A woman screamed—Eloise—her voice mixing with her son's in a high-pitched cacophony of panic.

Blood. A child watching. Predator male.

This time, Lena thought, I will not let it happen. This time I'll get there first.

In her mind's eye she saw Hayes—curly black hair, cold blue eyes, jawline edged with five o'clock shadow. Pressed black pinstripe suits, a voice in the middle of the night, seashells on the pillow.

The door was ajar. Lena went through.

The folded laundry had been knocked sideways and strewn across the floor. The stool was overturned, the magazines scattered.

"No, no, Archie!"

Eloise's voice.

A gurgling cry made the hair stand up on Lena's neck. She ran.

It was close, tight, and dark in the hallway. The walls were spattered with blood. Valetta held a broken bottle, the jagged green edges clotted with tissue. Blood oozed over the Coca-Cola trademark and coated his fingers bright red.

Eloise had one hand clamped over her eyes. She was jammed against the wall, shirt torn open, hair every which way, lips split and puffed. Black blood ran between her fingers. In her other hand she clutched the phone receiver, the broken cord trailing over her shoulder. Eloise's mouth was open, but she made no sound. She slid down the wall and crumpled to the floor.

Charlie stood in the bedroom doorway, belly pouched forward, finger in his mouth. A paralytic stillness had settled over him; a child turned to stone.

Archie Valetta moved toward Lena, wary but unafraid. He was

muscular—a prison weight lifter. An inverted silver cross hung from his right ear. He looked at the bat and smiled.

Probably figures I don't have the nerve, Lena thought.

She swung the bat sideways and cracked it solidly against the side of Valetta's left knee. He roared and fell backward. She swung the bat up over his head.

Valetta rolled. He snatched Charlie's legs, knocking the child to the floor. Charlie sobbed, scooted sideways, and curled into a ball.

Lena reached for him.

Valetta was there ahead of her, gathering the child close, tucking the small head under his chin. Static electricity mingled Charlie's fine blond hair with Valetta's coarse red beard.

The stink of sweat was thick.

"Back off, bitch." Valetta squeezed and Charlie whimpered softly. "I don't know who the *fuck* you think you are, Wonder Woman, but if you give a shit about this kid, you better back off now."

Sweat rolled down Valetta's temples, and his breath came in great heaving gulps.

"Put the kid down," Lena said. "Do it now." She arced the bat toward his knee.

Valetta put a huge hand on Charlie's throat, covering the small neck from sternum to chin.

"Just a squeeze, little girl. That's all it'll take."

A wet stain spread across the front of Charlie's blue cotton shorts, and urine ran in a trickle down his leg. The little body sagged in Valetta's arms, as if the child could take anything but that final shame.

And Valetta was on his feet, moving sideways, crablike.

"Don't call the cops, bitch. I see a cop and I'll throw the kid off the bike."

Lena was still holding the bat when Mendez came. He was there, as always, in time to pick up the pieces. Lena saw him take everything in; the laundry, so carefully washed and folded, now strewn across the couch and the floor; the empty pizza box, crumpled on the side where it had been trampled; the torn coloring book.

He almost came to her, then held back. Perceptive, she thought. In her mind she saw her sister in the driveway.

Don't think about it. Don't think.

60

Lena bounced the bat on the carpet. Mendez went into the kitchen. Eloise had been starting another cake when Archie had arrived. There were blood splats on the kitchen floor. Lena had seen them when she went to call for help, forgetting, in her panic, that the phone had been ripped from the wall. A bowl full of batter had overturned and dripped down the side of the cabinet, drying like beige enamel. One of the kitchen chairs lay on its side. Someone had set the pieces of the telephone neatly on the chipped Formica table. GenTel was going to be pissed.

Lena saw Mendez pass from the kitchen to the hallway.

Eloise had lost a lot of blood. The thick oval stain would be drying to a brown crust on the fringes of the worn shag carpet.

Lena shifted her weight, back aching, uncomfortable on the stool where Eloise Valetta had faced her this afternoon. She heard the bedroom door open. One of the uniforms frowned when she got up, but didn't say anything. The lab techs were in the hallway, so she could only stare down the tunnel of darkness at Mendez's back. He stood in the bedroom doorway, then turned and faced her.

"Too late again," Lena said. And saw, from the look in his eyes, that she'd scored a hit.

13

Lena's hands were trembling. Patrolman Geer leaned close and showed her how to buckle the seat belt as if it were a new form of technology. Lena fumbled it twice before the latch snapped home.

A woman's voice, wrapped in static, crackled from the radio. Something to somebody—call dispatch.

Lena felt strange in the police car. Strange, cold, important.

They had driven her crazy, asking how she felt—the ambulance crew, Mendez, even the woman from next door. Ms. Kilmer in 1B, kind but ridiculous in pink bicycle shorts and a black tube top. She had come immediately at Lena's knock, and had called for help while Lena tried to staunch Eloise's bleeding.

Lena looked at her hands. Clean now; she'd washed them. But there were dark brown stains on her Royal Robbins hiking shirt, on the front of her blue jeans, and on the tops of her shoes.

"He gouged her eye out," Lena said.

The patrolman glanced at her once, and kept driving.

"Mendez will get him," he said. "You be sure of that."

The radio crackled again.

"Getting busy out tonight," Geer said. "Usually not like this till the weekends. Gets going around eleven, then tapers down around three A.M. Nobody seems to sleep these days."

White swirls of fog drifted across the headlights.

"Foggy," Geer said.

Lena sat forward, trying to see the road ahead.

"Where I used to live, in Virginia, it would get foggy sometimes in the morning? We'd have forty- or sixty-car pileups on the interstate." He shook his head. "People are funny. Some slow way down, and others speed up, and nobody can see a thing."

"Which is it you do?"

A stoplight burned red through the haze and Geer eased the car to a stop. A Cadillac with dark-tinted windows and throbbing speakers paused, then went left, trailing irritation into the night.

Lena leaned her head against the side window, feeling cool glass on her right cheek.

"What I do is pull off," Geer said. The light turned green, and he eased the cruiser forward.

Lena glanced at his face, young and tired in the glow from the dash.

"You carry a baseball bat everwhere you go?" Geer asked.

Lena pushed hair out of her eyes. "In the trunk of my car. And one under the bed."

"Gun be easier," Geer said.

"We were afraid to have guns," Lena said softly. "With Kevin in the house."

The patrol car cruised the familiar territory of her neighborhood. It was odd to find her street looking just the same. Her house was dark.

"Kevin your son?"

"Nephew."

"I got a niece in Wilmington."

"No, don't," Lena said, when Geer opened his door. "Just drop me right here. And thanks."

"Sure you're okay?"

She'd been dying to tell someone how okay she was. That it felt pretty good, swinging that bat. Strong. Controlled. Scared shitless.

"I'm fine," she said, and slammed the door shut.

Officer Geer kept his cruiser poised at the curb, engine idling, while she walked through the grass to the porch. The illumination from the headlights gave her just enough light.

Lena held her right wrist steady with her left hand, so she could fit the key in the lock. Four tries and she got it. Geer didn't leave till she shut the door and locked it.

Lena took a deep breath. Her mind flashed a vision of Charlie, eyes dull, glazed with shock. Mendez would have to find him. If anybody could, it would be Mendez.

Mendez, Mendez, Mendez.

Her impulse was to get in the Cutlass and go looking. Do *something*. But the Cutlass was out of gas on Birken Street, and her knees felt like jelly. She leaned against the doorjamb and closed her eyes.

She was aware of the faintest trace of sweetness in the air. Men's cologne—something or other by Calvin Klein. She smelled it every time she went into Glenden's Department Store, and she had smelled it on Mendez, up close.

Mendez would find Charlie. *She* would find Charlie.

Lena went to the kitchen for the last of the Clos DuBois. She got a glass from the top shelf of the cabinet and tucked the wine bottle between her ribs and her elbow. She would curl up on the couch and drink it all.

The living room was dark and still, oddly tense in the dimness. The smell of cologne was stronger. The light from the kitchen showed an empty room, but Lena stopped, then took one step backward.

A dark head rose from behind the couch. Even in the dark, she knew him. Lena dropped the bottle of wine.

"Surprise."

The wineglass broke between Lena's fingers, and her hands grew wet with blood. Hayes switched on the three-way lamp—snap-snap-snap to the highest brilliance, then snap-snap back to a dim yellow glow.

He wore a new suit, expensive, deep gray. His hair looked soft, dark, and full, and his eyes were blue, cold, and still.

He took a black silk handkerchief from his left breast pocket, and stepped close to take hold of her hands. His skin was sallow, unhealthy. Lena jerked her hands away.

"Get the hell out of my house."

The stem of the wineglass fell to the floor. The handkerchief fluttered behind it.

Hayes smiled. "Don't be afraid, Lena." He picked up the soiled handkerchief, tucked it into his pocket, and settled on the edge of the rocking chair. "I'm just here to talk."

He held up a finger, stained with her blood, and slowly licked it clean.

Lena sat on the edge of the couch, close to the phone. There were slivers of glass in her fingers and palms. Tiny ones. Big ones. They hurt.

Blood dripped down her wrists to her lap. Hayes watched the red trickle with something like rapture in his eyes. Lena wondered if he'd looked at Whitney that way, when she'd died by his hand in the driveway.

He rocked gently in the rocking chair. Lena found herself riveted by the familiar slow rhythm—the comforting creak of old wood, and the memory of Whitney and Kevin, right before bed.

She pulled a shard of glass from the palm of her hand and held it between slick red fingers.

"Hope you haven't spent all that life insurance money, Lena. Got it locked up tight in the bank? I like to think that you know it's not yours. So you won't mind me taking it back."

Lena looked at him, her eyes narrowed. "*Seed* money. You and Archie are looking for seed money."

The smile he gave her was almost sheepish. He spread his hands wide.

"I took out those policies, Lena. On my wife and my child. I paid the premiums. I was beneficiary."

"You can't collect for a killing."

"It should at least have gone to my family. Not *your* bunch, not you Padgetts."

"We let the courts decide, Hayes."

"The courts were wrong."

"It happens. They let *you* out."

Hayes smiled. "How would you like me to go away, and you never see me again? Give me the insurance money, and I'm out of your life."

"Tired of selling cars already?"

He smiled, just a little, and rocked back and forth. His mind seemed elsewhere. "Maybe I don't want that money, anyhow. I like it here, with you. Like old times. Old, old times." Hayes kept smiling. "How you getting along with Eloise? I told Archie the two of you had your heads together. I hope Eloise is smart, and gives him what he wants."

Lena winced, remembering Charlie. "She doesn't have it."

Hayes raised his left eyebrow.

"She doesn't."

"Archie won't be happy."

"Listen, Jeff. You get me Charlie back—"

"Charlie?"

"Eloise's little boy."

"Didn't know she had one."

"Yes, you did. Archie took him tonight."

"Definitely not part of his plan, I *don't* think."

"Get me Charlie back from Valetta. And I mean unhurt and in one piece. Then you can have the money. Everything from Whitney and Kevin's insurance policies. Ninety thousand dollars."

"One hundred and fifty. Thousand."

"Legal fees, Jeff." Lena smiled sadly. "Funeral expenses."

"Yes, you did a nice job there, but you got soaked." He stopped rocking and cocked his head sideways. "Why do you care about getting the kid back?"

"Why do you care why I care?"

The doorbell rang. It rang again. Lena stood up.

"Just let whoever it is go away," Hayes said.

The doorbell rang again. Twice.

"I'll get rid of them." Lena waited for Hayes to object, but he stayed in the chair, rocking.

Lena undid the locks and flung the door hard, smacking it into the wall. Mendez stood, frowning, on her porch. He saw the blood on her hands.

"He's in the living room!"

She turned, shoes skidding on the plank floor, Mendez running past her.

The rocking chair was empty. The sliding glass door was open, and a breeze rattled the wooden miniblinds. The wind chimes rang, like tiny silver bells.

14

"You're not going to catch him."

"Let *go*."

"Lena. Come on. Back in. He's—"

"You don't believe he was here, do you?"

"I believe he was here." Mendez led her back through the living room and up the stairs.

"He's not up *there*."

"No, but your bathroom is. Just a minute, I'll be right back."

Lena glanced around the bathroom, wishing she'd put up the shampoo, the wet washrag, and particularly the red lace bra that hung on the towel bar. She followed Mendez's progress by listening to his footsteps—going down the stairs, into the kitchen, then back up the stairs again. He came back to the bathroom with a green ceramic bowl.

"I make meatloaf in that," Lena said.

He filled the bowl with warm soapy water. "Soak your hands in there. You have any gauze, bandages . . . first-aid stuff?"

"Medicine cabinet. Yank hard, it's kind of rusted shut."

He pulled once, then again, harder.

"Mendez?"

"Hmmm?"

"Would you mind just—"

He sighed. "This is it?"

"What'd you expect, General Hospital?"

"Every home should have . . . at least more than a dried-up bottle of peroxide and two crumpled Band-Aids. Dinosaur Band-Aids. Never mind. I have a first-aid kit in my car."

"I just bet you do."

His voice floated back from the stairs. "Plain bandages, though. Mine don't have little dinosaurs on them."

"Hey!" she yelled. "*Beth* got those on *sale!*"

The front door slammed, then a car door opened and closed. The water in the bowl was turning pink. Lena's hands throbbed. She leaned her head against the wall.

Mendez came through the door with a blanket tucked under one arm, a white plastic case, and a disconcerting air of purpose. He set the case on the bathroom counter, scooting three brands of skin lotion and a Lowila cleansing bar up against the wall. One of the bottles of lotion wobbled, fell off the counter, and landed in the overflowing trash can. Mendez leaned down to pick it up.

"Don't bother."

"No? Going to grow old gracefully?"

"Be still my heart, you made a joke."

He tucked the blanket around her shoulders. She rubbed her cheek against it.

"Scratchy," she said.

"Wool."

"Cotton is softer."

"Wool is warmer."

"You better take it off me, for real, Mendez. I might get blood on it."

He took off his sport coat and hung it on a brass hook on the back of the bathroom door.

"Won't be the first time."

Lena eyed the blanket and pushed it away from her face. Mendez unfastened his cuff links, set them on the back of the toilet, and rolled up his sleeves.

"You're starting to make me nervous," Lena said.

He selected a needle out of the white plastic box, and doused it with alcohol.

"What's that for? I've got tweezers somewhere."

He smiled at her. "Only take you a week to find them."

"I think they're with my makeup stuff."

"I have tweezers. I like a needle better. My wife used to go barefoot all the time. I dug out a lot of splinters."

He sat on the side of the tub, his knees touching hers. He took a red towel off the rack and folded it on his lap. He patted the towel.

Lena laid her hands down on the ridged terrycloth.

"Ow."

"I haven't touched you yet."

She peered down at her hands. "Think I need stitches?"

"No. Lena?"

"Hmmm?"

"You're in my light. Sit back now. Relax."

"Why do people always say that?"

She sat back and let her head rest against the wall. Her shoulder knocked the top of the toilet tank and the cuff links fell to the floor.

"Damn."

"I'll get them later. Be still."

"How bad was Eloise, Mendez? Did you hear anything from the hospital?"

"She's still in shock. He hurt her, Lena, but she'll live. Somebody's there now, waiting to talk to her."

"He stuck that bottle, that broken bottle, into her eye. Doesn't that get to you?"

"Would it depress you to know I've seen worse?"

"I can't stand it, thinking about—ouch, oh, stop a minute, *Mendez*."

"Be still. Okay. I got it."

"Thinking about Charlie. He's such a sweet boy, he shouldn't be in the middle of all this."

Mendez held her wrists, his gaze steady. "In the middle of what?"

"Of this *mess*, Mendez."

"Go on. Tell me the whole story."

"I already told you everything."

"No."

Lena stared at him, deciding he had the steadiest, most penetrating brown eyes.

"She's my client," Lena said finally.

"You want Charlie back? Give me everything, so I can find him. We don't have much time."

"What do you think Archie will do with him?"

Mendez raised one eyebrow. Lena thought of Hayes.

"It would help," Mendez said, "if I knew why he took him."

"He . . ."

"Lena. I've been a cop a long time. I've seen a lot of women, too many women, get beat up by husbands, ex-husbands, their boy-friends. Like you said, I pick up the pieces." He looked down at her hands. "Some men want to hurt, some want to humiliate. A lot of them hit in places people won't see. Some just lash out, blind rage.

"Eloise Valetta's injuries were systematic. Inflicted with maxi-mum pain in mind. What was it he wanted? The robbery money?" He leaned forward. "You're running a big risk, Lena. If this beating gets kicked to Domestic, that means no manpower on the kidnap-ping. And if and when we do catch up to Valetta, Family Court. *Mediation* instead of criminal prosecution. It's in Charlie's best interest to connect this up to the robbery."

Lena leaned against the wall. She began to shake.

"Okay, Mendez, you're right. God, you got that glass out yet?"

"It's out."

"I'm going to be sick. Go away, would you?"

He moved quickly, dumping the bowl full of bloody water into the sink.

"*Go.*"

He slipped the bowl into her lap and pulled her hair back out of the way, then was ready with a cool rag when she was done.

She took the rag with trembling fingers and bathed her face. Tears streamed from her eyes.

"It just hit all of a sudden."

"It does that." He took the bowl from her lap.

"Give me that."

He ignored her.

"I want out of these clothes, they're *bloody*. I want a shower."

"Wait on that. Get undressed, sponge off. I'll get you something to wear."

He left, shutting the bathroom door behind him.

She sat cross-legged on the floor and took off the brown-spat-tered shoes. There were stains on the cuff of her left sock. Blood had stiffened on her jeans and shirt, and she peeled out of them and tossed them in the trash. She heard the sound of dresser drawers opening and closing, the squeak of her closet door.

"There's a big T-shirt," she yelled through the door. "Football jersey. Second drawer, left-hand side."

The closet door closed and a drawer opened and shut. Mendez knocked.

"Lena?"

She opened the door a crack and he handed her the shirt.

Lena slid the T-shirt over her head. It hung to her knees, loose and baggy. She rinsed her mouth and brushed her teeth. The telephone rang.

"Mendez?"

"Got it."

His feet pounded the staircase.

"There's an extension in the bedroom!" She opened the bathroom door, strained her ears for the murmur of his voice. She went back in the bathroom for the blanket, avoided looking at the clothes she had tossed into the trash, and padded down the stairs.

Mendez was sitting in her chair, phone to one ear.

"Yes," he said. "No, he hasn't checked in. Stay on it. I'll send you some relief around six."

Lena curled up on one end of the couch and tucked her feet up under her.

"What?" she said.

"There are two—what would you call them?—under-the-counter doctors, locally. We've staked them out. Valetta may try to get his knee looked at."

"I think I broke it."

Mendez nodded. "I'm going to make you a cup of tea, Lena. Then I'm going to give you a couple of tranks—"

"No, I don't want them. Hayes might—"

"He won't come back tonight, and if he does I'll be here. I had all my calls routed here when I left Eloise Valetta's apartment. Any news, I'll wake you up. Okay?"

Lena nodded. Mendez got up and headed for the kitchen.

"Mendez? I don't think I *have* any tea."

"You do."

15

Lena woke up on the couch, mouth cottony, head pounding. Mendez was asleep in her chair. He'd taken off his shoes and put his feet up, and a legal pad and a pen lay in his lap. His hands were folded and his head was tilted sideways.

Lena swung her legs over the side of the couch and rubbed the back of her neck.

He even slept neatly.

She went upstairs and got in the shower, adjusting the water to the highest heat she could stand. She stood under the shower head, letting the water run, while steam misted and swirled.

She still felt groggy from the pills.

Lena toweled her hair dry and found a pair of clean jeans. She put the football jersey back on, grimacing when her hair, still wet, made a cold spot on the back of the shirt.

She went to Kevin's old room, sat on the dusty carpet, and wrapped her arms around her knees.

She had meant to think and plan, but dozed off instead, head on the top of her knees. A soft knock and the creak of wood woke her. Mendez stood in the doorway, the hallway dark behind him. The morning sun, rosy pink, filtered in through the animal-print curtains.

Mendez came close and looked down at her.

"What did you mean the other night? When you said it was supposed to be a nice evening?"

Lena shrugged. Mendez sat across from her on the floor. He crossed his legs and put his chin in his hands, looking, Lena decided, as though he would be content to sit in that one place forever.

72

Lena reached out and traced the line of his jaw. Her finger was thick, padded with gauze and white surgical tape. She touched the stiff white collar of his shirt. "You dress very neatly. You even sleep neatly." She undid the top button of his shirt. "And you're always prepared. First-aid kit. Blankets. Tell me, Joel, do you also have condoms?"

He leaned forward and kissed her slowly. She took a breath and tugged him down on the floor.

He touched her cheek and pushed her hair back off her shoulder. The hair held his interest. He took a handful of the black coarse curls, then put his hand behind her neck and brought her closer. Lena hooked her leg over his, feeling his warmth, smelling the faint scent of cologne—the same kind Hayes liked to wear.

She grimaced. All the men in my life.

He put both hands under the back of her shirt, fingers massaging the tight muscles. His hands moved up to her shoulders and down her spine—then around to her waist and up to her breasts.

Strong warm fingers. His touch went from firm to delicate.

She kissed him, eyes closed, and undid the other buttons on his shirt. She lifted the jersey up over her head. It tangled in her hair, then came off.

He rolled her gently to her back and settled his weight onto her. She wrapped her arms around him and he buried his face in her hair and neck, kissing her throat, cupping her breasts in his hands.

Over his shoulder, the child's mobile was dazzling behind dust motes and sunlight.

"Lena? What is it?"

She scrambled to get out from under.

"What—"

She twisted sideways. "I can't do this."

Abruptly, he let her go. She snatched the jersey and pulled it over her head, inside out.

"It was your job to protect my sister." She looked at him. "It was my job to protect my client."

He reached for her hand, but she yanked it away. She was out of the room, down the stairs, and out the front door in seconds.

The phone was ringing as she went.

16

His car was still in front of the house.

Lena shivered, hesitating at the edge of the porch. The grass was ice cold and the bottoms of her jeans sagged with dew. Her ankles itched and her hair was still damp on her shoulders.

She went in, closing the door softly.

It was warm inside, and she sighed deeply. The house was rich with the smell of coffee.

Go on, Joel, she thought. Make yourself at home. Don't be a stranger to my kitchen. She took a breath and headed for the living room. Definitely going to be awkward.

Mendez was on the phone. He glanced at her over his shoulder, and she veered into the kitchen. Mendez had her favorite black mug, so she took the white one and filled it with coffee. She sat on the couch and waited for Mendez to quit talking. His shirt was only slightly wrinkled, and his tie was neatly knotted.

The coffee scorched her tongue, and was warm going down. Mendez hung up the phone and looked at her.

"Developments?" she asked.

"Valetta's been spotted in Tennessee. Knoxville. With the boy."

Lena put the coffee cup down. "Where exactly?"

"Doctor's office. One of those places I told you about, bad part of town. Specialize in bullet and knife wounds that people don't want reported. He was seen by an Alfred Ritterman—Knoxville PD. He'd been on duty all night and heard the APB. On his way off shift this morning, he stopped to meet an informant at a Dunkin' Donuts place across from this office. And he saw Valetta and the child."

Lena stood up. "So they've got him!"

"No. He met with his informant, but he didn't really register until Valetta had been in for a while. As soon as he remembered he called for backup, but they didn't get there in time. He kept watch on the place, but figures Valetta left from the back."

"Aw, hell."

Mendez looked grim. "Can't watch two doors at the same time. Knoxville PD has two detectives on the way right now, to question the doctor and her staff. I'm driving down this morning."

"I want to go with you."

Mendez nodded. "Lena, when exactly did Eloise Valetta divorce Archie? She *did* divorce him?"

"Sure she did." Lena stared at her feet. Surely, *surely*, Eloise had divorced Archie.

"Can you say when?"

"How would I know?"

"Listen. If this can in any way be construed as a custody fight, I'll be pulled off. I told my captain they were positively divorced before the child was even conceived."

Lena took a breath. "Thank you, Mendez."

"You need to find out for sure, Lena. Get the details, and make sure the paperwork is in order. If there is any question . . ."

"She's his *mother*."

"Eloise will be better off if she has a statement of custody. You know any lawyers?"

"One. But the guy to hit first is Rick."

"Your ex-husband?" Mendez glanced at his watch. "Better do it."

Lena picked up the phone. "This early, at least I know he'll be home."

The phone rang six times before a woman answered. Her voice was low and seductive, though all she said was hello.

"Judith? This is Lena."

"Lena. How you doing, cupcake?"

"I know I woke you up and I'm sorry, but this is kind of an emergency."

"You didn't wake me up, I haven't gone to bed. What's wrong? You need Ricky?"

Lena let out a sigh of relief. "Yeah, if you don't mind."

"It's him that'll mind."

"Asleep?"

"Ummm. Listen, cupcake, he told me about Jeff. I want you to know, you can come stay with us as long as you want."

"I always wanted to sleep three in a bed."

Judith chuckled. "Don't think Ricky wouldn't love it. Hang on while I get him."

Lena waited. Mendez looked at his watch.

"Lena?" Rick's voice was deeper, thicker than usual.

"What's . . . is something wrong?"

"Rick, I got trouble and I can't explain. I need a favor."

"Another one?"

Lena heard Judith fussing at him in the background. "Yeah, another one. I need you to check some courthouse records and the dissolution of a marriage—"

"The courthouse isn't even open yet."

"I'm on my way out of town. Do it when you can. As *soon* as you can." Mendez had shrugged into his suit coat. "Look, Rick, I got to go up and put on some clothes. You remember Sergeant Mendez? He'll tell you what we need."

"Put on some—"

"Here." Lena handed the phone to Mendez. "He can figure out the dates and stuff. Tell him what we need and I'll be right back."

Lena ran up the stairs.

She got dressed quickly—black leotard, another pair of clean jeans, a jacket. She did a genuinely fast job on the makeup—mascara, yes; blush, no. She was ready in fifteen minutes, but could not find her watch. Had she taken it off in Kevin's room?

The door was ajar. The curtains were open, for the first time in seven years. Something silver glinted in the middle of the floor. Her watch. She slid it over her wrist.

Something was off, besides the curtains. She glanced around the room, frowning. She slid her jacket over her shoulders, then looked once more in the far left corner.

The mobile was gone—no more red-checked lion, hippo, and giraffe. Mendez had taken it down. She went into the corner and examined the tiny scars on the wall. He'd even taken the hooks out.

Now the room was truly empty.

17

They stopped at a doughnut place for coffee, corn muffins, and raspberry doughnuts. Even with the coffee, Mendez was drooping.

"Pull over," Lena said. "I can get to Knoxville."

"You're tired."

"*I'm* bouncing off the walls. Switch over and let me drive."

Lena licked sugar off her fingers as Mendez pulled the car to the shoulder of the interstate. A tractor trailer truck went past, making the Mazda quake. They got out of the car and switched sides, both keeping a wary eye on traffic. Mendez was grim and unsmiling.

Men, Lena thought. Treat them like shit, they get huffy.

It was still early enough that traffic was thin for such a well-traveled section of road. Lena merged the car into the flow with no trouble. Mendez adjusted his seat to tilt backward. The engine vibrated gently.

"Nice car," Lena said flatly. "It always just start right up when you put the key in? Don't have to crank it?"

Mendez opened one eye, then closed it.

"Mendez. *Joel*. We need to talk."

"The whole idea was for you to drive, and me to sleep."

"I know, but I want to apologize about this morning."

"No need. I understand."

"I don't see how *you* understand, when I'm not even sure I do. I just—"

"Lena, it was a big mistake for both of us. Knowing how you feel about things, I . . . It was unprofessional of me."

"Unprofessional?" Lena raised one eyebrow. "Good *point*, Mendez. You should only make love to strangers you meet in bars."

77

He reached into the caddy behind the gear shift, selected a tape, and slipped it into the cassette player. Tchaikovsky's *1812 Overture*. Lena kept her eyes on the road.

Lena did not like the doctor, and not just because the woman was thinner than she was. Dr. Whitter had hard edges—too much eyebrow pencil, an overabundance of fragrance. *Aliage*, of all things. Lena curled her lip.

"I talked to cops this morning already." Whitter had the kind of deep Tennessee accent that would sound uneducated no matter how much schooling backed it up. There was lipstick smudged on her front tooth.

Brash Pink, Lena decided. Maybelline.

The doctor had received them, after a long wait, in a cramped office that smelled like mildew and gym socks. Lena's chair was hard orange plastic. Mendez's was aqua. Dr. Whitter sat in a padded leather chair behind an immense chipped wooden desk that was covered with a glass top. Dust was thick on the few clear places that were not cluttered with stacks of files, papers, and magazines.

Black wrought-iron shelves overflowed with books on women's health, abortion, tubal ligation, and triage, trauma, and bullet wounds.

"If I did have a patient like you say come in here, and he had an injury such as a badly torn meniscus, and a severely bruised kneecap . . ."

Lena smiled.

". . . it would not, to my knowledge, be a matter for the cops. And I do respect patient confidentiality. You talking bullet wounds, stab wounds—I report downtown. According to standard procedure."

Mendez looked at her steadily. "Let's cut the crap, okay?"

The doctor glared at him. She leaned back in her chair and it creaked as she swiveled from side to side.

"I've seen the report that was taken this morning," Mendez said. "You treated Valetta, and he had a child with him."

"Yeah, so? He had a little 'un along." The doctor's voice was flat. "People bring kids in here all the time."

"What condition was he in?"

"Knee was badly swollen and locked—"

"The *child*."

She shrugged. "Charlene says she gave him a sucker and he ate

78

it up so fast she gave him a whole handful. Most kids, you know, suck on it awhile. But she thought he was hungry, so she filled his pockets with 'em. Charlene's a softie." Whitter shrugged. "She be the one you want to talk to. I didn't see much of him.

"Now, if you don't mind, I got six abortions to do before—"

"How come you don't get picketed, like everybody else?" Lena asked.

" 'Cause I pay 'em off, that's why. They like to close down the places on the nicer side of town. Their big ole cars tend to suffer 'round my neighborhood." She winked. "I see lots of their girls in my office, though. Happens all the time."

Maybe, Lena thought, with the lipstick off her tooth, she might not be all bad. Lena glanced at the worn tile, caked with weeks of dirt, and wondered how she'd feel, coming in here. Probably prefer the places across town.

"Did Valetta say anything, give you any idea where he might be headed?"

"Nope. Paid in cash, and left out the back."

"You understand," Mendez said. "I'm not local. I won't be back to harass you, nobody will know you heard it from me. The child you saw has been kidnapped. Valetta has a bad reputation."

Whitter frowned. "I got nothing to say to you, Sergeant, and you got no jurisdiction here. One thing I *know's* the law. You want to talk at Charlene, you go on ahead. But she don't know nothing either, and she's tender of heart, so keep the scare stories down to a minimum. She's got work to do too, so be quick."

"If I find out you knew something, I'll see you get picked up as an accessory."

"Yeah, you cops scare hell out of me."

Charlene turned out to be a heavy smoker—bleached blond hair, tired blue eyes, an intriguing sweetness in her hesitant smile.

"She say it's okay for me to talk to you?"

Mendez nodded. "Let's go across the street. I'll buy you lunch."

Her eyes lit up, then dulled. "Oh, I can't."

"Charlene." He leaned close and spoke gently. "Did you talk much to the boy?"

She shook her head. "He wouldn't say nothin'. Just stuck a finger in his mouth and stared at me. Poor little baby. Had these big dark circles under his eyes."

Lena winced.

"Looked like he'd been crying. Or maybe had a cold." Tears filled her eyes and ran down her cheeks, streaking her makeup. "I knew something was wrong there, I just knew that man didn't feel right. Didn't feel like a *parent*." She shook her head. "I got to tell you, too, I don't think he'd been feeding the little boy."

She told them about the suckers.

"Did you overhear Valetta say anything at all about where he might be headed?"

"Nooo." She wrapped a strand of hair around her finger. "The phone was ringing like crazy, and I was tending to that. I did hear him yell once or twice. Whitter was ahurting him."

"You understand the boy's been kidnapped?"

"Oh, yes sir." Her eyes were bright.

"There's nothing else you can tell us?"

She bit down on her knuckles and shook her head.

Mendez handed her a card. "Call this number if you remember anything, or *think* of anything, that might help us out."

She took the card and studied it. "Yes sir."

18

They sat in the nonsmoking section of a Cracker Barrel restaurant. A huge stone fireplace separated the kitchen from the dining room. An old-fashioned enamel coffeepot sat on the mantel, next to a Coca-Cola sign and a poster advertising Dr. Wollum's Elixir. A waitress in blue jeans and a checked shirt offered Lena coffee. Mendez sliced a biscuit in half and took a bite.

"Eat something," he said.

Lena rattled her bag of pretzels. "I am eating something."

"Why don't you order the chicken and dumplings?"

"What are you, the nutrition police? I don't want to eat, I want to crunch."

"You missed lunch, didn't get much breakfast—"

"Did Charlie miss lunch? Did Charlie get breakfast?"

Mendez positioned his knife on the edge of his plate. "You never know who to be mad at, do you, Lena? Me. Eloise. Whitney." He leaned close. "All this time, I thought it was me. Because I'm a cop, and my hands are tied, and no matter what I do, men kill their wives and their girlfriends. And Lena, if I put every man or woman in jail who threatened to kill their husband or wife, the streets would be empty."

"Mendez—"

"But now I'm not sure. I know you hold me responsible—or you used to. And I think you're angry with your sister."

"I don't blame victims, Mendez."

"Yes, you do. But mainly you blame yourself."

"Crap, Mendez."

"Crap, Lena. You need to put the blame where it belongs."

81

"And where is that?"

"*On Hayes.*"

Lena wadded the pack of pretzels and jammed them into her purse. "I'm not riding home with you, Joel."

A beeper went off. The woman at the next table reached into her jacket pocket. She frowned, shrugged, and looked at the man sitting across from her.

Mendez wiped his mouth with a white paper napkin. "Are you going to walk? Sixty-seven miles?"

"Sixty-*seven* miles, Mendez? Are you sure it's not sixty-seven and four tenths? Is that to my house or yours? Where are you going?"

"My beeper went off. I have to call the office."

The pay phone was just outside the bathrooms. Mendez rummaged in his pocket for a quarter, and dropped it in the slot. Lena wondered if he always had a quarter when he needed one, because she never did. One way to look at it was that Mendez had all her quarters.

She leaned against the wooden doorjamb and touched the gingham skirt of a cornhusk doll that hung on the wall. Mendez talked very little and listened a lot. She couldn't tell much from his face. She wondered if he had a facial-expression disability.

He hung the phone up and stared at a point on the wall over her right shoulder.

"Mendez? What is it?"

His eyes came back into focus. "Knoxville PD called my office. Archie Valetta's been hit."

"Charlie?"

Mendez's shoulders sagged. "No sign."

"But—"

"I don't know, Lena. I want to go back and take a look around before they close up shop. That our waitress?"

"I think so. Joel, Charlie has to be there somewhere. You're not keeping anything back? They didn't find his—"

Mendez put a hand on her arm. "Nothing."

"Where the *hell* could he be? What if he got lost? Jesus, Joel, he's four years old."

"I know."

*   *   *

The Tabor Road Inn was a tired-looking building—one-story cinder block that had been painted brown as recently as the sixties. An orange neon sign promising Air-Cooled Rooms, Tee-Vee-n-Vibrating Beds was barely readable in the sunlight, though Lena could see that it would flash cheerfully enough after dark. Each room had a porch light and a screen door enabling the guests to enjoy the muggy pleasure of summer nights in Tennessee.

There were three patrol cars and an ambulance in the oil-stained parking lot, and a small knot of onlookers. The guests were surprisingly uninterested in police business. Four uniformed cops were poking through the weeds on the side of the road. Mendez wedged the Mazda between a dark green trash Dumpster, and a white van with droopy red curtains in the windows and a PTL bumper sticker on the back. Somebody had spray painted Christ Is Lord on the Dumpster.

Lena recognized Valetta's bike in the parking lot. The screen door of room 17 was propped open, and yellow crime-scene tape barricaded the sidewalk in front. Mendez paused behind the tape.

"Sir?" The patrolman had long sideburns and fleshy red cheeks. Mendez showed his ID.

"This is my associate." Mendez nodded toward Lena. "Detective Hackburton should have cleared us."

The patrolman nodded. "He'p yo'self."

Metal wheels clattered on linoleum. A gurney came partway through the door, then stuck. A fat man with thinning reddish blond hair waved to Mendez from inside the room.

"Wanna take a look?" He motioned for the ambulance attendants to wait. "Come on in. Techs have finished their business."

Lena leaned against the front wall, taking in every detail—Mendez fishing rubber gloves out of his jacket pocket, the squeak of stretching rubber, the snap as the gloves snugged into place. Mendez peeled back the wet red sheet.

Valetta had been shot repeatedly at close range, several times in the face. The curly blond hair and beard were blood soaked.

Mendez looked at Hackburton. "Thirty-two?"

Hackburton shrugged. "Didn't find no weapon, but that'd be my guess. Shot at least eleven times. Maybe more. The fuc—" He glanced at Lena. "The shooter had to reload."

"You'll find thirteen bullet holes," Mendez said.

"Think he reloaded twice?"

"Thirteen."

Lena swallowed. Mendez peered into Valetta's mouth. Lena closed her eyes, trying not to hear the rustling sheet.

"Nasty, i'n it?" Hackburton said.

Lena opened her eyes. Mendez was pulling the sheet back over Valetta, and he glanced at her.

"What?" she said.

Mendez hesitated. "Took the tongue, the . . . genitals. And the heart."

Lena took a breath. "Do you think Charlie saw . . . saw them . . ." She took another breath.

Hackburton was shaking his head. "Ain't no sign of any little boy, honey."

"I want to see." Her voice sounded steady enough, very controlled. Normal to someone who didn't know her. She was relieved that it did not break in front of Hackburton, who had called her honey.

The attendants moved the gurney out to the ambulance, and Lena followed Mendez into the room.

The bed was unmade, rumpled, stained. Lena stared at the back wall.

"Figure he was standing 'bout there," Hackburton said, pointing to a spot next to the bed, about six feet from the wall. "The first slug knocked him backward." He fished a bent pack of low-tar Merits out of his jacket pocket and lit a match. For the first time in her life, Lena was grateful for the smell of tobacco. "See about three bullet holes, there in the wall. The killer was pumping it, firing one-two-three. Scared, I betcha, Valetta was a big son of a bi— . . . son of a gun. Took the rest crumbled up there on the floor. May *not* be thirteen holes in him, Mendez. Guy might have missed a couple times."

Lena turned away from the blood-splashed wall, the soaked carpet.

She was not exactly sure what she was looking for, but she wandered from corner to corner of the small room while Mendez talked to Hackburton. Hackburton and two other men in uniforms surreptitiously watched her looking.

She didn't find any little boys hiding in the shower stall, or a crayon in the corner. No diapers, or wet pants, or Batman T-shirts.

84

No half-eaten crackers with tiny tooth marks on the edge. No scared little four-year-old boys. No Charlie.

"Are you through?" Mendez asked her.

She shrugged and looked at Hackburton. "You didn't find any hairs, or anything? On the pillowcase or in the bathroom? He was blond, and—"

"Some gray hairs, and a few black ones. And a long brown one I don't think was his." Hackburton was patient and polite. "These rooms don't get cleaned real good, between customers. We been finding a lot of stuff, but nothing that points to a little boy. Going to be a while, though, before we know. Got to run some tests."

"FBI lab?" Mendez asked.

"State. FBI's dragging their ass, thinking custody fight."

Lena took a final look around. The back of her head felt tight.

"What about that photo," Hackburton said. "Still don't want to run it?"

"No," Mendez said. "Better not."

Hackburton lit another Merit and nodded slowly. "I 'spect you're right."

Lena turned and faced them. "Why not? Why not run his picture? Maybe he ran away and he's lost and somebody found him. If he's dead—"

"If he's dead, honey, won't matter anyway. And if somebody found him, they'll turn him in. People don't just run across little boys and keep them. Otherwise, you plaster his face all over the tee-vee and everwhere—"

"And they'll kill him," Lena said. "Good point." She rubbed a hand across her eyes. "Wait for you outside," she said to Mendez. The men stared as she left the room.

Her gait was slow and unsteady, and she headed for the car but did not get in. The sun had faded and it was getting dark. She leaned her forehead against the Dumpster, feeling the scratchiness of flaking paint and sun-warmed metal. The rancid smell of old garbage finished her off. She stepped behind the Dumpster and vomited neatly into the weeds. Out front, the neon sign flickered to life, sending orange pulses across the asphalt.

19

Darkness. Headlights. The vibration of the engine. Lena laid her head back and closed her eyes. Her mind brought forth the image of Archie Valetta on a gurney, and the vision of a blood-splashed wall.

"What's going on, Mendez?" Her voice sounded flat.

"I don't know." His face was lit by the glow from the dashboard. He stroked his mustache. "According to Hackburton, the place is owned and run by a couple named Cooper. Early yesterday morning, Mrs. Cooper saw a man in a blue raincoat knock on Valetta's door and go in. She thought it was odd, because the man was dressed well, a businessman. She wondered about him going in to see somebody like Valetta. The guy wasn't there long, just stayed a few minutes. Went in with a briefcase, came out without it."

"Did she see a child?"

"No. No one saw a child. Mrs. Cooper says the man left the parking lot on foot, and that made her curious. Then late last night—or early this morning—her husband was up doing the night audit. He'd fallen asleep, and something woke him up. He looked out in the lot, but didn't notice anything. Went back to his books. Then he heard tires squealing. He went to the window and saw a car tearing out of the parking lot."

"What kind of car?"

"Too dark to tell for sure, but he thinks the hubcap spun off as soon as the driver turned onto the main road. Hackburton's people are looking for it."

"Jesus, Mendez, this doesn't make any sense."

"We've got Valetta's killing, the business with the man and the briefcase, and the negative sleeve. If that's what it is."

"The what?"

"Hackburton found it wadded in the trash. One of those glassine sleeves photographers store negatives in."

"Any negatives?"

"It's never that easy, Lena. But—"

"Blackmail."

"One of Archie's old sidelines."

"But why did he take Charlie, and where *is* he? If I hadn't been there. If I hadn't—"

"Then Archie might have killed him. Or taken him anyway. Grabbing the little boy was an impulse thing. Valetta probably figured he'd use him to pry the money out of Eloise. We'll have to see what Hackburton comes up with on the physical evidence, but I don't think the boy was ever in the motel. Somebody would have seen him."

"Nobody heard Valetta get shot."

"Hackburton thinks the killer used a silencer."

"Okay. We *know* Valetta had Charlie at the clinic. So somewhere between the motel and the clinic he lost him."

Mendez was quiet.

"You think he killed him, don't you?"

"I'm not ready to quit looking."

20

It was raining when Mendez dropped Lena in front of the house. She didn't go in. It would be too tempting, once inside, to put off going to the hospital, to put off seeing Eloise, to put off telling her about Charlie.

The Cutlass—gas tank full—started on the third try. Mendez flashed his lights at Lena and drove away. Lena laid her head on the steering wheel.

It was the kind of weather she hated—wet, drizzling rain, thick humidity; too hot for a sweater, too cool for mere sleeves. The hospital parking lot was empty after dark on a weeknight. Lena parked near the entrance, avoided walking through a clump of sodden leaves, and passed through the automatic doors into the lobby.

The gift shop was empty. Lena stood in front of the elevators and breathed the thick miasma of cigarette smoke that drifted out of the snack bar.

Eloise Valetta was out of ICU and in a semiprivate room. The bed next to her was empty, no sheets. Lena stuck her hands in her pockets. She took a breath.

"Eloise?"

Eloise's legs moved under the sheets. Lena pulled a chair close, but did not sit down. Her purse slipped off her shoulder, and she caught it before it dropped.

"Eloise?"

"Lena?" Eloise turned sideways, moving stiffly. A thick white bandage covered her left eye socket, and her right eye was swollen and black. Her nose was swathed in gauze. She put a hand out and touched Lena.

Lena sat down. She cleared her throat.

"You find him, Lena? Did you *find* him?"

"I . . . no. Not yet."

Eloise's hand went to her mouth. Her lips trembled and tears streaked her right cheek.

"Eloise, we . . . the police traced Archie to Tennessee. Knoxville." Lena put a hand on Eloise's arm. "Archie is dead."

"Charlie?"

"No. Charlie wasn't with him."

"But—"

"Archie was killed in his motel room. Somebody shot him. As far as we can tell, Charlie wasn't there. He wasn't in the room; he wasn't there when it happened. Nobody at the motel ever saw him."

"Then *where* is he? You think he got away?"

Lena bit her lip. "I don't know. Archie stopped in at a clinic the day before. He had Charlie with him then. One of the people there gave him a whole handful of suckers."

Eloise sobbed. "He'd of liked that." She hiccuped. "How many times did I say no to all them sweets, poor little thing? I wished I said yes. I wished I said yes."

Eloise's shoulders quaked. Her breasts sagged under the print hospital gown, and her hair was a knot of tangles. She hid her face in the pillow. "What are the police doing?" Her voice was muffled, barely audible.

"They're looking. They're working on it."

"I just bet."

"No, now. Remember I told you about Detective Mendez? He's the best there is, Eloise, he's helped me before."

"He's really . . . he's really good?"

"Honest. And he cares about finding Charlie."

Eloise sank deeper into the mattress. She pulled the sheet up over her head.

"Eloise, I don't blame you, for being mad at me. But I need to . . . what?"

"Not mad at you."

"Pull the sheet down so I can hear what you say."

"No, no, I don't like you to see me like this. I'm so . . .

89

embarrassed. I don't like you to see me like this, I swore I'd never let any man ever—"

Lena sat back in her chair and bit her lip, remembering Whitney, after Jeff had hit her—her refusal to look Lena in the eye, her shame.

"Eloise, I need you to think. It looks like Archie might have been blackmailing somebody. Do you know anything about that? It's probably tied up with the killing, and whoever it was may know something about Charlie."

"Why did he take him? Jest to hurt me? Charlie isn't his kid. Oh, why did I let him go to the door? Open it a crack, and he . . . oh, God. . . . He shoved and I fell back and stumbled over Charlie. We was baking! Just baking a cake and listening to the radio."

Lena pulled the sheet down, uncovering Eloise Valetta's bruised, swollen face.

"Think for me, Eloise. How does the location fit into this? Was there anybody in Tennessee Archie might have been blackmailing?"

"Blackmail?" Eloise quit moving. "Oh, God. I wonder."

"Wonder what?"

"This cult, this group that your brother-in-law run? They used to take pictures of people, during the ceremonies, doing . . . things, you know. Things they wouldn't want other people seeing. And I think sometimes Jeff and Archie would ask for a 'donation,' you know what I mean? Backed up by a picture showing what a good worshiper the person they wanted money from was. You understand what I'm saying?"

"I understand."

"And some of them, some of them may be from around there. Archie and Jeff used to go down there a lot." Eloise pulled the sheet up under her chin. "Archie's dead."

"Yes."

"That feels funny. He . . . he held Charlie over the burner on the stove and turned it on high."

Lena took a breath.

"And I screamed and begged. Swore I didn't have that stupid money."

"Did he burn him? Did he burn Charlie?"

"I don't know, I don't think so. Everything runs together. . . . Charlie was crying, but not like if he was burned, you know, not that scream he has. And suddenly Archie put him down. Down soft,

90

like, you know, maybe God was listening to my prayers. And he . . .
he *grabs* me by the hair, and says . . . says *why* you make me do this
to you? And he took a bottle off the cabinet and broke it, and said,
'Here's what'll turn the trick and open your fat mouth.' " Eloise
took a deep, uneven breath. "And that hurt my feelings. It hurt my
feelings that he called me fat. Isn't that stupid? Isn't that stupid?"
She sobbed loudly, then her voice dropped to a whisper. "Stupid."

"Eloise?"

Eloise stared straight ahead.

"Eloise, I want you to listen to me. I'm going to find Charlie for
you. I'm going to. And when I find him, he's going to need his
mama. You understand me, Eloise? Do you hear what I'm saying?"

Eloise moved her head just a little. Lena decided to count it as
a nod. She watched Eloise for a long moment, then headed for the
nurses' station.

The nurse behind the counter did not look up. Her hair was
yellow blond, neatly flipped under. She sat sideways in the chair,
and she wore white hose that made her heavy legs look thicker.

"Eloise Valetta," Lena said. "The patient in three thirteen."

The nurse looked up and frowned. Her name tag said Steward.

"Mrs. Valetta is . . . she's upset. She needs something, I don't
know. Something to get her through—"

"That the one got beat up? She's about due, anyway." The nurse
shook her head. "Tell you the truth, honey, you look like you could
use something yourself."

21

Lena sat in the dark and hoped she was alone in the house. She wiped dust off the answering machine with the tip of her finger. A luminous green 2 heralded her messages.

Mendez had left his tie on the end table. Lena ran a finger across the cool blue silk. She pushed a button and the tape on the answering machine rewound.

"Lena? Rick. Eloise Valetta's divorce from Archie went into effect two months after her kid was born. Charlie. Is that what you need? And listen, Lena, your *cat* ate an entire begonia yesterday. Then he threw up *four* times in the living room. And once in the kitchen! Does he need to see his pediatrician? Talk later, sweetheart."

The machine whirred and beeped.

"Ave Satanas."

Lena sat up.

"All glory be unto the dark lord, Abaddon. All condemnation to the weary child of God. Dear dying lamb, spill thy precious blood."

Lena bit her knuckle.

"Suffer the little children to come unto me, for of such is the kingdom of hell."

Lena's finger trembled over the Save button.

She went to the kitchen and took the steak knives out of the drawer. They had come in a set of six, but she could only find five of them. She hid one under the middle cushion of the couch, one in the drawer of the end table next to the rocking chair. There ought to be one in the bedroom, and one next to the shower in the bath. She started up the stairs.

The phone rang. Lena leaned against the wall, and let the machine answer.

"Lena, this is Joel. I—"

Lena grabbed the receiver. "Hi . . . hi, Joel. I'm here. Joel, I think Hayes has Charlie."

Mendez's tone was sharp. "What makes you say that?"

"He left a message on my machine. He said, 'Suffer the little children to come unto me, for of such is the kingdom of hell.' "

Mendez was silent. Lena was aware of the hard beat of her heart.

"You can't be sure, Lena. But it bears looking into. What else did he say?"

"Some kind of mumbo jumbo stuff."

"How did he sound?"

"What do you mean?"

"Raving, amused, threatening?"

"Kind of, I don't know, intense. Like he was enjoying it, but was serious."

Mendez was quiet.

"Why don't you come over?" he said. "I'm tied up here at home, with paperwork. But I'd like to hear the tape."

"I can't, Joel. I have something I need to do."

"Okay, then." Mendez paused. "Good night, Lena. Be careful."

She left the knives by the phone and headed for the basement, not her favorite place at night. She moved down the stairs slowly, guided by the light from the kitchen. She wondered what Mendez was working on, what he was thinking about. She had never seen his place—was it a house or an apartment? She pictured him in a stark, nearly empty room, sitting behind a massive wooden desk.

Lena pulled the cord that hung in the center of the basement, and the bulb flashed on. The light was yellow and harsh, bright against the night-filled windows.

Suppose Eloise was right. Suppose Archie was blackmailing members of the cult.

Lena chewed her lip. She knew they were looking for seed money, Archie and Jeff, a business stake. And business was selling drugs and pornography to the cult. Drugs, pornography . . . and negatives?

The hit was a cult hit. Thirteen bullets. Mutilation. And Charlie, somewhere in the middle.

The box of Jeff's old things was still upended on the floor. The *Book of Shadows* was at the bottom, buried beneath old bank statements.

Somewhere, there might be a name. A name she could use. She flipped to the first page, the references to M.

Who was M?

Whitney had told her about a cousin that Jeff seemed attached to. Whitney had mentioned it because Jeff sent her birthday cards and Easter cards care of a state mental institute.

Was M the cousin? If she had the kind of childhood Hayes described, it made a lot of sense. M would know who was in the cult. If she could find M, maybe she could find out who they were dealing with, who Hayes and Valetta used to "worship" with. Which might lead to Valetta's killer, and maybe even to Charlie.

Lena closed her eyes and put her head in her hands. What was M's full name? Whitney had told her at least once. And where was the institution? She seemed to remember that the cousin had moved from the state hospital to a private facility.

Lena squeezed her eyes shut and tried to remember.

22

Lena put a hand on the radio knob, then changed her mind. She drove steadily, about ten miles over the speed limit, grateful for the sunlight that poured through the car windows. Farmland lined both sides of the interstate, and frost glittered in the matted brown grass.

She'd stopped at a Cracker Barrel and had sourdough toast, one of three slices of bacon she'd ordered, fresh orange juice, and coffee. She'd woken up in a panic at least three times last night, thinking about Charlie. She hoped Eloise was getting lots of drugs.

It took her two hours to get to LaRue County. She spent another forty minutes on a two-lane road that was a downhill succession of ninety-degree turns, coming at last to the outskirts of Nash, where Jeffrey Hayes had been born and raised. Every hundred yards was a poster that said Clump for Sherrif. She hoped Clump was better at law enforcement than spelling. Most of the posters had been used for target practice. Probably by English teachers.

The Clump posters thinned out, and Lena realized that she was back to farmland on both sides of the road. A brown sign with an arrow pointing left said Ray Lake Recreational Area, 20.4 mi.

She hadn't been on the outskirts of Nash. That had been Nash.

Lena put her turn indicator on and waited for the tractor that was inching down the left lane. She'd be fifteen minutes getting back into town.

The tractor, driven by a teenage girl in a Cardinals baseball cap and a Motley Crüe sweatshirt, rolled to a stop. The girl nodded laconically, chewed gum, and waited while Lena did a U-turn in the middle of the road.

Lena waved. "Thanks."

She passed a cement-block building that proclaimed itself The American Primitive Church of Jesus. An ancient gas pump was rusting in a concrete island in the center of the church parking lot.

Lena passed a Hardees, Cal's Shoe Repair advertising Cloggers and Stompers, a movie rental place that also sold Hunting Licenses and Live Bait-n-Nightcrawlers, and a boarded-up tin shed that swore it had Tanning Beds.

The LaRue County Courthouse, red brick and stately, was next to Horwald's Realty & Law. There were angled parking spaces down both sides of the street. Lena got out of the car. A huge American flag snapped and rippled over the top of the courthouse. Lena's hair blew in the wind. She put a quarter in an ancient gray parking meter, and bought herself two and a half hours of time.

Lena's feet tore through tangles of dried brown meadow grass. She kept an eye out for anyone who might object to her disregard of the Posted signs that were nailed to the trees at two-hundred-yard intervals.

Jeff Hayes had a cousin named Melody Hayes, born in the LaRue County Hospital in 1954. Cousin M. Melody's mother, Esther Gerrold Hayes, had died in 1956.

Esther had given her daughter a beautiful name. Melody, Melody, Melody Hayes. Where was Melody now?

Lena could see over the hill now, and she caught a glimpse of the house. Jeff had spent his young years here, before his family turned prosperous and moved closer in to town. The house was empty now, protected by a thick knot of trees so old that their lowest branches were on a level with the roof. The trees formed a horseshoe around the house, their limbs black and stark, the bark oddly smooth and impenetrable. The gravel drive was weed grown, full of hardened tire ruts, evidence that people still came here, often in wet weather.

It was a small house, a modest wood farmhouse, showing bare wood and peeling white paint. One of the shutters on the far right window had come unhinged, and now hung crooked, moving with the wind. The shutters had been painted red once, and they were all missing slats.

Lena climbed the boundary fence, holding the wood post with one hand, pressing down the top two strands of barbed wire with the other. She swung one leg over, then the other. A rusty knot of wire caught the inseam of her jeans. She plucked the wire loose,

96

wobbled from side to side, lost her balance. She grabbed the wire to keep from falling. Her left palm came down on a barb, but was protected by the thick bandage she still wore over the cuts on her hand.

Sunlight glinted off a rusty propane tank that squatted by the side of the house. A pile of bricks had fallen like rotten teeth from the chimney. Lena was surprised the house had no front porch. She headed up the crumbling concrete steps and tried the front door. Locked.

The windows had been covered from the inside with masking tape and brown paper sacks. Lena peered into a dirt-encrusted corner where the paper had sagged and curled. She squinted, making out an empty room with a linoleum floor. Something—garbage?—was piled in a corner.

Lena walked around the house, glancing once, then twice, behind her. Somebody was using a chain saw a couple of miles away. She noticed the latticework of wood that enclosed a dark dirt crawl space. Whitney had told her about Jeffrey's nightmares, how he dreamed about "under the house."

The back door was locked, too.

There was a rusty yellow swing set behind the house, and a sagging shed of silvery gray wood. The swings moved with the wind, and Lena thought of ghost children. The shed was windowless, and flat-topped, and had not been erected by any whiz at carpentry. The door was held shut with a simple hook and eye. Lena wrestled the rusty hook out of the loop, and tugged the metal hasp.

The door groaned, but stayed wedged in the dirt. Lena kicked the bottom and pulled again, and the door swung suddenly free.

The shed was dark inside, earthy smelling. Daylight came like smoke through seams in the slats of wood. There was nothing there to give her the tight feeling in her chest, nothing but four rough, splintery walls, a hard-packed dirt floor, and streamers of pale web hanging loose.

Lena's eyes adjusted. There were hieroglyphics on the walls—childish drawings, scribbles. A childish hand had sketched cats (horses maybe?), a couple of dogs. In the corner were the initials JH and 1963. Jeff Was Here. Lena inched closer. A tree, a circle, and a cat (or dog?) hanging from a noose. Something had been written at the bottom.

I HAF TO KEEP MY MOUTH SHUT OR THEY CUT OUT MY TUNG.

The wind smacked the door shut, leaving Lena in the dark.

23

She hadn't called to see if Mendez was in his office, and the empty chair threw her. Lena stood beside the desk, hands behind her back. She ripped a sheet of paper off a legal pad and sat down in his chair. CALL ME, she printed in large block capitals. She chewed the eraser and wondered if she should say anything else.

Jeff has a cousin, she wrote. *They grew up together. Trying to track her and will*

Lena realized that someone was looking over her shoulder. The pencil lead snapped, leaving crumbs of graphite on the paper.

"Mendez, what are you doing?!"

"Reading my message."

Lena took a breath. "Here. You can have your chair back."

"No. Sit. I'm on my way out." His jacket and tie were neat. He picked a file up off the corner of the desk. "Did you bring me the tape?"

"I forgot."

"What's up?"

"I just . . . I wanted to know if you'd heard anything. From Knoxville."

He nodded, frowning. "There's not much."

"They find the hubcap?"

"No. But the lab found trace elements of a hypo clearing agent on the inside of the glassine sleeve. That's what photographers use to clean negatives."

Lena chewed her lip. "Eloise told me that Archie and Jeff took pictures of people during, you know, *meetings*. Whatever. She said they used them to encourage 'donations' to the group."

Mendez scratched his chin. "The killing definitely looks like some kind of blackmail dodge. We may be seeing an internal squabble. Considering the nature of the hit."

"Were you right? Were there thirteen bullet wounds?"

"Eleven. But they found thirteen slugs. Looks like the shooter missed a couple of times."

"And the way they cut him up. Is that typical?"

Mendez shrugged. "There's not a rule book, Lena. Some of these groups make things up as they go along. But it's the right—"

"Flavor."

"That's one way to put it."

Lena put her chin in her hand. "How does Hayes fit in?"

"Don't know. But he used to lead a pretty hard-core group based in the area where he grew up. They may have members all over. Anywhere. Somebody had to run things while he and Archie were in prison. We may be seeing blackmail, or some kind of power struggle. There's no way to tell."

"Do you think Hayes has Charlie?"

"We've been watching his place, trying to pick him up since he showed at your house that last time. He hasn't been home."

"You'll get him."

"Maybe not." Mendez took a breath. "The captain pulled our man off. So unless we get lucky." He shrugged. "I'm on my way to Knoxville right now."

"Something going on?"

"Hackburton has a tip. Sounds remote, but you never know. What I'm interested in is the clinic. There are plenty of places Valetta could have gone. Why *this* particular one? Why Knoxville?"

"He got connections—family in the area?"

"None we know of. He's a Kentucky boy. From Jackson. Hackburton's checking on this Dr. Whitter. Getting a list of license numbers on cars in the clinic parking lot, for comparison to any numbers they can pick up at Valetta's funeral."

"When is that?"

"Coroner hasn't released the body yet. And nobody's claimed it."

"Eloise told me Archie and Jeff went down that way sometimes. On business."

Mendez nodded.

"What are you going to do down there, Joel?"

"Talk to Hackburton. Retrace likely routes from the clinic to the motel. See if I can figure out where he lost Charlie."

"You're looking for a likely place to dump a body."

Mendez was quiet.

Lena stood up. "I sure hope you're wrong, Mendez."

"I'll call you when I get back."

"You do that."

Lena turned left off Rose Street, onto the UK campus. She passed an empty guard booth and parked the Cutlass. It was dark out, raining. She locked the car and ran up twelve concrete steps to the sidewalk.

The Funkhouser Building was an old brown brick monster. There were at least six ways to get in—not counting the black metal fire escapes that ran down the ivy-covered sides. The Funkhouser had been built before security concerns tainted the architectural vision.

She went in from the side, up steps that were rain slick and worn. Inside, the black-flecked linoleum was muddy and wet, and Lena felt her shoes slide. She walked carefully up four flights of stairs to the second floor. Huge radiators, painted creamy white, hissed and emitted bursts of heat. The hall smelled like a laundromat.

Lena wandered down the hallway until she found room 207. She hadn't been in the Funkhouser Building since Psych. 102. She had gotten a C minus.

Dr. Caron looked younger than he sounded on the phone. He sat on the edge of an old wooden desk, cleaning a pair of wire-rim glasses while he talked to his students. There were circles under his eyes. He was clean shaven, though it was high time for another one, and his clothes looked as if they'd been slept in. He wore brown corduroy pants and a red-and-black flannel shirt. There were felt-tip pens in his pocket.

"Sounds like you guys had a better spring break than I did," he said absently. "Anyway." He frowned at the thick lenses of his glasses, then put them on. "Next week we get back to the books." He waved a hand at the board. "So be sure and get the reading down."

Page numbers and cryptic abbreviations were scrawled in small, knotlike handwriting at the top left corner of the board. On the other side of the board, someone had been playing hangman with red and blue chalk.

Murmurs broke out and chairs scooted back. Seven or eight students were packing up notebooks and scrambling for umbrellas. They watched as Lena approached the desk.

"Dr. Caron?"

"Hi. I'm Walt Caron." He took her hand. "You're Lena?"

"Yes."

He looked over her shoulder at his students. "See you next week."

They took the hint and left. He closed the heavy wooden door.

"Okay if we talk here? My office is across campus in the med. center."

"Sure," Lena said.

It was a large room, and it felt larger at night, with the lights bright, and darkness filling the gallery of windows that lined both outside walls. Lena shivered. The room was filled with tables and chairs. She sat down on a table and looked at Caron.

"I appreciate you seeing me on the instant like this."

He shrugged and leaned against his desk, cocking his head sideways. "Valerie said it was pretty important."

"It is."

"How do you know Valerie? Did you meet at . . ." Caron spread his hands.

"At the crisis center?" Lena smiled. "Not the way you're thinking."

"I meant as a volunteer."

"No." Lena looked out a window. "How do you know Valerie?"

"I did my doctoral dissertation out there. And Valerie and I used to see each other. Way back."

"You're that Walt."

"Yeah." He laughed. "Why? What'd she say?"

"Nothing bad, honest. She tell you anything about my sister?"

Caron blushed. "Actually, she did."

"Good. It'll give us a jumping-off point, because this is kind of connected. Jeff Hayes was my sister's husband. Her killer. He got out of prison a few weeks back."

Caron sat back on the edge of the desk. His expression was interested, alert without being avid, good eye contact. A good therapist, Lena decided, though she didn't think he saw patients. Talent waste.

"This is complicated, but a client of mine was once married to

101

one of Jeff's . . . associates. Cohorts. Partners in crime." Lena grimaced. "This man also just got out of prison. For reasons that are too complicated to go into, this man, this Archie Valetta, kidnapped my client's son. He's four years old and his name is Charlie."

"Is he Valetta's son?"

"No."

"Sorry. Go on."

"Valetta took the child with him to Tennessee, and a couple of days later got himself killed in a motel room."

Caron tensed. "And the boy?"

Lena shook her head. "Don't know. He wasn't in the room. We don't know for sure what happened to him."

"How can I help?"

Lena liked him for it. Why had Valerie let this guy go?

She gave him a small smile. "I have reason to think . . . I'll be honest with you, I don't know for sure. The killing was likely some kind of cult hit. And Jeff and Valetta were involved with a cult before they wound up in jail. I think maybe Jeff either has the boy or knows where he is. Did Valerie tell you anything about Jeff's involvement with cults?"

He nodded. "Yeah. It's in my line."

"I know. We're talking about an entrenched family type of group. One he grew up in."

Caron nodded.

"I found Jeff's old *Book of Shadows*. You know what that is?"

"A kind of occult diary. A journal of activity."

"Right. And he talks about a cousin of his. I know a little bit about this cousin. Her name is Melody Hayes, and she was born in LaRue County, Nash, Kentucky, in 1954. And she was, and may still be, in some kind of mental institution. Jeff's book talks about M being tortured in the ceremonies, and I think it's probably her. So I want to find her. Because she might be able to tell me some names of people involved in Jeff's group. I can't go door to door, you know, asking about devil worshipers. If I can get a lead on some of the people in the group, they may know about Charlie. They may even have him. I know it's a hell of a long shot. I know Archie may have killed the little boy and dumped the body. I can't tell you I have some kind of psychic feeling Charlie's alive, I can only tell you I hope he is, and I'm trying to find him any way I can. The police are following up the Tennessee end. But I think that Jeff knows where Charlie is. Anyway, does any of this make any sense?"

Caron frowned and walked around the desk, settling in a ladder-back chair. He took off his glasses and rubbed his eyes. "How much background do you have in satanic cults?"

"Only what I pick up from my relatives."

He smiled and leaned back in his chair. "This is something of a speciality of mine. I got involved about ten years ago, with students on campus. The kids, you know, they're usually just dabblers, misfits, plain curious. Mainly, they're a danger to themselves, with drug abuse, or suicide. What you're talking about, though, is a hard-core, long-term adult group. I haven't done any counseling in that area. But I've studied up. And you're closer on track than you realize. What's the date exactly? It's the seventeenth, isn't it?" He made a face. "You get your income tax done?"

"Yeah. Easy enough with my income."

He frowned. "There's a dangerous time coming up, if the cult really does have the boy. The end of April, around Easter. I think maybe the twenty-fourth, or the thirtieth. Let's see, there's St. Mark's Eve and Walpurgis Night . . . or is that February? I'm sorry, I'll have to check some notes. But the point is it's a very big event. One that particularly might pose danger to a male child."

Lena slid slowly into a chair.

"What do you mean, particular danger?"

Caron sighed deeply. "A pure white male sacrifice. Prized for this particular sabbat." He shook his head. "I don't know if I should have brought it up. Most satanic groups don't do sacrifices, certainly not human. But the kind of group you and Valerie describe, and considering Hayes's track record and Valetta's death. They sound like a serious bunch. I'm sorry."

"So." Lena swallowed. "Time's running out."

"I could be way off base."

"No. You just said out loud the kind of stuff I've been worrying about. But what about now? You think he's being hurt right now? Molested? Every minute he's gone, who knows what could be happening to this boy."

Caron chewed his fingernails, noticed what he was doing, and stopped. "You're right, anything *could* be happening. But if it *is* what you're worrying about, that he is in the hands of this cult Hayes ties up with, understand how it can work. A Satan worshiper

103

who molests children is different from the typical pedophile. In the typical situation, you have an adult who genuinely may love a child and can't comprehend that sex with a child is wrong."

"Crap. I don't believe that for a minute."

Caron's jaw tightened, then relaxed. "Okay, it's one theory, for certain situations. In any case, a pedophile wants to be around the child, and has constant urges. Let's say he knows it's wrong. He still has those urges. In this situation, though, with a satanist, there is no anger, and no abnormal love. The child is a means to an end. The abuse is *ritual* abuse. And done only in context of the ritual. It may satisfy their perverted urges, but they justify it as ritual."

"Can we cut to the chase here, Walt? You're saying that, if we're lucky, they may be saving him up? And if I get to him in time, they won't have molested him?"

"That's pretty much what I'm saying."

Lena grabbed the edge of the desk, clenching and unclenching her fingers. "All right. I need you to help me find this Melody Hayes. Do institutions specialize? Would any of your co-workers know where she might be? Patient lists . . ."

"This is very sticky, you know." He thought for a moment, absently scratching his cheek. "Here's what I can do. Some of the people I've worked with here, over the years, have been working in the area of multiple personality."

"So?"

"Understand. The kind of cult we're talking about here, where they take children, and subject them to ritual abuse from an early age, may create victims that are multiples. The theory is that the satanists are intentionally creating alter personalities—you could speculate forever on why. Paths for demons, whatever, who knows? But their methods of abuse, putting a young child through extremes of torture, often by a parent or grandparent, a figure of trust, will cause the child to fragment, to create alter personalities, because the child can't integrate their experiences of good and bad. So if you work with multiples—and there are still therapists who don't believe that multiples exist, by the way—but if you work in that area, a healthy percentage of the patients come from this kind of hardcore cult background. Not all children subjected to this sort of thing are multiples, of course. But there is a lot of networking, very informal, with colleagues who treat the multiples and other cult victims. I know some folks who do quite a lot of work in this area, and I consult with them when I work with my teenagers—whose problems are quite different, actually.

"So I can ask around about this cousin. Explain what's at stake. Just understand two things. Melody Hayes will not be put through anything that will hurt her. And she'll have to agree to talk to you. And if her therapist doesn't want her messed with, that'll be the end of it."

Lena nodded. "Remember, though. Charlie is four."

Caron narrowed his eyes. "That's the only reason I'm even considering helping you. That and Valerie, who twisted my arm, to tell you the truth."

"What's the second thing?"

"There is some risk, in me putting the word out, that information will get to the wrong person. I don't want to be overly paranoid, but you never know who might be involved in these groups. Some of them could be doctors and nurses. Some of them psychiatrists. Parents involved in these cults have ties to mental health people from day one. They want their child to have a record of mental disorders, or problems, so that if they do grow up and point fingers, they're labeled as being disturbed from a young age."

"I don't understand the *why* of all this."

He chewed a thumbnail. "It comes down sometimes to—are there evil people, or just very sick ones."

"You don't believe in evil, do you, Walter?"

"I didn't use to. I try not to. In my line of work, you know? But one thing I do think. These people, these hard-core ones. They're very angry folks. Doctors and nurses who see too many people die, and feel betrayed. They want to believe in something, but they've quit believing in a loving God. Some of them are ministers. Some are just people in pain who turned to traditional religions and got smacked in the head with the seven deadly sins. You find people who are trying to *control* their world. And satisfy all of the hedonistic urges. And there's plenty of the pathetic ones—ones who could never find acceptance, friendship, love, for whatever reasons. Dysfunctional people who get what they need from being one of the group. It's, forgive me, an exciting social outlet, that gives them all the no-nos their little hearts desire."

Lena stared absently at Caron's feet. He wore scuffed Hush Puppies, the left one untied, laces wet and muddy.

"I don't know how big a risk it is, Walt," she said finally. "But go with it and do what you can. We don't have a lot of time."

"One more thing I need to say."

Lena stood up. "What?"

"There's two ways to survive a childhood like that. Turn inward. Shrink. Disintegrate in alters. Or you can do what Jeff Hayes did. Go from victim to victimizer."

"I assume you're not asking me to admire the man?"

"Of course not. But like it or not, he's just as much a victim as Melody or Charlie."

"Jesus, you sound like a shrink."

24

The front porch light was out when Lena got home. Had she left it on that morning? She frowned. She'd locked the sliding glass door, checked the answering machine, turned the coffee maker off in the kitchen and . . . yeah. Turned on the porch light.

The bulb might have burned out. Or maybe . . . maybe Hayes had turned the light off. Maybe he was inside, waiting.

Mendez was in Knoxville. Next door, the Wilkses' house looked dark and empty. She didn't know the people on the other side of her house.

She got back in her car and drove to a gas station with a pay phone.

Lena sat in the Cutlass with the doors locked and watched the house. No lights had gone on, no face had peered through the windows. The light had burned out on her front porch, and she was being silly. So what if Hayes was inside? She needed to talk to him anyway. If he could get her Charlie, she could get him money.

Still, she had no urge to go into the house alone.

Rick's Miata pulled up in the driveway, headlights arcing across the garage door. Rick left the engine running and ran across the lawn to the Cutlass.

"Lena? Good girl, I was afraid you'd go in."

"Hi, honey." Judith waved. She was tall, five nine, with a full curvy figure and short blond hair. She was a presence, in black velvet leggings and a T-shirt that glittered. "We got a surprise for you, Lena."

"Yeah," Rick said. "Come on."

He took her hand and led her up the driveway. Lena heard a cat miaow.

"Maynard!"

She let go of Rick's hand and ran to the car. Maynard was in the front seat, nose pressed against the side of his kitty carrier.

"Oh, sweetie, oh, Maynard."

"Told you," Judith said.

Rick sniffed. "She was never that glad to see me."

Lena opened the carrier and picked up her cat. Maynard purred loudly and butted his head under her chin.

Rick cleared his throat. "You girls stay here where it's safe. Call the cops if I don't come back in a half hour."

Lena hugged Maynard and Judith tugged his tail. The cat miaowed. He licked Lena's thumb.

"Oh, Lena, he's giving you kisses."

"Maybe a half hour is too long," Rick said thoughtfully. "Probably fifteen minutes is plenty." He patted his pockets. "Where's my key? Okay. Here it is."

"Sorry about the bathroom rug," Lena said to Judith.

"I never liked it. Rick just had it when we moved in together."

"I picked it out," Lena said. "I was in my geometric phase. Rick took it when we split."

"Me and my mouth, sugar."

"Girls. Could I have your attention, here? I'm going on up now."

"Not by yourself," Lena said. "Let me go with you."

"No, it's too dangerous. Give me ten minutes. If I'm not back, you call somebody. Somebody big. Call Arnold Schwarzenegger."

"Be still my heart," Judith said.

"Rick, who are you doing? It's not Mel Gibson, is it?" Lena scratched Maynard behind the ears.

"It's not Mel Gibson," Judith said. "When he does Mel Gibson, he winks a lot. Is it Michael Douglas?"

"No," said Lena. "When he does Michael Douglas he sticks his chin out."

Rick, two steps away on the driveway, turned and glared at them. "Thank you very much. It's not enough for the two of you that I might get killed by this psychopath—"

Judith leaned close to Lena. "Sugar, is he serious or is he doing righteous indignation?"

"Did he change clothes before he left?"

108

"No."

"Serious." Lena put Maynard back in the carrier. "Rick, I think we should all go together."

"Not a chance."

"Rick, if there are three of us Jeff will just run off, he won't hang around. And the phone's inside. We could call for help, unless he cut the line."

"He didn't," Judith said. "Rick thought of that. He called to see if your phone was working. The answering machine was full, but your line was okay."

"Rick," Lena said. "You thought of that?"

"Yes, I did. I've done Agatha Christie, you know, on the dinner theater circuit."

"I know. Look, Rick, let's just go in together, okay?"

He bounced up and down on the balls of his feet. "If you really think it's for the best."

"I do."

"Avoid that phrase, Lena. It's gotten us in trouble once already."

Maynard miaowed. Lena picked up the carrier. They went together in a knot to the dark front porch. Rick looked at the scattered leaves and the corner full of dirt clods and spider webs.

"Fire your gardener, sweetheart."

Lena turned her key in the lock and pushed the front door open. Rick and Judith walked in a step behind her. The hallway and living room were dark. The light over the sink in the kitchen was on, just as Lena had left it.

Lena left the cat in the foyer and turned on the living room lamp.

"Anybody home?" Rick breezed past her and ran up the stairs, turning on lights as he went. "Hayes? You here, you bastard? Come out, come out, wherever you are! On Dasher, on Dahmer, on Hayes and Bundy. Manson and Gacy and . . ."

His voice trailed off. Lena opened the carrier and let Maynard out.

"*Lena!*"

Lena and Judith looked at each other.

"Lena, come quick!"

"The bedroom," Lena said. She ran up the stairs and skidded to a stop at the doorway. "Rick? What's the—"

"That bastard ransacked your bedroom!" Rick circled the room, shaking his head. "Don't come in here, honey, it's awful."

Lena took two steps into the room. "Rick, cut it out. Nobody's been in here."

"You mean you left it like this?"

"Shut up, Rick."

He picked up a pair of red silk panties. "I don't remember these."

Lena snatched the panties out of his hands. "Get out of here."

"Maybe he's under the bed." Rick got down on his hands and knees.

"He's not under there. What are you doing?"

"Looking for used condoms."

Judith grabbed his arm. "Come on, sugar, let's go find something to eat."

"Not here. Lena doesn't shop. Anything in her refrigerator will be a hundred years old. Around here it's safer to order out."

Lena tossed the panties on the bed and followed them down the stairs.

"Either of you girls got any money?" Rick said. "Let's order a pizza. Lena, you *do* have beer?"

"Yeah, I think. Only Beth and Mendez know for sure." She headed for the telephone in the living room. The answering machine was blinking. Twenty messages.

Rick paused in the doorway. "Sweetheart?"

Lena quit chewing her lip and looked at him over her shoulder. "Yeah?"

"What?" Judith said.

Rick grinned. "Lena, where are your spare light bulbs?"

"Under the sink in the kitchen."

"Jude, hon, make sure and get extra cheese on the pizza." He turned away. "I'm getting both of you a beer, so holler if you *don't* want one."

"Rick, the beer's in the door of the refrigerator, so be sure and open it slow."

There was a crash in the kitchen. "Booby traps!" Rick shouted. "I said *slowly!*"

Lena pushed the Play button on the answering machine. The strains of piano music sounded tinny.

"Who cleaned out your pantry, Lena?" Rick cruised through

110

the room, handing Lena and Judith each a bottle of Corona. A light bulb was tucked under his arm. "This is expensive beer. How do you afford it?" He cocked his head to one side, listening to Jeff's voice coming from the machine. "This is criminal, Lena! That man can't sing." He headed toward the hallway, muttering something about amateurs. The front door opened and his voice faded.

The music stopped and the machine signaled the onset of another message. The piano started up again.

"God, that's creepy." Judith took off her boots and curled up on the side of the couch. "Why don't you turn it off?"

Lena took a sip of beer. "May be something else in there. From somebody else. Or he may say something about Charlie."

"He—"

The doorbell rang three times. Lena jerked.

"Just Rick," Judith said.

Lena took another swallow of beer. The front door slammed.

"Lena." Rick stood in the doorway. "You say you just changed that light bulb?"

She nodded.

"There's no bulb there."

Lena frowned. "None at all?"

"Nope. I unscrewed the fixture to change the bulb, and there wasn't one in there at all. You think you just forgot to put the new one in?"

"That's a two-pack you're holding. Is there one missing?"

"Yeah."

"Then I didn't forget."

"You know what I think, babe? I think Jeff came and took it. That's what I think."

"That's bizarre," Judith said.

Rick sat beside her on the couch. "That's what *I* think." He put an arm around Judith. "Either of you order pizza yet?"

25

"Rick," Lena said. "Don't let Maynard eat off the plate. You're getting him in bad habits."

"Lena, girl, you need another beer."

Judith gouged soft white bread balls from the belly of her pizza crust. "I can't get the little boy out of my head. Rick, let's go to Knoxville and look for him."

"Look for him where, Jude? Lena's right, Mendez has to handle that end."

Maynard stepped delicately from Rick's lap onto the kitchen table. Lena scooped him up. The cat purred and wrapped his paws around her neck.

"Hugs *her* when I give him pizza." Rick shook his head. "Lena, did you listen to all those messages on the machine?"

"All of them."

"You said you tried to set up a trade. Insurance money for the kid. Hayes say anything about it?"

"Nope. I'm kind of surprised. I figured he'd of set something up by now. I don't like waiting around for him."

Rick scratched his head. "Why don't you leave him a message?"

"With who? Satanists-R-Us?"

"On the computer, sweet bee. Electronic bulletin board. Something Uncle Rick can help you with. The kiddie diddlers have them. The satanists will, too."

Lena looked thoughtful. "Can you do that, and them not know where to find you? Otherwise you could attract all kinds of nut cases."

He shrugged. "Shouldn't be a problem. If it's a dial-in link nobody will know where I'm calling from. I can set up a shadow for information dumps. There may be passwords." He shrugged. "There could be complications getting things, but should be no sweat leaving a message."

"He may not be tied into that computer stuff," Judith said.

"You can bet he knows somebody who is," Rick said. "Be blunt, use his name, he ought to *love* that. Somebody will get it to him."

Lena leaned back in her chair. "How about this. 'Jeff Hayes. I have what you want. You have what I want. I can give you ninety thousand reasons to take care of the merchandise and make me a trade.' "

"I s'pose it gets the job done. You could use a writer, hon."

The doorbell rang.

"I'll get that, Lena," Rick said. "Write that message down, so I won't forget."

Lena scrounged a pen from her purse and scratched the message out on a napkin. The front door opened and male voices sounded from the hallway. Lena frowned and looked up.

"Judith, do I look okay?" Lena tucked her shirt in and ran her fingers through her hair.

"Your hair's fine, leave it alone. Unbutton the first two buttons of your shirt."

"*Judith*. Listen." Lena fiddled with her buttons. "I'm having trouble with . . . I think it's body language, Judith. I want to be saying yes, but I think he's getting no. What I have to figure out is whether he's *getting* no, or *telling* me no."

"Stick to cleavage, Lena."

"It's the fuzz." Rick came back into the kitchen. "Lena, babe, you're coming apart at the seams."

Mendez paused in the doorway. His tie was loose, his hair rumpled. Lena stood up.

"Joel. Come in. You know Judith Barnes?"

Judith leaned toward him and offered a hand. "Hello."

"Get you a beer?" Rick said. "There's pizza if you're hungry."

"Thanks."

Lena guided Mendez to the chair beside her. "You okay?"

He nodded. His face was tight with exhaustion.

"Give me a plate, Rick," Lena said.

"Sure, hon. Just like old times, you giving me orders."

"You weren't such a big help back then."

"So, Sergeant Mendez." Rick put a plate on the table. "Where do we go to report a stolen light bulb?"

"A what?"

"Somebody took the light bulb out of the socket on the front porch."

Mendez looked at Lena.

She shrugged. "I know I had the light on when I left. Somebody took it out of the socket."

"And we know who that somebody is," Rick said. "So what you going to do about it?"

"Such as?"

"Can't you dust for *prints* or something?"

"Shut up, Rick," Lena said. "What's the point?"

"And what about all those messages he left on your answering machine? Surely that proves something."

"Yeah," Lena said. "Intent to sing."

"With a voice like his, honey—"

"Nice to meet you." Judith leaned across the table and shook hands again with Mendez. "Come on, Ricky, it's time to go home."

"What's the hurry? I want another piece of pizza. You want another—"

"Come *on*, Ricky."

"Take the cat," said Mendez.

"Be glad to," said Judith. She snatched Maynard off Lena's lap and tucked him gently into the carrier. " 'Bye, Lena. Be sure and call if you need anything."

" 'Bye, Judith."

Lena and Mendez were silent until the front door opened and closed.

"Come home with me tonight," Mendez said.

26

Mendez lived on the north end of town in a neighborhood that had hit bottom, but was bouncing back. His apartment was on the third floor of an old house that had been subdivided. Lena followed him up a black metal staircase that ran alongside the house.

Mendez went in first, turning on lights.

The wooden floor of the great room was dark with age and glistening with polish. On the right was a stone hearth and fireplace; straight ahead, windows shuttered against the night. A worn love seat and a rocking chair faced the fireplace. Behind the couch, against the outside wall, was a massive, scarred oak desk, flanked by old wooden file cabinets. A horseshoe of counters set off the kitchen, and a short length of hall led from the left.

"Coffee?" Mendez asked.

"Sure." Lena peered through the wooden slats of the miniblinds. The sky was black, speckled with the lights of downtown. "How'd it go in Knoxville?"

Mendez put coffee beans in a grinder. "They found the hubcap."

"Yeah? Nothing else?"

"No."

"But you were looking."

"Yes."

"Enlarge on that, Joel. What *did* you find?"

"Found a family of four, living in the dump. Mother, two kids, and a baby."

Mendez ran water, and the coffeemaker bubbled. Lena took a deep breath. "That smells good."

"Be ready in a minute."

Lena sat in the rocking chair. It was old, mahogany, and it made a comforting creak when she rocked. Something moved on the arm of the chair.

"What *is* this?" Lena narrowed her eyes. A lizard wandered onto her wrist and stared at her, its left eye rolling in a complete circle. "*Mendez.*"

He came over with a cup of coffee. "Garcia? What are you doing out?"

"He's a resident, I take it. Get him off me, okay?"

Mendez picked the lizard up. "He won't hurt you."

"This is your pet?"

"Garcia. A Senegal chameleon. Stroke his back."

Lena touched the lizard. It was soft and dry, like suede. The lizard's eyes closed, but his sides heaved with the quickness of his breath.

"He's scared," Mendez said. "I'll put him up."

Lena followed Mendez to the bookshelves that lined the wall behind the desk. On the bottom shelf was a glass terrarium, with a water bowl and a few dry branches. Mendez opened the lid and put Garcia inside.

"There are bugs in there," Lena said.

"Crickets. That's what he eats."

"How come they're hanging out on that rock? Why don't they hide?"

"It's a hot rock," Mendez said, pointing to a cord that ran from the bottom. "It's the big social spot. They hang out there all night."

"You have to go and catch them?"

Mendez grinned. "I buy them at the pet store. Eight cents apiece."

"That's cute, Mendez. That my coffee over there?"

"Yes."

Lena went back to the rocking chair, and held her mug with both hands. The coffee was very good. Mendez raised the blinds and turned off the lights.

"It's kind of like being in a planetarium," Lena said. She looked at the array of city lights in darkness. She could hear Mendez moving around, settling on the couch. She pictured him sitting here at night, thinking through his cases.

"You were supposed to sit on the couch," Mendez said.

"Why, this your favorite chair?"

116

"For reasons of seduction."

"I can move."

"I'll manage."

She could track him moving in the darkness. He squatted in front of her chair and took her hands.

She pulled them away. "It's not good to be too happy, Joel. People can take it away from you."

He pressed his hands on her thighs and the rocking chair tipped forward. "There are no ghosts here, Lena." He leaned close and kissed her.

Lena sighed and laid her head on his shoulder. He loosened his tie and eased it out of the collar. Lena slid her hands under his shirt and across the warm flesh of his back, scratching lightly with her fingernails.

He whispered her name. He unbuttoned her shirt, then reached up underneath to unhook the catch of her bra.

Lena tilted her head sideways and looked at him. "Can we really do it in a rocking chair?"

He stood up and took off his shirt, undid his pants, stripped. He was solid, compactly built, and she ran her fingernails across his belly to his hip, then down the side of his leg to his thighs.

He bent down and unbuttoned the cuffs of her blouse, and pulled it away from her arms. Her bra sagged loose and she took it off, letting it drop to the floor.

"You aren't going to run away this time?" he said.

"No."

He pulled her close and kissed her, unfastening her jeans, pushing them down her legs. She moved away.

"Shoes," she said, stumbling, off-balance. He knelt down and unlaced her tennis shoes, fingers precise and competent, the laces whipping from the closures. She took off her shoes and socks and jeans, letting them heap at the front of the chair. He shoved them aside, and held her again, his hands running along the top of her panties. He hooked a thumb under the elastic and eased the panties over her hips.

"Sit down," he said, pressing her into the chair. He pulled her forward to the edge, and knelt in front of her. "This is how it's done."

*   *   *

"You're not sleeping."

"Strange house, strange bed," Lena said.

Mendez rolled to his side and scratched her back. "Strange man."

"I like your house," Lena said. "I like your bed."

"Anything else you like?"

"I've been mad at you a whole long time, Mendez."

He kissed the back of her neck, pressing his body into hers. "Are you still mad at me?"

"You know that time I told you all that stuff about my house? How it was my family's place, and I got my strength there?" She rolled onto her back. "It's not true. Hayes took all the good things, the good years of growing up. It's all overlaid. One bad night, Joel. One bad night can kill years of good memories. And they can come and get you anytime."

"Who are 'they,' Lena?"

She was sleepy. "I like your house better than mine."

"You're welcome anytime."

"Joel, what if we never find Charlie? What if we *never* know what happened to him?"

"Lena."

"Hmmm? Don't stop, that feels good."

"We've had developments."

She opened her eyes. "You said you *didn't* find a body."

"I think we have the shooter. Valetta's killer."

"Mendez, that's *good*. Isn't it?"

"He's a high school kid, from Louisville."

"A *high school* kid? How'd you find him?"

Mendez rolled onto his back. Lena turned her head so she could see him.

"He talked about it when he got back to school. Told all his friends, and word got around. One of the parents called the police. Since it had that old cult flavor, it hit the desk of a Detective Casey. She's the Louisville ghostbuster. She called Knoxville last night."

"Are they sure this kid did it?"

"They have the gun, the car, and a confession. Hackburton is going up tomorrow to get a match on the hubcap."

"Why'd he do it? Why'd he talk about it?"

"It's stupid, but not out of line. The kids that get into this stuff, working cult crime for an adult group, they're easy to catch. For

118

exactly that reason. They brag about it at school. Don't destroy the evidence. They have the ultimate protection, the devil on their side. And when they get arrested, and it all falls apart, they're children again and they go to pieces."

Lena took Mendez's face between her hands, and made him look at her, not the ceiling. "Why did he do it?"

"That he won't say. They have to go easy, he's a juvenile. Seventeen. They may try him as an adult, or go after bigger fish."

"Somebody put him up to it."

"Casey thinks so. I agree. So does Hackburton."

"But the kid won't say who?"

"No."

"Does he know anything about Charlie?"

"I don't know. I'm going up to talk to Casey tomorrow. We've filled her in. She's doing what she can."

"Can I go with you tomorrow?"

"I ought to say no."

"You won't." Lena smoothed hair out of his eyes. "What does this mean, then, for Charlie?" She propped her chin on her fist. "You think this kid is involved with Hayes somehow?"

"I'm not sure. I think they're connected to the same people. I think Hayes and Archie were deeply involved with the top hierarchy of a hard-core, generational, satanist cult—based somewhere in the area where Jeff Hayes grew up. And I think Hayes has tried to get back in a position of leadership. And that Valetta wanted to skim off some blackmail money, and got killed for his trouble. He was looking for a stake when he got out of jail. He didn't get it from Eloise, so he tried to burn off some quick cash from the cult."

"Poor little Charlie. Right smack in the middle."

"It's always the kids in the cross fire." Mendez was quiet a moment. "One of two things has likely happened, Lena. Archie killed him, and we haven't found the body. Or he got taken up by the cult."

Lena rolled sideways and stared at the wall.

"Hackburton is watching the clinic in Knoxville," Mendez said. "There must be some reason Archie went there, instead of somewhere else."

"You think somebody there is part of this cult?"

"Consider the sequence. Archie goes straight to the clinic. Hours later, he has a meet. And then he gets killed—thirteen bullets and sacrificial mutilations. I think there's no doubt of a connection. Hackburton is checking out that doctor, taking down plate numbers of patients and employees. And we may get more from this boy who killed Valetta."

Lena put her hands over her eyes. "Which is worse, Joel? That Charlie is dead? Or that he's in the hands of this cult?"

Mendez didn't answer.

27

The lion blinked and smiled benevolently across the deep pit that separated him from his admirers. There were almost no visitors at the Louisville Zoo—it was midweek, lunchtime, off-season. But the weather was cool, and the animals were alert and amorous.

"He can jump over that pit anytime he wants," Lena said.

She and Mendez sat side by side on a stone wall. Mendez looked at the lion and nodded.

The tap-tap of heels caught their attention. A woman approached, smiling but wary. She was slender and tall, and wore black flats, a navy skirt, and a soft wool jacket. Her hair was short, blond, and curly.

Mendez stood up. "Detective Casey?"

She shook his hand. "Anita."

"Joel Mendez. This is Lena Padgett. She's private. From Lexington."

Casey frowned slightly. "I see."

"She's okay." Mendez held up a grease-spotted paper bag. "Chili from Ralph's."

Casey grinned. "Who set this up?"

Mendez smiled. "Clint Rosenburg told me that if I wanted a minute of your time, I should get you a quart of chili from Ralph's and offer to meet you at the zoo."

"God, the man knows me too well." Anita Casey laughed and sat on the edge of the stone wall. "Why am I being bribed? Something to do with the Skidmoore kid? You from Knoxville PD?"

"Lexington. I'm working on the kidnapping."

"That kid Valetta took?"

Lena quit swinging her legs.

"Did you question the Skidmoore boy about it?" Mendez asked.

Casey shrugged. "We got a lot on the murder itself, that's what he wanted to talk about. He about died when he went in there and saw how big Valetta was. That's why he missed a couple—or so he says. He's supposed to be a pretty good marksman. Done a lot of hunting with his dad." Casey grimaced. "But nothing on the kid that's missing. I don't think Skidmoore knew Archie Valetta from a hole in the wall. Valetta was an assignment."

"Assignment?" Lena said.

"From some man he calls his mentor. That's all he'll say. He was mixed up in cult stuff with some other kids, and then he got recruited at a hell party."

"Excuse me?" Lena said.

"Adolescent satanism," Mendez said. "Get together around a bonfire. Take drugs, chant to the devil, maybe sacrifice an animal."

"Typical sock hop," Casey said. She looked at Mendez. "This kid you're looking for. He's five years old?"

"Four," Lena said.

Casey looked at her thoughtfully.

"His mother hired me," Lena said.

Anita Casey pushed hair out of her eyes and looked at Mendez. "You got anybody on the bulletin boards?"

Mendez nodded. "One of the guys in vice."

"Good. Probably nothing will show up, but you never know. I watch the boards myself. If I see anything, I'll get with you. And I've got some people and places I can check into. But I'll tell you now, Skidmoore doesn't know anything about the kid. I've got the whole statement on video, though. It can't go out of the office, but you're welcome to take a look."

"I'd like to see it," Mendez said.

"Looks like a match on the hubcap. Eyeball, anyway." Hackburton took a pack of Merits out of his shirt pocket. "Assuming the lab backs us up."

Lena yawned and propped her chin in her hands. It was after seven and they still had the drive home. Casey had wanted them to wait until certain administrative personnel went home. She slid the video into the VCR and pushed the Play button. The television screen showed static, then a case number. The picture blossomed, showing a small interrogation room—yellowing ivory walls, scarred linoleum, a battered wood table.

Hank Skidmoore was young and nervous. He wore a black suit, white shirt, and brown tie. His eyes were blue, he wore round, thick glasses, there was acne around his temples. He had a thatch of brown curly hair that he pushed out of his eyes. He looked up and focused on the camera.

"State your name please," came a female voice. Casey's.

Skidmoore turned away from the camera, and stared across the room. "Henry P. Skidmoore. I go by Hank."

"What does the P stand for?"

"Umm. Peter." He took a sip of water from a glass that sat on the table.

"That's fine, Hank."

The boy smiled.

"Hank, where'd you get the camera?"

He shrugged. "I found it."

"Found it? It's got Archie Valetta's initials on it. Where'd you find it?"

"I saw it in the motel room. Valetta's. It was kind of neat. It has its viewfinder thing on the top. Like those old-timey cameras, you know?"

"So you took it?"

Hank shrugged. "Spoils of war."

"Okay, let's go back some, Hank. I want to understand, okay? I want to know how all this got started."

Hank frowned. "It was—" His voice cracked, and he cleared his throat. "I was kind of into Scientology. This was after my mom left. And me and Dad—I guess, you know, we weren't, we weren't getting along. And one of the Guardians noticed me."

"Who are the Guardians, Hank?"

"They're kind of like spies for the group." Hank grinned suddenly, looking young and attractive. "The CIA of Scientology. This guy introduced me to one of the bitches. This was just, you know, because he kind of liked me. He said I had potential. And shouldn't be stuck in that kind of chicken-shit Scientology stuff. That there was more to life."

"Do you know the name of the Guardian?"

Hank's face seemed to close up. "No."

"Who were the bitches?"

123

"Girls, you know, prostitutes. Only they're different, you know. They're not part of the Scientology stuff. They do it for Satan. Bring their money for the group. Anyway, this one, she calls herself Wendy, and me Peter Pan." Hank smiled bashfully, then stared at his hands.

"Tell me about Wendy, Hank."

"We . . . She liked me. She was even younger than me. But it didn't seem like it. She had lots of neat experiences. Like she'd been with this rock group awhile? They're real famous. But now she does this. She didn't like being with them after a while, 'cause they hit her a lot. And one of them liked to hold her under water. So she didn't like that.

"But we were friends and like. She . . . We could talk, you know? She was always so interested in everything, like what I did, and movies I saw, and gave me books to read. And I mean, she really did like me. She took me places to eat and stuff, and she paid for it. And she got me in with the kids, but then she said, you know, they were pretty small stuff. Kid stuff, and she said she had lived, and like they hadn't. And she knew things, she was what you call street smart, and she told me all kinds of stuff you can't believe." He shook his head from side to side.

"Then what?" Casey's voice.

"There was going to be a hell party, but I wasn't sure I was going. I told Wendy that was just kid stuff, and I wanted something . . . and wanted real stuff. And she said go to the party. That there might be somebody there I could, like, you know, talk to. Who might tell me things."

"And did you go to the party, Hank?"

He nodded.

"When was that?"

He shrugged.

"Do you remember what day of the week?"

"I think . . . I think it was Thursday. 'Cause I know I had school the next day. But I skipped."

"How long ago was this?"

"A few months."

"Do you remember which month?"

He shook his head.

"What kind of weather was it? Was it cold? Was it around Christmas?"

124

He slumped back in his chair, eyes downcast.

"Did you meet someone at the party, Hank?"

He put his elbows on the table, rocking it gently back and forth. He leaned forward. "I met this guy. And he said I had something. Like charisma, or magnetism, like that. And I asked him about the Black Cross. 'Cause those guys are so cool, and I really wanted to be in that. And he wanted to know where I heard about it. And it was Wendy told me, but I didn't tell him, 'cause I didn't want to get her in trouble."

"What's the Black Cross, Hank?"

"They're like murder for hire. They're bad. You haven't heard of them? I guess they're secret. No police could ever catch up to those guys. Those guys want you"—he snapped a finger—"and it's over, man. You're history."

"Do you really believe that, Hank?"

"Oh, yeah. Wendy, see, she told me about this rock guy. This other guy was bothering him and stuff. Said he owed him money, or something, and was getting like to be a pest. Real pest. And said he was going to the cops and stuff. And he knew some people kind of high up. So the rock guy, he calls this dude who calls the Black Cross. And next thing you know, this pesty guy, he gets it. I mean, all you got to do is pick up a phone. Talk about, you know, reach out and touch someone."

"Was this guy that you met at the hell party, was he part of the Black Cross?"

"I don't think he ever did things. I think he kind of like made arrangements. Or recruited. Your navy recruiter."

"Can you give me a name?"

Hank shrugged.

"Come on, Hank. You must have called him something."

"It wasn't his real name."

"What did you call him?"

"Enoch. Mr. Enoch." Hank stared down at the table.

"What did you-all talk about?"

Hank shrugged. "He told me that the Black Cross was like this elite kind of cadre. Like navy SEALs. Only the best. And that they wouldn't even consider a guy like me, 'cause I was so young. But he said sometimes they made exceptions, if somebody vouched for you."

"Did he say he'd vouch for you?"

Hank nodded.

"Say yes or no, Hank."

"Yeah. He said he would."

"Just like that? No strings attached?"

"I would have to prove myself."

"How would you have to prove yourself?"

Hank shrugged.

"What kind of things did he want you to do?"

Hank looked at his hands. "Just things."

"What did Enoch ask you to do, Hank?"

Hank mumbled something Lena could not catch. Anita Casey turned up the volume on the VCR.

". . . to be initiated."

"What did that involve?"

"It's a secret ceremony!" Hank almost stood up, then settled down in his chair. "If I tell you it all, I'll be struck dead, and the spirit will leave me to burn alone."

"What happened after the initiation?"

"I had to earn ten thousand dollars. It was like a token, for Satan, to prove I was sincere."

"How did they want you to earn the money?"

Hank's chin sank down to his chest.

"Hank?"

He took off his glasses and wiped his eyes. "I just did it, okay? I earned it."

"How long did that take?"

"I don't know. A few months. Three months."

"And then what?"

"I earned an assignment."

"What was the assignment?"

"To kill that guy in the motel. Archie Valetta. See, they knew I could shoot. And that I could get guns."

"Who gave you the assignment?"

"Mr. Enoch."

"What did he tell you?"

"That this guy had turned on the group, and that they had to, like, make him an example. And he wanted me to drive down there. But I couldn't."

"Why not?"

Hank looked up. "I never drove that far by myself. I was afraid

I'd get lost. So Mr. Enoch drove down and I followed him." Hank grinned. "I did pretty good till we got to the city. Boy, that Knoxville is confusing to find your way in."

Hackburton blew smoke.

"When we got to Knoxville, Mr. Enoch showed me the motel. Then he told me to go to McDonald's and get something to eat. And he'd tell me when to go. I ordered stuff, but I wasn't really hungry, so I threw it away and waited. And he came and said to shoot this guy, Valetta, thirteen times, and to cut him, like. Like they'd already showed me. Put his balls in his mouth and like that."

"Had you done that before?"

Hank shrugged. "And then I was supposed to get the briefcase and go."

"What happened to the briefcase?"

"I gave it to Mr. Enoch."

"What was in it?"

"I don't know. He told me not to look."

"And you didn't? Come on, Hank. You must have been curious. Nobody would know you'd peeked."

Hank looked up steadily. "Satan would know."

Casey turned the television off and hit the Rewind button on the VCR. Hackburton tapped a Merit out of his pack and lit it.

Anita Casey sat on the edge of the table, skirt hiked high on her thighs. "Okay." She looked at Mendez and Hackburton. "I've given you all I've got. Like I told Mendez, I'll be looking around for the kid, and watching the boards for anything that might come up. I think this group you're after may be connected to a child-porn ring I'm looking into. They're called the Five-to-Nines. Ever heard of them?"

Hackburton shook his head. Mendez frowned.

"There was a kiddie porn movie out by that name."

Casey reached for Hackburton's pack of Merits and helped herself. "That's where they picked up their title. According to one of my sources, there's some crossover between them and a heavy-duty cult in LaRue County. There can't be two damn cults in that area, surely. So it sounds like your people. If your Hayes shows up again, I'd like to know when and where."

Mendez nodded. "He's due to see his parole officer in about three weeks. If he shows, I'll grab him then."

Anita Casey pointed a finger at Hackburton. "I want a list of the license numbers you pick up at that clinic in Knoxville."

"Yes ma'am," Hackburton said. He looked at Casey, then at Mendez. "She tell you what they found in the kid's freezer? When they searched Skidmoore's house?"

Casey blew smoke. "Testicles, heart, and tongue. Done up in white butcher paper, just like at the deli. Our boy Hank's been this route before."

Hackburton looked at Lena. "You got kids?"

"No."

"Lucky you."

28

Lena trudged up the steps of Eloise Valetta's apartment building, checking the dark corners on her way up. She heard a footstep and glanced over her shoulder. Nobody. She knocked on Eloise's door.

For once, the television wasn't going next door. It was early. Most people were off to work, or huddled in bed.

Lena knocked again. Louder.

The door swung open. Eloise Valetta still had the patch over her gouged eye, but the swelling was down on the other. Her bruises were fading from blue to yellowish green. Her good eye seemed unfocused, till she squinted at Lena.

"Lena! Come in."

Eloise wore ragged pink bunny slippers and slid her feet along the carpet. She led Lena around two columns of square white boxes, stacked a foot over her head. She waved Lena to the chair, then sat down on the edge of the couch, her hands in fists.

"*Anything?*"

Lena looked at the boxes and sat down. "We haven't found him yet."

Eloise nodded dully.

"But we've got Archie's killer."

Eloise made a tiny, high-pitched noise.

"He didn't hurt Charlie. He never saw Charlie."

"You sure?"

Lena looked at the floor, then back at Eloise. "No, I'm not sure. But I don't think so."

Eloise covered her face with her hands.

Lena swallowed. "I'm not going to ask how you're holding up.

That's stupid, I know. But hang on, will you? Charlie's going to need you when I bring him home. Look, I got things I'm looking into—"

"What things?"

Lena was quiet.

"What things you looking into?"

"I think Jeff may know where Charlie is."

"Jeff *Hayes*?"

"Yeah."

"He killed your sister." Eloise's voice got small and whispery. "He killed his own little boy."

"Eloise. Either Archie killed Charlie and hid the body, or the cult that Hayes and Archie were involved with from before, they've got him."

Eloise reached out blindly, and Lena took both of her hands.

"It's best you know what's going on." Lena licked a tear that dripped down the side of her face.

Eloise burst out laughing. "Charlie used to do that! Lick his tears when they rolled down." Eloise put her head on her knees. "I want my baby back."

"Eloise, you shouldn't be here, facing this by yourself."

"No one. I don't want no one."

"What are you doing? Are you eating? Getting any sleep?"

"Eating? I'm eating *cake. Cake.* I'm baking." She pointed. "Look at all them boxes. They're all full of cakes. I can't . . . If I bake it's the only way I can stand being in my head. Lena, you got to take those cakes with you. *Please.* Take the cakes."

"Okay, Eloise. I'll take the cakes."

Eloise sighed deeply. "You take them."

"I will."

"I'll help you load them in the car."

"Fine. That's good. And, Eloise, I want you to come home with me."

"No. I got to be here in case Charlie comes home."

"You sure?"

"I got to bake."

"Okay," Lena said softly. "You bake."

"I'll help you load them in. Is it cold? Do I need a sweater?" She looked at Lena, but her good eye would not hold contact. Eloise looked at the floor, then at Lena, then at the floor again.

"Better slip on a jacket," Lena said.

Eloise stood up. She frowned and glanced around the room.

"Need a jacket," Lena told her.

"Jacket."

"Eloise. Mendez is working night and day on this, and so am I."

"Let's get them cakes loaded in," Eloise said. "I got to bake."

Lena cradled the phone on her shoulder, keeping her hands free to unplug the lamp and wrap the cord around the base.

"Help line," said a female voice.

"I need to speak with Valerie."

"She's in conference."

"Please tell her Lena Padgett is on the line, and it's urgent."

"Ma'am, are you all right? Can someone else help you?"

"It's not about me. Just give her the message, can you?"

"One moment."

The doorbell rang.

"Shit," said Lena.

The doorbell rang again.

"Shit. *Just a minute!*" Nothing to worry about. Hayes didn't ring the bell.

The bell rang three times, quickly.

"Hello?"

"Yes?" Lena said.

"Valerie will be right with you. Can you hold?"

"I *am* holding." Lena rubbed her temples. She heard the snap of the deadbolt unlocking, then the creak of the front door.

"Lena Bina?" Rick's voice. "You in there?"

"I'm in here, Rick!"

"Are you naked?"

"No, I'm not naked!"

"Hello?" came a puzzled female voice from the phone.

"Valerie? It's Lena."

"Hi, Lena. What's up?"

"This Valetta case—"

"Have you found the boy?" Valerie asked.

"Not yet."

"Lena Bina, where *are* you, sweetie?" Rick again.

"I'm in *here*. Shut up, I'm on the phone. Sorry, Valerie. We're still looking for Charlie. It's Eloise I'm worried about."

131

Rick stood in the doorway. "My God, what have you done? Did Hayes come for the furniture?"

"Rick, be quiet," Lena said. "Sorry, Valerie."

"Lena, what's this about Eloise? I've talked to her before, at the shelter. How's she holding up?"

"Not good. I . . . she . . . Could somebody, could you drop by and just talk to her some? Make sure she's okay?"

Rick put his hands on his hips. "This place looks worse than when we split. *What* have you done with the couch?"

Lena put a hand over the mouthpiece of the phone. "It's on the staircase to the basement."

"That's odd decorating, even for you, Lena."

"I couldn't get it all the way down."

"Lena," Valerie said. "Is Eloise Valetta alone?"

"Yeah. I tried to get her to come here, but she won't leave the apartment. She's in trouble, Valerie."

Rick left, and Lena heard him go into the kitchen and open the door to the basement. A loud thump and scrape sounded from the staircase.

"Why don't I go by there on my way home? Just check on her. Get her to talk," Valerie said. "That be okay?"

"*Thank you*. I'm sorry to ask. You sound tired."

"Up all night. Got a bad one going right now. With a husband who knows where we are."

"How'd he find you?"

"Sent his sister to us on a trumped-up thing, so she'd get delivered to the shelter and find out where we were. Bastard."

"Bitch."

"Yeah, both of 'em."

"Hell," Lena said. "Can you leave?"

"For a while. We're crawling with coppers right now. How'd it go with Walt?"

"Walt Caron, Mr. Empathetic Psychologist? What a sweetie. He blushed whenever your name came up. And he said he'd help, but I haven't heard from him yet."

"I'll call and give him a prod."

"Like you haven't got anything else to do."

"I wouldn't mind an excuse to call him."

"Go for it. Listen, I got to deal with Rick, or he won't go away."

"Lucky you."

"Let me know about Eloise." Lena hung up.

Rick stared at her from the doorway. "This room is so empty, it echoes. Lena Bina," he shouted. His voice was amplified by the emptiness. "Are you moving?"

Lena scratched the back of her head. She'd kept the rocking chair in the room, and a side table. The phone was on the floor.

"No, I'm not moving. I'm just trying to breathe."

"Get rid of the clutter, huh? Okay, Lena Bina, I gave up trying to understand you forever ago."

"Would you quit calling me . . . What is it, Rick?"

"Let us just say the audition went well. I was . . . ahem . . . brilliant."

"The . . . Rick, did you get the part?"

"Not yet. Call-back, though. I'll go up again next week."

"Rick, I'm happy for you."

"Don't get too happy yet, you'll jinx me."

"I jinx everybody these days. Did you do that thing for me?"

Rick sat on the floor. "How conventional of me to want a chair," he said absently. "Yeah, it's done. No nibbles yet, but it's early. I've set up a couple of shadows, and I'm trying to ferret things out, but somebody is being careful."

"Make sure they can't track you."

"They can't. What are you going to do with that lamp?"

"Put it somewhere. I can't put it in the basement, the couch is in the way."

"Want me to help you move it?"

"I'm going to leave it there, so Hayes can't sneak up on me from below."

"New ideas in home security."

"Rick, I've got a name for you."

"No insults, please, I *am* doing you a favor."

"To use on the bulletin board. Mr. Enoch. Put Mr. Enoch in there too, okay?"

"Mr. Enoch? Why does that make me think of that guy in *The Legend of Sleepy Hollow*? You know, the headless horseman one. What was that guy's name?" Rick shut his eyes. "Archibald Leach."

"That's Cary Grant's real name."

Rick cocked his head sideways. "Did you ever see *Penny Serenade*? But my favorite Grant movie is—"

"Rick, I got things to do. Can I walk you to the door?"

He stood up. "I'm going. I just . . . You'll be okay, won't you? While I'm out of town?"

"If I'm not, I'll call Judith."

"Good move, she's bigger than I am. Be good, then, Lena Bina."

Lena opened the front door. "Let me know what you find out."

Rick nodded. "Testing, one-two-three." He flicked the porch light on. "Hell, Lena, did it burn out again?" He stood on his tiptoes to unscrew the fixture. It was cool out, and the wind ruffled the carefully honed muss of his hair. "Hold the screws, Lena." He handed her the nuts and bolts that held the glass bowl of the fixture. "Sounds like a fast-food whorehouse."

"Ha ha. Oh, hell."

The light bulb had been broken off in the socket.

"Think it was Jeff?" Rick asked.

"Hope so," Lena said. "Me and him got business."

"Be bold, be bold," Rick said. "But not too bold."

29

Lena sat on the rug with her back to the wall. A stuffed bear, the top of its head barely visible, was propped up in the rocking chair. The bear's ears were held down with clothespins, and it wore a ball cap and sat with its back to the sliding glass door.

The television was on, the sound low but distracting. There was an open can of Coke on a table beside the rocking chair, but the bear never reached for it.

The phone sat on Lena's left, the baseball bat on her right. She had spent the last two nights alone in the living room with the bear.

Hayes would come. Sooner or later, he'd come.

The cop who had taken her home the night Valetta attacked Eloise was right. A gun would have been better than a baseball bat. If she'd had a gun that night, Charlie would be home with his mother. And she might not be so afraid right now.

Rick had bought a gun after Hayes had killed Whitney and Kevin. And had gotten rid of it, when he found her stroking the barrel against her temple.

Some people, Lena knew, felt dizzy when they stood up high, so sure they would fall that they felt the urge to bow to the inevitable and jump. She had never heard of anyone else who had that same kind of suicidal feeling about guns.

The phone rang. She wondered if it was Mendez. He seemed to have a sixth sense when she was up to something.

She would bring him in on this, when the time came. Right now there was too much risk he would not approve. And for all his help and consideration, she knew better than to rely on anyone but herself. Cops moved too slowly and had too many rules.

"Hello?"

"Lena Padgett?"

The voice was familiar.

"Speaking."

"Walt Caron. You remember we—"

"Of course. Hi. Any luck?"

"Yeah, pretty much. I have it set up for you. To go and talk to Melody Hayes. She is very . . . She is doing well, actually. She just checks in, as a resident, around Easter. Easter is a hard time for her because . . . of various reasons. Usually she's an outpatient. Unless there are bad spells. Her doctor is Delores Criswold, and she said it would be okay for you to come, but please get there in the afternoon. Don't wait until dusk."

"Don't wait until dusk?"

"That's what she said. She didn't explain. Melody is very . . . keyed up. About talking to you. She wants to get it done right away. They asked if you could come tomorrow. I said I'd . . ."

Something moved outside, at the corner of the sliding glass door. Lena squinted, but saw nothing through the darkness. She had set the blinds at half mast so Hayes could see in and she could see out. He was supposed to keep his attention on the bear.

"I'm sorry," she said. "What again? They want me to come tomorrow?"

"Yeah. If that's okay, I'll call them back."

"That's fine. Where is she?"

"It's a place on the outskirts of Nashville. Got a pen?"

She did. But no paper.

"Go ahead."

"Rolling Ridge," he said.

Lena wrote the name on her palm. "Rolling Ridge?"

"Right. Get on the Bluegrass Parkway, then take 65 South to Nashville."

"Got that," Lena said.

"Okay then, best way I think is, when you hit Nashville, take the Old Hickory exit—it's right after Goodlettsville. Stay on that till you get to Little Creek—you'll be going west past U.S. 41—then take Shaw Branch Road."

"Is it on Shaw Branch?"

"Yeah. Be sure and—"

Something moved, outside the door. A large dark man-shape. Lena glanced at the bear. One of the ears had come unpinned.

"Got it, Walt," she said quickly. "Don't worry, I'll find it. Thanks a lot."

"Uh . . . okay. I'll call and—"

"Good. Thank you."

Lena heard a squeak. The sliding door opened a crack.

"Don't forget, then," Walt said. "Before dusk."

Lena hung the phone up gently.

The sliding glass door eased open, moving slowly along the tracks. The usual stick and scrape were gone, and Lena pictured Hayes coming into her house, oiling the tracks.

He moved very quietly, gently thrusting the blinds to one side, his head turned to the back of the bear. Lena's fingers shook as she picked up the flashlight.

Hayes wore a large black overcoat that swayed against his legs. He moved quietly, until he stood just a couple of feet behind the chair. Lena switched on the huge black flashlight.

"Hello, Jeff."

She heard him catch his breath. He stepped back, squinting, throwing his arm up in front of his eyes.

Not Hayes. A bald man, with his face painted—diamond patterns, black and white.

"That you, Lena?"

It was Hayes. He had shaved his head.

"Going to a costume party?"

He stared into the dark corners of the room, then at her. He knew where she was.

He smiled. "Welcome to the theater of cruelty."

How like Rick he was. Give him a spotlight, and he would perform.

"The bread of life is broken." He held up a hand. "And it is death. The rock shall crush thee, and thou shalt perish in the fount."

"Gee, Jeff, I would've made popcorn if I'd known you were putting on a show."

Hayes frowned. "So, Lena. How did you find out about Mr. Enoch?"

"You'd be surprised." Lena held the baseball bat.

Hayes walked to the lamp and turned it on. Yellow light pooled in the center of the room. "*Mr. Enoch* is surprised. And unhappy.

137

But I didn't tell him who *you* are, because I don't want anything to happen till I get all my reasons. Ninety thousand reasons, Lena. We still on for the deal?"

"Yeah."

"Then get the money. Have it at hand."

"And then what?"

"I'll let you know. You still bank at Commerce, don't you? Go to the Valley Road branch, and see the teller at the second slot from the front door. His name is F. Breeding. He works ten to five. He'll have to let one of the vice presidents know."

"Know what?"

"Banks get funny sometimes, Lena, when people take out large amounts. I don't want some perky little teller calling the police, or checking to see if you're paying a ransom. So do as I tell you. Make sure and go to F. Breeding. He'll talk to a Mr. Franklin, and you won't have to answer embarrassing questions. You got that?"

"Breeding and Franklin. And then what?"

"And then I'll let you know." Hayes cocked his head to one side. "I *don't* want Mendez in on this, Lena. If I see him, or any cops, or see you go to the cops, the deal's off. The money's what I want, so I'm willing to trade you the kid.

"And believe me, Lena. You don't want Charlie going to the Easter services. They can be . . . draining. For now he is very sanguine. Afterwards, he will be exsanguine. You understand me?" Hayes did not smile.

Lena considered a dictionary.

"Be ready," Hayes said. "And I hope Rick is good at covering his tracks on the boards. Mr. Enoch is looking. You don't want him to find you. He is very hard on lambs."

30

Rolling Ridge was a private hospital, likely expensive, consisting of one-story yellow brick buildings that were old but well kept up. A wide expanse of lawn surrounded six or seven low buildings and a network of interlacing sidewalks.

Lena checked her watch. Three-thirty. She'd come straight from the bank to Nashville, and she glanced at the canvas bag of money. Ninety thousand dollars. A bit much to fit in her wallet. If she and Hayes weren't careful, the money would be stolen.

Should she leave it in the trunk, or carry it with her? Hayes might be watching for just such a chance. She'd carry it with her.

She parked her car—there were plenty of spaces. There were always too many or too few. Organ transplants might be possible these days, but parking lot design was still beyond societal skills.

Lena passed through the double glass doors at the front of the main building. The windows were threaded with wire mesh.

What would it be like to be inside looking out?

The receptionist was young, male, and solidly built. He wore a pair of chinos, a sport shirt, and a heavy leather watchband that made Lena think of restraints. His arms were thick and muscular, and Lena wondered if he did other things besides answer the phone.

Delores Criswold met Lena in the hallway. The beige-and-black-specked floor tiles were getting the once-over from a depressed-looking woman in a blue work smock. She swung the heavy buffing machine left and right, putting a shine on the ingrained dirt.

Criswold was short, rounded, with black, gray-flecked hair. Her eyes, behind steel-rimmed glasses, were alert and kind. She shook hands with Lena.

"I 'preciate you letting me come," Lena said.

Dr. Criswold looked at her speculatively. "Walt explained about the little boy. I hope you find him."

"I'll find him."

Criswold narrowed her eyes. "Melody is very strong. She'd have to be, to survive the things she's been through. But this is a difficult time of year for her. Please use good judgment when you talk to her."

Lena nodded. "I don't want to bother her. I don't want to cause her problems. But Charlie is four years old."

"That's what Walt said. And Melody's staying overnight for a while, so she ought to feel as safe as she can, this time of year. But don't stay past five-thirty or so, okay? That will give her plenty of time to wind down and get her mind on something else well before dusk."

"Sure," Lena said.

Delores Criswold nodded. "You'll find her just down the corridor. Take a right, then a left. First door you come to. Just go on in. She knows you're coming."

"Right, right, left," Lena said.

"If you get lost, Zack will show you." Criswold nodded her head at the man at the front desk, turned, and headed down the hall.

"Dr. Criswold?"

She stopped.

"What's the problem with dusk?"

Criswold looked at the woman buffing the floor. She moved close to Lena, her voice low. "That's when they used to come get her. At night after supper. Just as the sun went down."

The sign on the door said Do Not Disturb Any Further. Lena heard voices and music. A burst of laughter. She knocked.

No one came to the door. Probably, from the noise level, no one heard the knock. She closed her eyes for a moment, her grip easing on the canvas bag of money. She was tired. No sleep last night. Just Hayes, Hayes, pulsing in her head. And Whitney. And Kevin. And Charlie.

Lena opened the door a crack. The music and the voices stopped.

Rolling Ridge was not a mental institution in the sense of restraints and state auditors, but it was a residential facility for the

140

mentally ill, and Lena regretted that the knowledge made her look more closely at the people in the room.

There were seven of them. Four men and three women, all lounging in chairs and holding instruments. Lena saw a cello, a banjo, a violin, a guitar, a mandolin, another guitar, and a flute.

The woman with a cello between her legs wore Mickey Mouse ears and was blowing a large pink bubble. She frowned at Lena. The bubble gum lost air and sagged onto her chin.

"Excuse me," Lena said. "I'm looking for Melody Hayes."

No one said a word. Everyone watched her.

"I'm her."

A girl in a blue wheelchair with an empty IV pole looked at Lena. A violin rested in her lap. She clutched the bow tightly.

"Lena Padgett."

The girl stood up. The wheelchair had been a place to sit, no more.

"Y'all go on and play," she said to the others. "I'll be back in a while." None of them moved or spoke. Melody looked at Lena. "Come on with me."

She was slender. Skinny, actually, and no taller than five feet four, though her thinness made her seem taller. She wore heavy Levis, snug over the tiny bump of her hips, but gaping at the waist. She wore a short-sleeved knit blouse, faded pink, and her tennis shoes were cheap, dirty, and scuffed.

Standing up, she drooped like a flower blasted by the sun. Her arms hung to her sides, the elbows dry and knobby. Her hair was brown and long, thin and wavy. Her face was tiny and heart-shaped, her chin pointed, her eyes heavily made up.

She had a woeful, bedraggled look.

Lena followed Melody Hayes down the hall. Behind them the room stayed silent.

Melody headed for a door marked Exit and pushed the bar handle. Lena looked over her shoulder, half expecting someone to stop them.

"It's okay," Melody Hayes said flatly. "I got the run of the place. They don't keep us locked up or nothing." She paused by a white concrete bench and sat down. "It's a little damp," she said. "Must of rained here earlier. This okay with you? We could go back in."

Lena sat on the bench. It was cool on the back of her jeans. "This is okay."

The wind blew Melody's hair in her face, and she pushed it out of her eyes. She looked at Lena, her expression an appeal for something.

"You sure you want to talk to me?" Lena asked.

"It's okay," Melody said. "I talk all the time to Delores. I'm what you call desensitized. Or getting that way." She leaned forward. "I wanted to come outside so nobody can hear us. I think it would be all right, but you never know. Sometimes it's hard not to be paranoid. Everbody knows everbody, and things seem to get back to Jeff."

"Have you seen him lately?"

"Not *seen* him, exactly. But even in prison . . . he finds ways to let me know he's around."

Lena nodded.

"*You* seen him? Since prison?"

"Last night," Lena said.

Melody caught her breath. "What about?"

Lena shrugged, not wanting to give away the arrangements for Charlie. "He was strange. Wore a black overcoat, and he'd shaved his head. And he'd painted his face. In four diamond sections."

"White and black," Melody said softly. "Getting ready for the big show. Practicing, probably. Did he say anything?"

"It's hard to remember the exact words." Lena frowned. "Life listens, death speaks. The bread of . . . something, I don't know."

"That's all?"

"He said something about a Mr. Enoch. Do you know who that is? He said Mr. Enoch is hard on lambs."

Melody's face went from pink to white. "*Lambs?* He said lambs?"

"Yeah. Why?"

"Just—" Melody took a deep breath. "That's what his mama used to call us kids. Lambs. I went to live with them after my own mama died. I was pretty little. And my uncle Shep and aunt Lisa took me in. Shep and Lisa Hayes. My daddy couldn't care for a kid, 'cause he worked in the mines all day. I don't remember a lot about my mama, but she was a real good woman. I have her picture." Melody turned away from Lena, her voice low and flat. "You should of known Jeff's mama, though. She was something to see. Little and pretty, black curly hair. I used to love her hair. All dark and shiny

142

and thick. She had long black eyelashes, and she wore White Shoulders perfume. Dressed real nice."

Melody clasped her hands tightly together, and Lena noticed thick red scars crisscrossing her wrists.

Melody looked at Lena. "She used to call us her lambs. She had this big ole bentwood rocker. And she'd rock us, and love on us, and used to sing that song about little lambs who's lost their way. And she told us all about these watchers that lived in the wood. And if we try to run off, they get us."

"Did you ever try to run away?"

Melody nodded. "A couple times. They made me stop."

"How'd they do that?"

Melody's face was expressionless. "I had a pet goat. That's the kind of pet you wind up with, when you live way out of town. First time I run away they said don't, or we'll kill Jester. But they . . . Something happened real bad, so I run off again. When they brung me back, they killed Jester. Cut his throat and caught the blood in a big blue bowl. Uncle Shep was doing it, but my Aunt Lisa made me hold the knife. She made Shep put his hand over mine, so I'd do it. I quit running off after that. Even though I tried not to have no more pets."

Melody shook her head. "Sometimes Aunt Lisa—she could be so sweet. She'd talk nice to you, and you'd want so bad to make her happy. But she was always the one to make me do the things. Things I didn't want to. And Jeff was her boy, and she made him do things, too. But they seen real early that he was special. Later he was kind of set apart, and doing things with the grown-ups.

"But when we were littler, me and Jeff used to be real close." She cocked her head sideways. "They started taking us to what they call the picnics when we was about four." She frowned. "One time in school some boy asked me to go on a family picnic, and I 'bout clawed his eyes out."

They were silent a long moment.

"This was how it would go," Melody said. "Aunt Lisa would give us our dinner first, real early. Then when Uncle Shep would come in, they'd tell us to go on out back and play. And we'd go out and play till dark. We had an old rusty yellow swing set. Musta' been a hundred years old, but we loved it. The slide was bent, and you had to be careful, 'cause one time Jeff cut his hand on the metal, and Aunt Lisa got real mad.

143

"We'd get sticks and dig in the dirt under the swing set. Didn't have much grass back there. And some nights they would come and get us. After supper, they'd drive us in this old green Buick. The seats were so deep down in the back, that even though I usually got set in somebody's lap, I could hardly see out the windows.

"There was always lots of people crammed in the car, and we got pretty hot back there, even with the windows down. Some of them people didn't smell too good, but you could always get a sniff of Aunt Lisa's perfume.

"And we'd head out for the woods somewhere. State parks sometimes, or campgrounds. Maybe somebody's farm. There was always lots of people there, and they was all busy and excited. They'd bring the altar in back of a pickup, and a whole bunch of men would have to lift it off. They had fires to start up, and people was changing clothes. Jeff and I had to stay out the way. When we got bigger they made us look for sticks and stuff to help keep the fires going.

"But when we was real little, me and Jeff, we'd kind of go and hunker down by a tree and hope they'd forget we was there. Sometimes they'd make us go in a barn till they called us out. Me and Jeff used to get along then. We'd stay side by side, and pretend we was hiding in mine tunnels, and if we wasn't quiet, the timbers would come crashing down.

"But sooner or later, they'd call us in. And at first, all we had to do was watch. Listen and learn, they told us. And Jeff, he was real smart. And they saw that. And then one night they buried him alive."

Lena winced.

"They'd do that to some of the kids. They did it to Jeff a bunch of times."

"Did they ever do that to you?"

Melody looked at her feet. "Once they did. It was supposed to prepare you. Me and Delores talked about that. When they meant prepare a kid, what they had in mind was breaking them.

"It was real bad for Jeff. 'Cause when we was kids, him and me, we use to have to go get locked in the shed when we was bad. Or they put us under the porch of the house, and they was lots of spiders under there. And he would have a terrible time. Breathe real hard, and cry a lot. When they saw he was special, they took him in a separate car from me, that first time, I think. And what they did was they buried him in a coffin, with some kind of a tube thing to help him breathe."

Melody shivered. "He wasn't the same after that night. He quit minding being in the shed. And they let him do things—to us other kids. I would go to sleep and wake up with him standing over me, and blood all over. Then they'd let me go somewhere and sleep, and this fat lady named Mira would clean me up. And Aunt Lisa made sure our clothes covered up the cuts."

Lena glanced at Melody's wrists.

"I did those myself," Melody said.

"This Mira," Lena said. "Is she still alive?"

"I guess. I don't go back home. But she called me a couple years ago. You believe that? Wanted me back."

"You remember her last name?"

"Farley. Mira Farley. Her common-law husband was Alfred Ginty."

"Was he part of the group?"

"Yeah."

"How about your aunt? Is she still alive?"

"No. She died when Jeff was fifteen."

"What happened?"

"I don't . . . I don't remember."

"I need names, Melody. People who might still be involved with Hayes."

"I made you a list." Melody dug in her pocket and pulled out a folded piece of orange construction paper. "I don't know if all these people are still around. And I'm not sure how the names are spelled. I hope it helps."

"It helps." Lena looked at Melody. "Thank you for talking to me."

Melody grabbed Lena's wrist. "Just get the boy. Get him as fast as you can, and don't give up on him. Even if it takes a long, long time. Find him. And you come back if I can help you any more."

Lena stood up. "I'll let you know when I find Charlie. And I'll let you know when I see Jeff back in jail. Which I'm planning to do."

Melody frowned. "Delores told me he killed your sister and her little boy."

"He did."

"Someday he's going to kill me."

"No. He's going back to jail."

145

Melody looked at her seriously. "C'mere. Show you something."

She got up and walked to the base of a dogwood tree. It was a mature tree, just blossoming with white flowers. Melody picked up a stick, and squatted down to dig. She scrabbled in the dirt with her fingers, making a satisfied noise, finally, and bringing something up out of the sandy soil. She blew on it, and wiped it on her shirt, and held it up for Lena to see.

A seashell.

31

The Cutlass sat in the parking lot—grimy, rusty, reassuringly tacky. Lena had locked it, and it was still locked, but a piece of paper had been folded and wedged between the horn and the steering wheel.

Someone has been in my car, she thought.

There was something on the front seat. A tiny, blue-striped T-shirt.

Lena unlocked the Cutlass and reached for the paper.

RAY LAKE RECREATION AREA. CAMPSITE 49. YOU BRING ALL YOUR REASONS, AND I'LL GIVE YOU WHAT YOU WANT. BE THERE, TO-NIGHT, AT 8:30 P.M. JUST YOU AND ME.

BE ON TIME OR IT'S ALL OVER BETWEEN US.

HAPPY EASTER!!!

Lena recognized the shirt. Little Charlie Valetta had been wearing it the night Archie had snatched him. It was crumpled now, streaked with oily black dirt. There was a smear of dark red on the neckline.

Lena sat down hard in the front seat of the car. She closed her eyes and took a deep breath.

Bloodstains dried reddish brown, not red.

Lena looked at the shirt again, scraping at the red streak with her fingernail, sniffing the sweet scent.

Candy.

There was a map on the front seat next to the shirt. A LaRue County map. Lena opened it up and studied it. She checked her watch. Three-thirty. Figured mileage in her head. Daylight, and trails in the woods.

If she left right now she still might not make it.

She remembered Hayes talking about Charlie, Easter services, and exsanguination. She'd had to look it up—exsanguinated. It had been defined as anemic. Or bloodless.

Lena folded the map and started the car.

She stopped at Hooper's Gas-n-Go, and pulled to the side of the gas tanks. She opened her wallet and counted up her cash. Four dollars and seventy-eight cents.

Lena opened the canvas bag and took out a hundred-dollar bill.

She looked over her shoulder while she pumped gas. Was Hayes watching?

Maybe. Maybe not. She wasn't prepared to meet him at a lonely campsite with ninety thousand dollars in a canvas bag, and Charlie Valetta's life dependent on the outcome. She would call Mendez.

The pay phone was on the wall between the restrooms. An old man in baggy shorts and knee socks was headed right for it. Lena nudged him sideways and got there first.

Lena put a quarter in. The old man edged close.

"*Private* call," Lena said coldly. She wondered why she found it so easy to be rude.

The old man grimaced and went into the men's room.

Lena got a Detective Lester, who she thought she might have met at one time or another. She had the feeling she didn't like him. He knew who she was, and told her that Mendez was meeting with Anita Casey in Louisville. He gave her the Louisville number.

A desk officer in Louisville told her that Detective Casey was out and she didn't know who Mendez was, and hadn't seen him. She agreed that if she didn't know him, she couldn't know whether or not she'd seen him, but she was not inclined to pursue the matter.

Lena had one more quarter. She dialed Rick's number.

"Judith? It's Lena. Is Rick there?"

"Sugar, he's in Louisville. The call-back, remember?"

"*Fuck*."

Judith sounded wary. "Lena, honey, better tell me what's up."

Lena glanced over her shoulder. The guy behind the cash register kept looking her way, and smiling when he caught her eye. Lena turned her back on him.

"I'm meeting Hayes at the Ray County Recreation Area. Campsite forty-nine. I'm making a trade."

Judith sounded breathless. "Where's sweetie?"

"Who?"

"Mendez. Don't tell me he's not with you."

"He's not," Lena said, wishing her voice weren't quite so shrill. "I can't get him. He's in Louisville with that bitch, Anita Casey."

"Cupcake, what you going to do? You want me to come?"

"Try to get hold of Mendez for me. Maybe he can arrange something local, if he can't get there in time."

"Lena, you better not."

"Don't worry, Judith, I got my baseball bat."

"Lena—"

"Judith, Charlie is four years old."

"Right. But, Lena, sugar, you got to use your smarts on this. If you could sneak up, maybe, and bash Jeff's head in, do that, okay?"

"Stay with the phone, Judith. Nobody but Mendez."

"I hear you. Go, cupcake. Break a leg."

Lena hung up.

She wasn't hungry. She wasn't stupid either, so she cruised the grocery counters, found a chicken salad sandwich, a bag of Ranch Style Fritos, and a giant Tootsie Roll. She grabbed a can of Coke, a package of new batteries for the flashlight that she hoped was in the trunk of the Cutlass, and pulled out her hundred-dollar bill.

The clerk looked it over carefully.

"You wanna pay for this candy bar with a hundred?"

"Not just the candy bar. The sandwich, the chips, the Coke, the batteries, and the gas on pump nine."

The woman in line behind her pursed her lips. "The gas alone ought to do it."

32

It was cool, too cool, now the sun was sliding away. A brown wooden sign with yellow lettering pointed the way to campsite 49. Lena bent over a water pump, rinsing and refilling the empty can of Coke. Water splashed over the side of the can, getting her sleeve wet and drenching the top of her shoe. The Tootsie Roll crackled in her pocket. She tucked the flashlight under her arm, hefted the baseball bat, and headed down the trail.

It was lonely out.

There had been no one to meet her at the ranger station, though she had cruised by slowly two times. With the exception of an old man on a tractor, she had seen no one.

It was not possible to walk quietly. The path was wide and easy, covered with dry, wadded brown leaves. Winter had blasted the trees, though there were a few thinking about leafing out.

The trail narrowed and sloped steeply upward. The trees thinned, and on the right the land cleared. Lena could see quite a ways over the tangle of weeds and coarse brown scrub.

Something rustled. Lena stopped and looked, but saw nothing. She took a sip of flat, Coke-flavored water.

She was breathing hard when she crested the hill. She walked along the ridge top, keeping her pace steady. A black-and-white butterfly, attracted by her bright red sweatshirt, fluttered close to her waist, then skittered away. Three Canada geese flew overhead, complaining in odd hoarse barks.

Lena wondered if Mendez and Anita Casey were having dinner together in Louisville.

She wiped her forehead with the palm of her hand, and tucked

150

her hair in the back collar of her shirt. The air was damp and cloying and clouds were gathering overhead. Lena picked up the pace, wondering how much farther she had to go.

Dusk settled heavily and she turned on the flashlight. The wind swirled her hair. A light cascade of raindrops pattered on the leaves. Lena pulled on her jacket. A silvery can of Bud Lite had been squashed and left under a bush. Lena curled her lip.

She walked.

The path veered right and widened, almost into a road. A sign showed an arrow to campsites 45 to 53. Deep tire ruts, spaced closely together, led the way. Lena saw paw prints in the muddy dirt on the right-hand side of the road. Dog, most likely. Big dog.

Darkness came gradually, and the rain picked up. Lena shivered and adjusted the canvas bag under her arm. She had to go slower now. Every once in a while she stopped and killed the light, scanning the trees around her. No other flashlights. Was Jeff Hayes out there, waiting in the dark?

Charlie would be scared. If he was there. She was scared.

Mendez picked a fine time to be tied up in Louisville.

Moonlight poured through the trees, and white mist rose from the ground as rain-cooled air mixed with warm currents. The path narrowed again and swung left. The decomposed leaves were wet now, and slippery. Lena slowed her pace. It took all of her concentration to follow the trail. She stopped every few yards, waiting for streaks of fog to slip away so she could find the path.

Somewhere geese were honking and squawking loudly. Lena stopped and listened. About a mile away, she decided. The rain pelted her sporadically, gentle through the canopy of trees. She was wet through, and cold. Her shoulders began to ache. She left the Coke can on the trail and readjusted the canvas bag. Never thought she'd get tired of carrying money.

The insects got loud, stirred by the rain and the warmth of the day. Too early for mosquitoes. All was not lost.

Lena wondered if Charlie was cold. Or hungry. She was hungry. She thought about the Tootsie Roll, but decided to save it. Charlie could chew on that while she got him home and out of the woods.

If she got him out of the woods.

Her light caught one of the brown wooden signs, designating campsites 50 through 54. She'd gone too far. She doubled back, shining her light on the right-hand side of the trail, looking for markers.

A few yards away she found it—a circular clearing where the paths converged, an outhouse, and a marker that pointed to camp-sites 46 through 49.

She shone her light around the clearing and the woods, then shut it off and listened. Nothing out of the ordinary.

Lena opened the door of the outhouse. The hinge creaked. She went up two steps and inside. The smell wasn't too bad, all things considered. Not too good either. There was no roof, and the rain had saturated the roll of toilet paper and turned it gray. Spiderwebs hung in the corners, insects had left eggs on the walls. The toilet seat was held in the up position by a spring in order to provide maximum convenience for men, who usually used the woods. A small brown moth dashed crazily back and forth in Lena's light.

The light caught a flash of movement by her left foot. Lena aimed the flashlight at the floor. A baby garter snake, not much fatter than an earthworm, lifted its round, brown head lethargically, disturbed by the noise and the light.

Lena pushed the door open and backed slowly down the two steps. The door slammed shut and she headed for the trees.

A narrow gravel path led to campsite 49. Lena figured Hayes could hear her coming. She glanced over her shoulder, shining the light behind, beside, and in front. Maybe he was up in a tree. She checked her watch and bit her lip. She was thirty-seven minutes late.

The gravel trail ended in a clearing. Lena shone the light, illuminating a large, splintery picnic table, two stone steps that led to a squared-off tent site, and a concrete pit for campfires.

No sign of Hayes.

The dirt was flat and worn down. Lena walked the perimeter, shining the light into the trees.

"Hayes?"

An asphalt path sloped down through the trees to the water. She followed it.

The lake was huge, blue-black, and silent. A fish jumped, making a splash and a ripple. The sky was deep black and livid with stars. Moonlight touched the water, turning it milky white.

Lena shone the light on the reddish, pebbled wet soil. Every few yards was a landing, shored up with cement blocks, and a line post with a campsite designation. These were boat-in campsites, Lena realized. Somewhere between backpacking and Airstream trailers. There were three landings in the horseshoe-shaped inlet, but no boats. She headed back up the hill to the campsite. Somewhere close by came the hoot of an owl.

Lena sat on top of the picnic table. Hayes had to see her, after all.

An enormous black ant moved across the table. The ant was carrying something: the sagging corpse of another ant.

The picnic table was wet. Lena felt the seat of her jeans soaking up water. It struck her that there were people who thought it was fun to come out here. She frowned, watched the trees, and listened.

33

Lena sat in the dark, enduring wave after wave of shivers. Her ribs were getting sore. It was after midnight—well after one, actually—when she flashed the light on her watch. She sat on the edge of the picnic table, her shoulders slumped, back aching, arms wrapped around her sides.

She thought how the cold could exhaust you. She did not want to walk those miles back to the car. Earlier, picturing herself hand in hand with Charlie, she'd had confidence about finding her way back. Now, alone in the dark, she wasn't so sure.

"Time to call it a night, don't you think?"

Lena jumped off the picnic table and stumbled over a tree root. Someone stood at the edge of the circle, the magic circle of site 49. Lena shone her light into the woods.

A dog whimpered.

The man was black, tall, solidly built. There were touches of gray in his hair at the temples, and he had a serious, comforting face. He was in uniform—the olive drab of the National Park Service. A large black Labrador retriever stood close to his leg. The dog's nose twitched, and she yearned toward Lena.

"You mind?"

Lena turned off the light.

"You Lena Padgett? PI from Lexington?"

"Who are you?"

"Don't be afraid. Anita Casey radioed me from Louisville. I'm Ted Moberly. I'm here to see you're okay."

Lena took a deep breath. "I'm okay." It was hard to talk when your teeth were chattering.

"Sound cold to me. You been out here long enough. Don't think he's going to show tonight."

"I was late getting here. I may have missed him."

Moberly shook his head. "Don't think so. I haven't seen anybody but a few night fishers. Local boys I know."

"How long have you been here?"

The dog whimpered.

"Hold on, Sally." Moberly looked at Lena. "You like dogs okay?"

"Sure."

"Okay, girl," he said to the dog. "Go make friends."

Sally bounded forward and shoved her head at Lena's leg. Lena staggered sideways, glad that Sally was too polite to jump. She patted the slick black head and Sally pressed closer, wagging her tail and panting.

"Good girl," Lena said. "Good dog."

"What time was this meet set up?" Ted walked closer. Sally wagged her tail, and he scratched her ears.

"Eight-thirty."

"What time you get here?"

"Ten after nine."

"Close enough." Ted leaned against the edge of the picnic table and the wood creaked. "Uh. Getting too old for this." He shook his head. "I don't think he ever showed."

Lena frowned. "How much did Casey tell you?"

"Anita? Pretty much everything. We've worked together before, same problem. Not your man Hayes, but others. Your Mendez wanted to call out the marines, but Anita convinced him that one marine was enough."

"So you're a marine, huh?"

"Used to be. Ex–navy SEAL."

"Vietnam?"

"Do I look old enough for Korea?"

"Hard to tell in the dark."

"Huh. Don't waste time trying to butter *me* up."

Something rustled in the woods, and Sally pricked her ears.

"It's okay," Ted said softly. "Go on, get it."

Lena put her chin in her hands.

"We need to check in," Ted said. "Last I heard, Mendez was on his way. Said they'd stop at my place. I got a big pot of chili on the stove. How about we go have a bowl while we wait."

"He's not coming, is he." It was a statement. No answer required.

Ted's voice deepened. "I been here since nine-thirty. Walking the perimeter, in a two-mile range. No sign of anybody. And I'd know if he'd been around."

"It doesn't make sense," Lena said. "I know he wants the money."

Ted straightened and stretched. "I got a canoe beached on the other side of the peninsula. No more than a half-mile walk. *Sally*." The dog came bounding back. "Ever taken a canoe out in the moonlight?"

"Nope."

"Tonight's your lucky night."

The canoe glided through the dark silky water. A tiny lamp on the right-hand side of the prow cast a narrow green beam of light. Ted sat in the back of the canoe and paddled. He had declined Lena's offer of help. Sally lay on her belly in the middle of the canoe, her head resting on the left-hand side of Lena's seat.

The shoreline was dark and quiet. Fog drifted across the water and shrouded the inlets.

"How do you find your way?" Lena asked.

"Polaris over my right shoulder."

The buzz of a gasoline engine was sudden and close. Lena turned and strained her eyes. The boat was almost invisible in the darkness, a hundred yards away to their right. It was built for speed and silence, and painted flat black. It ran without lights.

"That's no fisherman," Lena said.

"Businessman," Ted said laconically. He turned the boat until they faced the opposite shore.

Lena wondered what he was doing, then the wake hit and she understood. The canoe bobbed up and smacked down, rocked by violent ripples. Lena didn't like the way the canoe rocked from side to side, feeling no steadier than roller skates on ice. She put a foot on the canvas bag and pinned it to the bottom of the canoe.

The ripples passed, and Ted turned the canoe. A minute later, the ripples found the shore, smacking noisily against rock and tree roots.

"Pretty out, isn't it?"

"Umm," Lena said.

34

Ted Moberly's house was brown fieldstone, a snug two-story, set on a hill in a thicket of trees. Ted led the way across a broad porch, his feet thumping on the hard wood. Lena could smell chili cooking all the way outside. Sally lifted her head and sniffed the air.

The house was small and immaculate, like the one in Lena's childhood book of fairy tales, *Goldilocks and the Three Bears*. She stopped just inside the doorway.

"Don't be shy," Ted said. "Come on in."

"My feet are muddy."

Sally groaned and shook vigorously, spattering Lena and the floor with water droplets and mud.

"As you can see, we don't worry about such things. But take your shoes off, if it bothers you. That chili smells good, don't you think?"

Lena nodded. She set the baseball bat in the corner, and put the canvas bag on the floor. She bent down and unknotted the laces of her shoes. The leather was wet and they were hard to pull off. Her socks were like sponges, so she took them off, along with her wet jacket, and piled them in the corner with the shoes. She shivered. Her shirt and jeans were damp. The floor was much too cool on her feet, but the house was warm. The heat pump ran, giving off a homey background hum.

Ted disappeared through an open doorway on the right. Lena followed and found herself in the kitchen.

The cabinets were dark polished pine. Lena's feet made soft slapping sounds on the warped yellow linoleum. A round rag rug, shades of amber and red, rested in the center of the room, cushion-

157

ing a rectangular wooden table. The refrigerator was white, humming loudly, and the stove and sink were harvest yellow enamel. There was no dishwasher in the small square kitchen, and clean dishes were drying in a plastic holder on the right-hand side of the sink.

Ted stood at the stove, using a large wooden spoon to stir a copper-bottomed pot. He sniffed deeply.

"Ummm." He looked over his shoulder. "How wet are you? I got some dry clothes I could lend you."

"I'm okay."

"Sit down. I'll get some coffee going."

"Think we should give Mendez a call?"

"He's on his way."

The dog nosed an empty stainless-steel food bowl, pushing it under the cabinet. She looked at Ted, who ignored her. She lapped from the water bowl, slopping water onto the floor and wetting her chest.

"You're still looking cold," Ted said. "Why don't you grab that jacket? Over there—hanging by the back door."

Lena took the black leather jacket and put it over her shoulders. The leather was cracked and worn, and gave off the vanilla-molasses smell of rich pipe tobacco.

Ted picked up the pot from his Mr. Coffee and poured cold brownish black coffee down the sink. He glanced over his shoulder at Lena, huddled on the edge of her chair.

Sally, toenails clicking on the linoleum, padded onto the rug, leaving muddy paw prints. Her tail wagged vigorously and she shoved her head in Lena's lap. Lena noticed white hairs in the dog's wet muzzle, and around her neck near the worn leather collar. Sally's eyes were kind and knowing, and Lena realized this was no young dog. Lena scratched Sally's ears, and the black Lab sighed, snuggled close, and made a high-pitched groaning noise back in her throat.

"You got a friend for life," Ted said. He poured water through the coffee filter and the heater sputtered and steamed. A thin stream of brown liquid filtered into the glass pot, and the coffee smell mixed pleasantly with the garlic-tomato smell of the chili.

"You told me you and Anita Casey have worked this problem before. Did you use to be a cop or something?"

Ted grinned. "Naw, now." He dipped a ladle in the pot of chili

158

and filled a brown ceramic bowl. "There you go. Let me get you a spoon." He fished a large serving spoon out of a drawer that rattled with silverware. "Be careful now, it's hot."

Lena dipped the spoon into the thick red chili, churning onion, beans, and plugs of sausage. Sausage? It *smelled* good. She blew a spoonful until it was cool, and took a small taste.

"How is it?"

"Wonderful. Could I . . . could I have a glass of water, please?"

" 'Course. Kind of spicy, I hope that's okay."

"Fine. It's good. Great."

Ted set a large glass of icewater on the table in front of her. Lena took a deep swallow.

"Naw, I never been a cop," Ted said. He sat down across from Lena, dipping a large spoon into his bowl of chili. "Coffee be ready in a minute." He took a bite of chili. "You want any Tabasco?"

"No. Really."

Ted jumped up and opened a cabinet. "I go through more Tabasco. My wife—my ex-wife, that is—she keeps some around, just for when I'm there. Same bottle, year after year. Sauce is turned kind of green and dirty brown. Got an interesting flavor, that's for sure, but don't tell her that. I must go through a bottle a month. Guy that runs the grocery store keeps it in stock just for me. Says if he had a nickel for every squirt I use . . ."

Lena took another bite of chili, avoiding the thick chunks of sausage. Sally whined softly and drooled onto her leg.

"I see things sometimes," Ted said. He stared into a corner of the kitchen. "Like one time, I came across three or four tiny little nooses, hanging in a tree. Strange, that night. And right by the nooses were the ashes of a fire. When I rooted through it, I found bone fragments."

"Human?"

"Small animal. Rabbit, maybe, or cat. Sometimes what I find is pretty obvious—blackened circles of ashes, candle stubs, pentagrams."

Lena fished a piece of sausage to the top of the bowl. Ted was not paying attention. She slipped the sausage under the table to Sally. The dog opened her mouth, and the sausage disappeared swiftly and silently. Sally graciously licked the excess chili from Lena's fingers.

"Where do you find these things? Just out in the woods?"

"Off in the remote sections sometimes. Or sometimes not. Some people won't walk very far. Depends on who you're dealing with. Lot of times it's just kids. Bored, middle-class white kids—kids who ought to know better. Trying to make sense in a senseless world, I guess." He shook his head.

Lena slipped another piece of sausage under the table, and Sally politely snapped it up.

"What do you do about it?"

"You don't go running to the head of the Park Service telling stories about devil worshipers, that's for sure. Not if you want to keep your job."

"Is it something about this area, do you think?" Lena ate a spoonful of chili.

"Aw, no. This is going on all over. Some of my buddies in the Park Service, they got similar problems. Same things happening, just nobody says much. 'Cept maybe when we're together, having a couple beers."

"So you don't do anything about it."

"I keep tabs," he said. "See what kind of groups I got. It's not like I run across something every week. But you can usually tell how many you got. If they're kids or not. I see their bonfires sometimes, over the hills. I do get upset when they start rooting in the cemetery. That we can prosecute, but they're hard as hell to catch."

Lena flinched. "What do they do?"

"Dig up graves," Ted said softly. "Steal bones."

Sally put a paw on Lena's leg, and Lena fed her a chunk of sausage.

"How does Anita Casey fit into all of this?"

"Had us a pretty serious group some time back. About eight years ago. And Anita had a missing girl, a teenager, that she tracked to this area. We thought for a while she might be with them."

"Was she?"

"Don't know. Never found her."

"That when you and Anita met?"

"Yeah. She calls me in on her missing persons, if somebody disappears in the woods."

"You track them or something?"

"Me? No. That's Sally's job. She's an air-scent dog."

"What's that?"

"Trained to find people. She can even find them under water, sometimes."

Lena patted Sally on the head. Sally gave her a sloppy doggie smile, then perked her ears and stood at attention. A second later Lena heard the sound of tires on gravel.

"She never barks," Lena said.

"Trained not to." Ted stood up and looked out the window. "Looks like somebody called the cops."

Lena stood beside Ted and rose up on her tiptoes so she could see. A Buick Skylark was pulling up next to the shed out back. Behind it was a navy blue Mazda. Mendez.

The door opened on the driver's side of the Buick and Detective Casey got out.

Ted headed out of the kitchen to the front door. Lena stayed at the window, though she could see very little in the dark. Now would be a good time to feed Sally the rest of the sausage. But Sally was outside, saying hello to Mendez. Lena watched as Ted and Anita shook hands, and the three of them stood talking.

They were moving toward the house now. Lena smoothed back her hair. The rain and fog had turned it to corkscrew curls and tangles. The front door opened and closed, and she heard Sally's toenails on the wood floor.

Anita Casey stopped in the doorway of the kitchen. "So you lost him," she said, coming into the room. The rain and humidity had reduced her hair to limp strands that hung close to her face.

Lena turned her back to the sink and folded her arms.

Ted walked into the kitchen. "He never showed, Anita."

"Can you really be sure, Ted? I know you're good, but it's a big area out there."

"Pretty sure," Ted said. He opened the corner cabinet and reached for two more bowls.

Anita cocked her head sideways and glared at Lena. "Even my greenest rookie wouldn't walk into something like this alone."

"I'm not your rookie. I'm not a cop."

"No, you're worse. You're an amateur who's likely screwed everything up."

Ted snorted. "You told me yourself, Anita, she's a private investigator."

Anita Casey laughed. "You know how you get to be a PI in Kentucky, Ted? You get a tax license from the state like any other business, then you put an ad in the yellow pages. You could hang out a shingle tomorrow, Ted, if you were so inclined."

Lena folded her arms. "Tell you what, Anita. If being an amateur means not sitting on your butt until there's nothing left to do but pick up the pieces, then, yeah, that's me."

"And what exactly have you accomplished?"

"Find all your missing people, do you?"

Anita gave her a sharp look. "If you're talking about—"

"Anita." Mendez stood in the doorway of the kitchen. "This gets us nowhere."

"Come on, folks," Ted said, looking at the knot of uninvited people in his kitchen. "Have a bowl of chili. Sit down. It's Miller time." No one answered. "You folks sit down and behave. Little boy's still missing, and this doesn't help."

Anita Casey sat down.

"Lena?" Mendez said.

"I'm tired, Joel, I want to go home. If Ranger Rick here will give me a ride back to my car—" Her voice was thickening and getting out of control. She swallowed hard.

"*Ranger Rick?*" Ted shook his head. He filled two bowls with chili and set them on the table. No one made any move to eat.

"Tell me what happened," Mendez said.

Lena leaned against the counter. "He came to my house. Jeff did. He told me to get the insurance money together, and he would trade for Charlie. He would let me know when."

Anita frowned. "Why didn't—"

"Let me finish." Lena narrowed her eyes. "I was in Nashville."

"What were you doing there?" Anita said.

"Auditioning for the Grand Ole Opry. Hayes left a note on my car. Told me where and when to pick up Charlie. There was just barely time for me to come straight here. I tried to call you, Joel. They said you were in Louisville."

"Why didn't you call my office?" Anita said.

"I did." Lena looked at Mendez. "Judith finally get you?"

He nodded. "Then what?"

"I came here. Did just what Hayes told me. I was late, maybe forty minutes. I waited, but he never came."

"I got Anita's message about eight-thirty," Ted said. "I got right out there. Walked the perimeter constantly two miles out. Your man never showed up."

"You can't be sure."

"Sure as I can be. Don't tell me my business."

Anita sagged in her chair. "Sorry, Ted. You're right. If you say he didn't show, he didn't show. It just doesn't make a lot of sense."

"Come on, people," Ted said. "Eat up. You'll all feel better."

Anita studied Lena. "Who did you tell about Mr. Enoch?"

Lena frowned. "What do you mean?"

"I mean that information, that name, has been leaked. It's come up on the electronic boards, and I want to know who put it there."

Lena shrugged. "Could be any number of reasons it came up on the board. Maybe it's been there all along, and you just know to look for it now."

Anita studied her. "Maybe."

Ted picked up Sally's bowl and filled it full of chili. He set it down on the floor. "Come on, Sally, come on girl."

Sally dutifully got up and sniffed the chili. She turned away from the bowl, walked in a circle three times, and lay down, head on paws, near Lena's feet. Ted frowned.

"Now, why isn't that dog hungry?"

35

Lena's footsteps were loud in the gravel. Mendez walked beside her, Anita Casey a step behind. Anita put a hand on Mendez's arm.

"I'll be in touch, Joel."

He nodded. "I appreciate your help. Let me know if you hear anything. About that other business. There could be a lot of reasons he hasn't called."

Anita Casey nodded glumly. "That's why I'm worried." She seemed about to add something, glanced at Lena, and changed her mind. "Good night, Joel."

The Mazda was unlocked. Lena got in awkwardly, slowed by her baseball bat and the canvas bag of money.

"My Cutlass is on Old Indian Road. You go back out to the main road, the turnoff's a couple miles east."

Mendez touched Lena's hand. "I'm sorry this didn't work out tonight, Lena."

She shrugged. "Thank you for coming, Mendez. I wish I could have arranged it better. But Hayes fixed it so I'd be off-balance, you know?"

Mendez nodded.

"Thanks for sending Ted Moberly. I'd probably still be stuck out in the woods, without him. And it was good, him scouting around. I just wish I knew why Hayes didn't show. I *know* he wants this money."

Mendez started the engine and backed the Mazda onto the gravel drive.

Lena was quiet while they found their way out onto the main road. She was thinking. Debating. She'd slept with him, after all.

164

"One thing you better know," Lena said.

Mendez glanced at her, then looked back at the road.

"That business about Mr. Enoch. That really was me."

"I know."

"You . . ." She looked at him. His face was hard to read in the darkness. Hard to read in broad daylight, too. "I had Rick throw it out on the bulletin boards. That's how I got set up with Jeff."

"I see."

Lena frowned. "That all you have to say about it?"

"Kind of latc to say anything else."

"God forbid, Joel. Don't waste words."

He put an arm around her. "Let's go home. We'll leave your car here—pick it up tomorrow or something."

"Why?"

"Because you're carrying nincty thousand dollars. Because you look exhausted, and you could sleep all the way home." He paused. "Because I've been missing you."

"Sounds nice, Mendez, but I got to get home, and with my car. I got some names. People who Hayes may be involved with."

Mendez raised an eyebrow. "Where'd you get the names?"

"Jeff's cousin, Melody Hayes. She thinks Hayes will kill her someday. She may be right. He sends her seashells and she keeps them."

"So do you."

"Yeah, Mendez, you know how women are. So sentimental."

"I'd like a look at that list of names."

"Sure. What were you doing in Louisville?"

"Anita was questioning the Skidmoore kid again. She asked me if I wanted to be there. See if he came up with anything to help with Charlic."

"Did you get anything?"

"Not really. Hackburton's come up with a list of license numbers from the clinic in Knoxville. Anita's people will be on the lookout. See if we can get any matches on names her informant comes up with."

"Is that who she was worried about calling in? She got an informant?"

Mendez sighed.

"Come on, Joel. Does she?"

"Yeah. We think there may be a connection with some of the people she's onto in Louisville, and the LaRue County group."

"The LaRue County group. Hayes's people. You got any names?"

"Not yet. That's what the informant's for. He's going to—"

"What?"

Mendez shook his head.

"Will you cross-reference the names I got from Melody? Compare the license numbers?"

"Yes."

"Maybe we should give them to Ted. To check with cars parked around here."

Mendez nodded. "Lena, do me a favor. Keep off the bulletin boards. I don't like the sound of this Enoch."

"I don't either."

"Promise?"

"I won't do anything to compromise your investigation."

He took her hand and kissed her fingers. "You're not making me feel better."

"I can think of lots of ways to make you feel better."

"Come home with me tonight."

Lena shrugged, and cocked her head sideways. "Mendez. Suppose Hayes never intended to show up here tonight? Suppose he's waiting back at the house?" Lena sat up. "Maybe there's still a chance. Maybe he has Charlie."

"Maybe and maybe not. He might be planning to kill you and take the money."

"Let's go see," Lena said. "Got to have the Cutlass now. And show up alone—"

"Lena—"

"I mean *look* like I'm alone. You can be down in the seat. Or on the floor or something."

Mendez nodded. "I want to send some people out there. Backup."

"No, Mendez, they'll scare him off and screw it up."

"Lena, you don't go into these things without help. Stupid cops are dead cops." He glanced at her. "Only people I trust. They'll keep their distance and stay in the background. Okay?"

"It's not really up to me, is it?"

"No."

36

"Let me off here," Mendez said.

Lena eased the Cutlass to a stop. "What if he sees you sneakin' up?"

Mendez switched off the interior light. "He'll be watching the car." He took the socks full of money and tucked them inside his jacket.

"Almost as good as a bulletproof vest," Lena said.

"And about as expensive." Mendez squeezed her hand and got out, staying low to the ground.

Lena drove slowly into the driveway. Mendez hadn't shut the door all the way, and the buzzer was going. Was she being watched? She hesitated over the baseball bat, then left it in the car. Lena hefted the canvas bag, filled with rocks, trash, and a top layer of bills, and got out of the Cutlass, slamming the door.

The porch light made her a target in the darkness.

The house was just as she'd left it—a light on over the sink in the kitchen, downstairs curtains closed, the stuffed bear watching TV in the living room.

Lena opened the door to the basement. The couch was still wedged on the staircase. No Hayes, as far as she could see.

She went into the living room. No Hayes. And no furniture for him to hide behind.

The front door shut softly. Lena swallowed hard. "Who's there?"

Mendez moved swiftly and silently into the living room, gun drawn. He put a finger to his lips, pointed up the staircase, did a double take when he passed the bear.

Lena paused in the upstairs hallway, waiting for what, she didn't know. She peered into the bathroom. Mendez went in around her and checked behind the shower curtain. The rings scraped across the metal bar.

Lena checked Kevin's room. It was empty, dusty. She'd left the curtains open, and the night sky pressed, beginning the morning fade from black to ash gray. It would be sunup soon. Lena took a deep breath. The house felt empty.

She left Kevin's bedroom, Mendez still at the ready behind her. Her bedroom door was open and she switched on the light.

Mendez caught his breath. He motioned Lena back to the hallway, and disappeared into the room.

Lena heard the familiar creak of the closet door opening, the slide of hangers across the bar.

"Clear," Mendez said, finally. He took his handkerchief and wiped sweat from his forehead. He waved a hand at the room. "He might have been looking for the money, but he must have known—"

"Mendez."

"—*you* had it. I don't—"

"*Mendez*. Hayes hasn't been here." Lena cleared her throat. "I've been busy, Joel. I haven't had time to clean up."

"You haven't . . . oh. Oh."

Lena sighed. "It's been a long night. I'm going to grab a shower, okay?"

"Okay."

"How come you didn't wait like you said? You weren't supposed to come in till I signaled all clear."

Mendez shrugged. "Did you check the basement?"

"First thing."

"I'll take another look. Then I'll send my people home."

"You're coming back?"

He nodded.

She smiled and shut the bathroom door. She wondered if he would be cleaning the room when she came out.

She turned the shower on hard and hot. Soap ran off her body in runnels of water. Had it been her imagination, or had she heard a yell? She turned the water off and listened. Nothing. She turned the water back on and washed her hair.

No bathrobe, and her clothes were dirty. She wrapped herself in a towel and went into the bedroom. Mendez was not cleaning up. He was crouched on the edge of the bed, face racked with pain.

"Joel? What—are you okay?"

He winced and held his knee.

"Joel?"

"Why is your couch on the basement staircase?" He spoke to her through clenched teeth.

"Mendez, you should have turned on a light."

"I had hoped to sneak up on him."

"Was he down there?"

"Not unless he's dead of a broken neck, or . . . this is not funny, Lena."

"I'm sorry, Joel, really. Is your knee okay?"

"No."

"At least you didn't hurt anything else."

"My shoulder."

"You know what? You've had a long day." Lena headed for the bathroom. "What you need is a good hot bath."

"Lena."

"Quit arguing, Mendez." She turned the water on, then opened her cabinet under the sink. She shoved a bottle of shampoo to one side, causing a chain reaction of falling clutter.

"What are you doing in there?"

"I'm looking for the bubble bath."

"No."

"Mendez, it'll relax you."

"*No* bubbles."

"I got some strawberry bath salts. Beth got them on sale."

"*Plain hot water.*" Mendez's voice came loudly over her left shoulder.

He had stripped off his shirt and was working on his pants. Lena sat on the side of the tub and watched him undress.

"Get in the tub, Mendez." Lena touched his knee. "You got some bruise coming up."

He stepped into the water, then eased down slowly in the tub. Lena turned off the taps.

"That feel good?"

Mendez leaned back and closed his eyes. "Yes."

"Mendez?"

"Hmmm?"

"I'm sorry about the couch. I was trying to move it downstairs and it got stuck. Then I thought, well, no way Jeff can sneak up through the basement with this in the way."

"Why were you moving it downstairs?"

"So he couldn't hide behind it in the living room."

Mendez opened one eye. "What bothers me the most, Lena, is that you make sense to me."

Lena threw a washrag at him. "Scrub your own back." She gathered up his clothes and left. Something in his back pants pocket clinked. Lena stuck a finger in the pocket to see what it was.

Mendez wasn't long in the bath. He stood in the wedge of light from the bathroom, then turned off the switch.

"Lena?" he said softly.

"In bed."

His footsteps were soft on the carpet. He pulled back the covers and eased into bed.

Lena held both his hands and raised his arms over his head.

"What are you doing?"

"You'll see. Go on, grab hold of the bed frame." Lena eased her body on top of his. "Feel good?"

"Uh huh."

"Now close your eyes." She slid her hands under the pillow, biting her lip at the telltale chink of metal. Mendez was tired, his reaction time slow, and even fumbling in the dark, Lena was able to snap the handcuffs in place.

He jerked his hands, hard, shaking the back of the bed.

"Too late, Mendez, I got you."

"*Lena*. What are you doing?"

"Interrogating you. Did you and Detective Casey have dinner together in Louisville?"

Mendez was quiet for a moment, and then he began to laugh.

"I don't know what you think is funny. Answer my question, Mendez."

"I think I'm flattered. And yes, we had dinner together."

There was an awkward silence.

"I guess you just went out for a quick sandwich. Something fast and easy—not to interfere with the work."

"She took me to Tattitores. Her favorite Italian restaurant."

"I see."

"Lena." His voice deepened. "Anita Casey is a good cop and an attractive woman. But I only have eyes for you."

"Mendez, that's sweet. Not that I care, you understand."

"I understand. Will you let me go now?"

"You sure you want me to? The thing is, Mendez"—Lena snuggled closer—"now I've got you this way, it's like . . . it's like having a big dessert all to myself, with nobody asking for bites."

"You are a deeply disturbed woman."

"Okay, fine, I'll go get the key."

He caught her legs between his. "Not just yet."

37

The phone rang, and Lena snuggled deeper under the covers. Mendez reached over her head and picked up the receiver.

"Mendez." He was quiet a moment. "She's here."

Lena raised up on one elbow and took the phone. "Yes?"

"Lena?" The voice on the line was vaguely familiar. "This is Dr. Criswold. Delores Criswold, from Rolling Ridge."

"Yeah, sure. How are you?"

"I'm sorry, did I wake you? I figured you'd be up after ten."

"I had a late night."

"Yes." Dr. Criswold sounded knowing, and Lena glanced at Mendez. "Lena, when you talked to Melody yesterday, did she seem odd in any way? Particularly agitated? I know that's difficult to judge, considering the nature of your conversation, but—"

"What's up?"

"She's gone. She left last night after dinner."

"At *dusk?*"

"Yes. And she hasn't come back or called in. This doesn't feel right and I'm very worried about her. Did she say anything to you? About going anywhere?"

"What is it?" Mendez asked.

Lena covered the mouthpiece of the phone. "Melody Hayes. She's disappeared." Lena rolled onto her back. "Dr. Criswold, Melody seemed about right for what we were discussing. Didn't seem like she was going over the edge. Steady, under the circumstances."

Delores Criswold sighed. "I thought so, too."

"Has she ever taken off like this?"

"Not for a while now."

172

"You think something's happened to her?"

"I don't know. I've got people out looking. They're gearing up right now."

"Can I help?"

"No point, Lena. The people looking are all locals. You don't know the area."

"One thing maybe I should mention. I guess you know as much about Jeff Hayes as I do. You know about the seashell? She said he'd sent her one. She dug it up and showed me."

"I know." Delores Criswold said. "She has them buried all over the grounds."

Lena closed her eyes. "Call me if I can help."

Gatewood Center was a down-at-the-heels shopping area, and parking was plentiful. Lena found a space near the front of the lot.

It had been a hard call, deciding whether or not to go back to Nashville and look for Melody Hayes. But Dr. Criswold was right, Lena didn't know the area. And the bottom line was that Melody Hayes had already given her the list of names. Charlie was only four years old. And Melody had said to hurry.

Lena walked across the crumbling asphalt. The sun was high, almost hot, early enough in the year to be considered friendly. Women were shopping in shorts. The doors of the grocery swung open and closed; nobody else was busy.

Benita's Shoppe of Beauty was dark and narrow and dirty, and it sat beside Ernie's Barber Shop. The glassed-in window was filled with curling yellow posters of ancient hairstyles. It was the only salon regularly open on Sunday. Lena had first gone in one Sunday afternoon several years ago, desperate after a very bad perm. It had been a tremendous risk, and she had stood outside the shop for a long time, watching the clientele. Men, women, well-heeled and rough-around-the-edges—all with beautiful hair.

The inside of the shop smelled like chemicals and hairspray. Business was slow. Only one man under the hairdryer, and a woman getting her hair frosted. A tiny Mexican woman, thick black hair layered back, looked up from the magazine she was reading.

"Lena! How you do?"

"Good, Benita. I'm good."

Benita offered an open pack of Lay's Sour Cream and Onion Potato Chips. "Here, you want one?"

Lena took a chip. "Thanks for working me in this morning."

"We not busy." Benita dusted crumbs off her hands. "Sit down, sit down."

Lena sat in a chair in front of a spotted mirror. Benita draped a plastic smock over Lena's shoulders and tied it behind her neck.

"Besides, I tell you before, I always got time for you." She glanced at the woman in the other chair and pointed to Lena. "She the one Annie was telling you about. You got a problem, you go to her."

The woman looked at Lena curiously. Annie, a tall, thin woman with short red hair, smiled at Lena as she pulled the woman's hair through holes in a heavy plastic cap.

"Hi, Lena."

"Hi, Annie. How's your little girl?"

"Just learned to ride her bike."

Benita smiled. "And Annie is going broke on Band-Aids."

"You should get her a helmet and knee pads," said the woman in the plastic cap.

The man under the dryer made a rude noise. "Just let the poor kid ride her bike."

Benita turned the chair around and tilted it back. "What you want today, Lena?"

"Just a trim."

"Want me to shampoo it?"

"Please."

"Annie, hand me that conditioner. Lena, you hair getting dry. You take some of this home. You take it home, and you use it two times a week. Okay?"

"Okay."

"You having any trouble with it?"

"The top part is getting in my eyes. Drives me crazy."

"I fix that."

Lena nodded. Benita could do anything. Benita lathered Lena's hair, and Lena closed her eyes.

"Lena, you got so many tangles all the time. I think you drive a convertible very fast before you come here."

"How's Georgie these days?"

"Lena, he and Manda are engaged. Married in two months."

"That's great, Benita. Tell him congratulations."

"She such a nice girl."

174

"What does your son do?" the woman in the cap asked.

"He major in journalism, but that not turn out," Benita said. "He thought he wanted to be on the TV news, you know? He got the looks for it."

"He *was* on the news," Annie said. "For a while. He interned with WBRC. He did good."

"Yeah, and that's when he got all that trouble," Benita said, shaking her head.

"What kind of trouble?" the man under the dryer asked. He spoke too loud, with the dryer in his ears.

Benita rolled her eyes. "Program director was a woman, and my Georgie, he very nice-looking boy. She like him, but he has a girlfriend, Manda. And Manda sweet girl, but she not going to put up with Georgie fooling around with no old lady program director."

"Oh, Benita," Annie said. "She wasn't that old."

"She too old for my Georgie. And he made her very mad when he wouldn't meet her like she wanted. After work, like, you know." Benita shook her head. "He come to me and say, 'Mama, what do I do, I don't want to go.' I say don' go. Nothing she can do. But then, she say she going to give him bad grade for college credit. Say he have bad attitude and not work so good. Nothing we can do. So I tell Lena about this."

Lena smiled and closed her eyes. Benita rinsed suds out of her hair.

"Next thing I know, she call up Georgie and say please excuse, she under personal pressures and not use such good judgment. And he get A because he did work hard while he was there. He did."

The woman in the cap looked at Lena. "What did you do?"

Benita giggled. "She call this woman up. She say—your maid service not come today? Too bad, huh. That plumber you call not show up? Tough luck. And I hear your hairdresser, she not remember you had appointment. That too bad. Life can get very inconvenient."

"You forgot the mechanic," said Annie.

Benita giggled again. "Yeah, him too."

"I had nothing to do with that," Lena said.

"It was coincidence, sure," Benita said. "But this lady, she thought it was part of the parcel. She not so nice on the phone, but after about ten days of this . . . this inconvenient life . . . she begging to give Georgie A plus. Myself, I would have accepted a B. But Lena, she said Georgie do good work, and deserve to be taken care of."

Benita wrapped a towel around Lena's hair and patted it dry. "Lena, you do this when you dry. I can tell you now, you stop scramble that towel in your hair when it is wet. You have nice hair, you take care of it."

Benita pulled a black comb from the pocket of her smock, and worked the tangles out of Lena's hair.

The haircut was unhurried. Benita turned Lena's head one way, then another. Annie answered the phone when it rang, which wasn't often, and the man under the dryer was unrolled and fluffed, and sent home happy.

Benita applied a round wooden brush to Lena's hair, and pointed the hand dryer.

"See how much nicer this look with conditioner on it?"

Lena nodded.

"Twice a week," Benita said. "Come back in five weeks for a trim and we see. Healthy, shiny hair." Benita untied the plastic cape from behind Lena's neck. "I be right back. Conditioner in the storeroom."

Lena folded the cape and set it on the counter. She followed Benita into the back room.

It was more a cubbyhole than a room, with black metal shelves, a small refrigerator, a sink, and a microwave oven. Benita glanced over her shoulder.

"You are two weeks early for this cut."

"I am not. You say to come in every five weeks."

"Yeah, but you too lazy to get in here."

Lena grinned and leaned against the wall. "I need a favor. A big favor."

Benita straightened and groaned. "Got to do something about this back." She twisted a bottle of conditioner in her hands. "What you need me to do?"

"Someone I know has a little boy named Charlie. He's been kidnapped. He's four years old."

"Ah, no! Somebody took him?"

"Yes."

"But what can I do?"

"Do you know anybody who does hair in Nash?"

"Nash, Kentucky? He get kidnapped by a hairdresser?"

"No. But do you know anybody that does hair around there? LaRue County, near Ray Lake."

176

"I don't think so."

"I have a list of names. Of people who live there. Sometime in the next couple of weeks there's going to be a . . . gathering. I think some of the women on this list, and maybe some of the men, are going to be spiffing up. And that means they're going to get their hair done." Lena leaned against the wall. "I need to know when it comes up. Say three of them call in and say they have to have an appointment before Friday night. How Saturday, or the next Monday, will be too late. All the appointments will cluster, you know? And then drop off."

"Ah, like before a home basketball game?"

"Can you do that? Can you find out?"

Benita frowned. "How will this help the little boy?"

"You'll have to trust me on it. Keep it quiet as you can, but find out. It's important, Benita. It could make the difference in whether or not I find him. It could save his life."

She took a breath. "Do you think you know who has him?"

"I think so." Lena folded her arms. "Will you do this for me? It's more important than I can say."

"You know, I am thinking of Georgie when he was so little. How long has the boy been gone?"

"Too long. His mama wants him back."

Benita nodded. "I need to call Alexander. He will know the right people. He knows everyone."

"Every minute counts, Benita."

She nodded, eyes dark and knowing.

38

Nashville was ten degrees warmer than Kentucky, and Lena took her sweater off. Ted Moberly stood beside a navy blue Jeep, Sally leashed and sitting quietly at his side. He leaned against the driver's side of the Jeep and lit a pipe, and made no move to get in on the conversation between Delores Criswold and the sheriff.

Dr. Criswold had her hands in her pockets and her shoulders jutted forward. The sheriff was looking down at her, his face red, his conversation doled out in slow, measured tones. Lena tossed her sweater into the front seat of the Cutlass and headed for Ted Moberly.

She held a hand out for him to shake, but was knocked backward by Sally, who demanded first greeting. Lena scratched Sally's ears and patted the smooth black head.

"Hey, girl. Hey, Sally."

"Sally, behave." Ted reached forward and shook Lena's hand. "How you been?"

"Craving your chili every time I get hungry."

It was the right thing to say. Ted smiled. He took out a lighter and went to work on the pipe again.

"What's up?" Lena inclined her head toward the sheriff.

Ted shrugged. "The usual. They got no faith in Sally here, and they don't understand how she works. They better make up their minds. They've had two days to find this girl, and haven't seen a thing. Time to let Sally have a go."

Delores Criswold held up a hand to the sheriff, and stepped over to Lena and Ted.

"Hello, Lena. Look, Ted. He wants to keep looking while you do."

Ted shook his head. "Won't work."

"He says—"

"Let me talk to him." Moberly clamped his teeth down on the stem of his pipe. He walked forward and Lena followed. "Sheriff?"

"Butcher."

"Sheriff Butcher. I'm Theodore Moberly."

Butcher looked at Lena.

"My assistant," Moberly said.

Butcher nodded. "If that dog can really find a scent"—he shifted his weight from one foot to the other—"what's it matter if we got other people in the woods?"

"She's an air-scent dog," Moberly said. "She goes after any human scent. So she'll track down your searchers. How many people you got out there?"

" 'Bout six."

Moberly grimaced. "How long you been at it?"

"Roughly twenty-four hours."

"You called the air force?"

Butcher took a deep breath. "Mr. Moberly, we can't call the air force every time a disturbed person takes it into their head to wander off. This isn't the first time this Hayes woman has done this."

Moberly smiled pleasantly. "I understand. Why don't you let me and my dog here give it a shot?"

"And then what? We come looking for you when you get lost."

Moberly stiffened, but he kept on smiling. "I'll be sure and have a radio with me. How's that?"

Butcher smiled. "My people know the area. They'll be back in around supper time. Since they're already several miles out, why don't we let them be for now? You and your dog can start fresh in the morning." The sheriff gave them a stern smile. "Excuse me just a minute."

Sally whimpered.

"Stay, girl," Ted said. "Good girl."

Delores Criswold watched the sheriff walk away. She folded her arms and shook her head. "Can't get him to come when I need him, and now I can't call him off."

Ted Moberly took a tobacco pouch out of his jacket pocket, and scooped tobacco into the bowl of his pipe.

179

"They won't find her," he said absently.

Delores frowned. "Why do you say that?"

Moberly tamped tobacco down in the bowl of the pipe. "I hope they *do* find her. But I think they're too far out. Most people are found a lot closer in."

"But they've already looked—"

Moberly shook his head. "I've seen grid searches, three or four hundred people trying to cover every inch of ground, go right by people. Mainly the searchers find each other. It's just too easy for people to miss things."

Delores Criswold wrapped her arms around her chest. "I don't like to think about her being out there at night in the cold. She's so thin."

"She wearing a sweater or jacket?"

"Blue sweatshirt, I think."

"Good. Too bad she didn't go in for red or something, like Lena here." Moberly lit the pipe and looked at Criswold. "This isn't much of a search, you know that."

Criswold's shoulders sagged. "I know."

"Supposed to get down below fifty tonight." Moberly sucked the pipe and blew a cloud of smoke. "Just hold on a little longer. Soon as those searchers come back, me and Sally are going out."

"At night?"

"Sure. Sally and I do this a lot at night, 'specially in the summer when it's hot. We neither one of us are getting any younger. Dog can smell as well after dark as in the day." He pointed at Lena. "Found you, didn't we?"

"You had a campsite number."

"You always picking on me."

"Do you need me to get something of Melody's?" Delores asked. "So your dog can track her scent?"

Moberly shook his head.

Delores swallowed. "What if she's dead? Will it make a difference?"

"Might in a couple months, but not this early. Scent cone will still be strong."

"Scent cone?" Lena asked.

Moberly eyed Delores, then looked back at Lena. "The body sheds millions of dead skin cells every minute. That's what gives people their scent. Air currents carry the scent through the air like

180

smoke, and the scent actually forms a cone shape. Strong and narrow near the person, wider and fainter the farther away the wind carries it. Death won't affect the cone, at least not at first. I've known dogs like Sally to find people buried in avalanches under twenty feet of snow." He scratched the dog's neck under the collar. "Sally's a good working dog. She's tracked plenty of people. She knows what she's doing. Dr. Criswold, if you can get the sheriff to get me a topographical map, I'd like to do some studying before Sally and I go out."

Butcher's people came in at dusk—dirty, tired, hungry. Ted Moberly waited till they were all checked in. He took Sally off the leash. The searchers, all men, watched the dog in curious, dubious silence. Sally eyed them warily, but did not bark.

Lena stood next to the Cutlass, hands in her pockets. Delores Criswold was deep in conversation with the sheriff. Ted looked over his shoulder at Lena. Sally whimpered.

"*Come* on."

Lena bounded after them. "Thanks, Ted."

"Look funny if I went without my assistant. You going to be warm enough?"

"Yeah. I'm in layers."

"Good."

They walked to the edge of the woods. Sally quivered, ready to bound off. She waited while Ted scanned the woods.

"This way." He turned away from the trees and headed southwest, toward the back of Rolling Ridge Hospital. "Far as I can tell"— Moberly stopped by the dogwood tree where Melody had dug up the seashell—"this is the PLS."

"Excuse my ignorance. PLS?"

Moberly took a puff of his pipe. "Point last seen."

"Even search dogs have jargon," Lena said.

"Lena, this woman. Would you say she was despondent?"

Lena frowned. "Are you thinking suicide?"

"Could be."

"Does it make a difference where you look?"

"Suicides usually don't go that far, maybe two-tenths of a mile at most. And"—he stared toward a ridge to the east—"they tend to climb."

"Why?"

"I don't know. Statistics."

"She was upset, Ted. But I don't think she was going to kill herself."

"What you think happened?"

"She was giving me some information. About this business with Hayes and Charlie. And Hayes was around, he trailed me to the clinic. Then that same night she disappears. Those kind of coincidences I don't believe in."

"Me neither." He pulled an altimeter from his jeans pocket and checked it. "We'll drift downhill. Easy enough to do." He looked at the dog. "*Go find*, Sally."

The dog hesitated, then bounded off toward the woods.

"You should have worn heavy boots," Ted said suddenly.

"Why?"

"Snakes."

"That makes me feel better."

The last of the sunlight filtered through the trees, making patterns on the forest floor. Lena tried not to think about snakes curling around tree trunks, sliding over fallen leaves, slithering around stones. Sally veered right suddenly, tail wagging vigorously.

Lena looked at Ted. "You think she's found something?"

"A squirrel, maybe. Or a bird." He smiled at Lena. "When she's got a scent, you'll know it."

39

As darkness fell it grew colder. Moberly was surefooted, watchful, tirelessly working his way back and forth through the trees. The arc of his flashlight made the woods seem all the blacker. Lena did not like to think of Melody Hayes, alone with the night and her memories.

What kind of memories was Charlie making?

According to Delores Criswold, Melody Hayes had received a phone call before she disappeared. The call was logged in at 5:37 P.M.—two hours after Lena was well on her way to LaRue Lake. Someone had seen Melody go out right after supper.

Lena pushed her hair out of her eyes. Melody hadn't come in at dusk, and she hadn't come in by dark—unthinkable, this close to Easter. Unthinkable at any time.

Moberly stopped, and Lena scooted sideways into a bush so she wouldn't run into him.

"Look," he said. He aimed the light at Sally.

Her head was up, her body stiff. She moved forward, her posture businesslike, but avid.

"She's got it," Moberly said.

The dog picked up speed, a graceful fluidity to her motions. Ted and Lena followed her through the brush, leaves crunching underfoot, thorn bushes catching their clothes. Sally began to zigzag back and forth, moving faster.

"She's hot," Ted said, picking up the pace. "Getting close."

A branch caught Lena's hair and she stopped to untangle it. Moberly glanced back at her.

"Go on," Lena said.

He went.

Lena pulled at the hair caught up in the spiny branch and tangled with a knot of budding leaves. The trees pressed, close and dark. And she knew, with absolute certainty, that Melody Hayes would never have come here alone, at night, by choice.

The light from Moberly's flash was swiftly moving away. Lena tore her hair loose, wincing at the hurt, and at what Benita would say next time she went in for a cut. Her own light was not as powerful as Moberly's, but she went quickly and noisily, trying to catch up.

The ground sloped down and grew mushy underfoot. Lena heard a splash. She ran forward.

The water gleamed black and shiny beneath the trees. Moberly was shining his light and Lena could just make out Sally's head as she swam across the creek.

"Hell," Lena said. "We going to have to swim across?"

Moberly frowned. "Let's see what she does."

Sally's head bobbed up and down with the strength of her strokes. She scrambled up the muddy creek bank, then stopped. She turned and looked toward the light, at Ted.

Sally jumped back into the water and swam toward them. She looked eager, happy.

"I don't understand," Lena said. "Does she want us to come across?"

Moberly shook his head.

Sally came up the creek bank and jumped at Ted, paws hitting his chest, knocking him backward. She turned back to the water, then back to Ted.

"Good girl," Ted said. His chest was wet and muddy, but he did not seem to notice. "Go find."

Sally whimpered and splashed back into the water. She weaved back and forth in the shallows, splashing water up on Moberly's calves. She veered left, and Lena and Ted followed along the shoreline.

Moberly flashed his light, catching a deadfall of trees and banked-up mud. Sally headed for the downed trees, and Ted splashed into the creek behind her.

Lena hesitated, then went in. The water was warmer than she'd expected. She went slowly. The creek bottom was sandy and uneven, and there were rocks and chunks of wood underfoot.

184

Sally jumped up on a fallen tree. Ted spoke in a soft, kindly voice, but Lena could not make out the words. He splashed through the water, shining his light. Lena saw him bending over.

"Good dog!" he said suddenly, his voice full of warmth and praise. "Good girl, Sally! I knew you'd do it. What a smart girl you are." He was rummaging in his pocket. Sally jumped forward and snatched something out of his hand.

Lena quit moving. She watched Ted pet the dog, watched Sally wag her tail and wiggle with pleasure.

"Lena," Ted said. It was a tone of voice she'd never heard from him. "Lena, I think we got her. I need you to come look and make sure."

It was strange, Lena thought, how vivid the night sky was in the forest. To her right was a blaze of light that was downtown Nashville. It seemed a long way away.

"Lena?"

"Coming."

The water got deeper as she went, up to her knees, then her thighs. The bottom dropped off suddenly, and Lena stumbled forward. Moberly reached out and caught her.

"Thanks," Lena said. She shivered, water up to her waist.

Moberly pointed his light.

The body floated just under the surface. A scuffed tennis shoe, dark and soggy, had snagged on the jagged V shape of a broken tree limb. Lena bit her lip. What kind of shoes had Melody been wearing? Tennis shoes, she thought.

Long brown hair billowed softly. The waterlogged body rocked gently, set in motion by the easy current and the rowdy dog who panted and smiled from her perch on the dead tree.

"This her?" Moberly said.

To be sure, Lena thought, she should reach down, turn the shoulders gently, and look into the face. She thought of Melody Hayes sitting in the wheelchair, clutching the violin—fiddle, Melody would call it. Sometime the day before she had sat down with a pen and a piece of orange construction paper, and made a list of people whose names she was afraid to write down. She had hidden seashells all over the grounds of the Rolling Ridge Institution. And her mother had died when she was two.

Her mother, Lena thought, would not hesitate to take those

thin, waterlogged shoulders, and raise her daughter's body up out of the cold black water.

"It's her," Lena said.

Moberly lifted the radio to his lips, then stopped. "You understand, don't you, about the dog? She has to be praised. As far as she's concerned, it's all a game. And she did her job. Like she's been trained."

"Of course," Lena said. She would have liked to pat Sally, and scratch behind her ears, but the dog was just out of reach, and Lena did not feel like moving closer.

It was warmer in the water than out. At least, Lena decided, it was if your clothes were wet. She stood out of the way on the bank of the creek, close to Ted Moberly and Sally. They weren't needed anymore, and nobody seemed to have any thanks or praise for Sally and Ted, who had brought bad news.

The sheriff and his people were surprisingly gentle with what was left of Melody Hayes, and for that Lena was grateful. She had half expected coarse jokes and rough handling, but the quiet was thick, and the only conversation was muted, emotionless instructions.

Delores Criswold hovered near the rescue team, getting in their light, standing too close. The body was noisy coming up from the water. Delores reached out, but found nothing to hold on to.

Melody Hayes, drowned and swollen, dripped streams of water. Her hair wrapped around her face like bandages, and she was settled onto a dark plastic tarp. Delores Criswold fluttered close, and the sheriff stepped back, silent and watchful.

Delores bent down and peeled the hair away from Melody's face, then plucked a leaf from the dead girl's mouth.

Lena waited for Sheriff Butcher to object. He didn't. He was thinking drowning, not murder.

Delores Criswold lifted Melody's head and shoulders and embraced the cold wet corpse. Lena thought of the mother that Melody had never known but always missed.

40

Lena had relieved the stuffed bear from sentry duty in the rocking chair, but left the TV on, picture, no sound. She rocked back and forth. She had changed to dry clothes—lavender sweats and a white T-shirt. She picked the phone up off the floor and set it in her lap. For once, there was no message.

She wanted to call Delores Criswold, though she wasn't sure why. Dr. Criswold had likely prescribed herself some medication and gone to bed. Maybe even enough medication to sleep. Unconscious would be nice.

Lena ran her fingers lightly over the telephone buttons. She could call Mendez. She could tell him, please, talk to the damn sheriff in Tennessee, make him see that Melody Hayes was murdered. But she didn't want to talk to Mendez just yet. Didn't want him to know that she had likely caused Melody Hayes to die in a cold black creek.

She missed Whitney. Some times more than others. This was a more-than-other time. She closed her eyes and thought of her sister, reading to Kevin in the rocking chair, storybook propped on her ever-expanding belly, maternity clothes culled from her pals in costume, so she wouldn't have to face the usual tiny bows and puffed sleeves.

Headlights shone through the foyer window to the living room, and Lena heard a car in the driveway. She waited. The doorbell rang three times. Rick.

She half expected him to ring again, or use his key and come in.

He didn't. A car door opened, then slammed. A car engine started.

And just like that she changed her mind—didn't want to be alone anymore. She ran to the door, fumbled the locks, heard the car back down the drive.

"Rick!" she shouted. "I'm home! Rick?"

His headlights pinned her, shivering, on the sidewalk. The brakes squeaked, the car jerked to a stop. The engine seemed loud in the middle of the night. The car backed and returned. Lena took a breath.

Rick came slowly up the sidewalk.

"I'm home," Lena said.

"So I see." He smiled with his mouth, but not with his eyes.

"Come in. You can have the chair." Lena sat on the floor, back to the wall.

Rick picked up the bear and absently plucked at its ear.

"Is Maynard okay?" Lena said. "Is he eating?"

Rick grimaced. "Is he *eating*? Yes, dear heart, he is eating. Off the kitchen tables, off the counters, everywhere we leave food."

"Damn, Rick, you're getting him into bad habits."

Rick fluffed up the loop of hair on the top of the stuffed bear's head.

Lena cocked her head sideways. "How'd the audition go?"

Rick settled back into the rocking chair and folded his arms. "I don't want to talk about that, Lena."

"Thank God."

Rick looked at her. "What is that supposed to mean?"

"I thought it might be something impor . . . What I mean is, Rick, that you're always like this after call-backs. You always get depressed. You didn't get turned down for the part?"

"Not yet. But I will."

"You *always* say that. Especially when you do good. This is one of the stages you go through."

Rick frowned. "Is it?"

"Yep."

"How come I don't remember?"

"You never remember. It makes no sense, but you do it every time."

"I do?"

"Yes. So quit worrying."

"You're *really* sure about this, Lena?"

188

"Jesus, I hate these postmortems." Lena winced and looked away.

"There are certain advantages to ex-wives." Rick was thoughtful. He tossed the bear up in the air and caught it. "What are the clothespins for?"

"To pin back its ears."

Rick sat the bear in his lap, settling him carefully on one knee. "Lena, did you know that you can arrange a child-sex vacation in Mexico? I didn't know that. I didn't *want* to know that. This takes a lot of shine out of hacking." He looked at Lena. "I have a message from Mr. Enoch."

Lena sat up. "Something off the computer boards?"

Rick rolled his eyes. "It didn't come UPS."

"What does he say?"

Rick fished a scrap of notepaper from his shirt pocket. "To Lawrence of Arabia—"

"To *who?*"

"That's my code name."

Lena wrinkled her nose. "Rick, that is so—"

"So what?"

"Nothing. What's the message?"

"Tell her—you get that, Lena? He said tell *her*." He looked back at the paper. "Tell her this: 'The pleasure of hell for the people of hell. I invite you to drink from the bowl, that you may know him. Know also, that it comes for lambs who inquire.' "

Lena sat back and closed her eyes. "Ask him when is the party. Tell him the lamb is inquiring."

41

The dank hallway and staircase were all too familiar. Lena knocked on Eloise Valetta's door. She had showered, used the new conditioner on her hair, changed to loose cotton khakis and a tailored shirt. She'd even cleaned up her bedroom.

She knocked again, teetering back and forth on the balls of her feet. She leaned close, ear to the door.

Eloise might be out, of course. Lena wondered if Valerie had stopped by, like she'd promised. Lena's mind conjured an image of Melody Hayes, body moving gently in the creek.

It had been stupid to leave Eloise Valetta alone.

The front door was no thicker than the inside doors in Lena's house. Lena put her shoulder to the door and shoved. The door popped open, scraping wood and snapping the lock.

The living room was quiet and empty. Matchbox cars were lined up on the coffee table, organized too neatly for a chubby-fingered child. Lena went into the kitchen. Dirty cake pans had been rinsed and stacked in the sink. She veered down the dark hallway toward the bedroom. The dry brown bloodstain had coarsened the nap of the carpet.

In her mind's eye, Lena pictured Eloise Valetta sprawled on the bed, gun in limp, stiffening hand, blood soaking into the mattress.

The bedroom was empty. On the right-hand side was a black iron bed made up with a thin chenille bedspread. On the left side was a matching iron bed, made up with a blue bedspread that had dinosaurs on it. In the corner was a stack of dirty, worn blocks, a coffee can crammed with broken crayons, and several coloring books—the thin giveaway kind. A pair of threadbare red pajamas was neatly folded in the center of the bed.

Lena checked the bathroom, picturing bodies in bathtubs, slit wrists.

The bathroom was clean and empty. A wooden potty chair with a yellow plastic seat sat opposite the toilet. There were two toothbrushes, one big, one small, on the counter beside a box of Arm & Hammer baking soda.

No one home.

Lena went down the hall to the kitchen and dialed the spouse abuse center.

"Lena?"

"Valerie, have you seen Eloise? Eloise Valetta?"

"Yeah, sure, she's here now."

Lena took a breath. She glanced at the front door, which now bowed inward.

"Sorry, Lena, I should have called you. But you know how crazy it is right now."

"How is she?"

"Hanging in, Lena. It's hard."

"How'd you get her to come down?"

"She wouldn't at first. So I went by. She was baking cakes, *dozens* of them."

Lena smiled.

"She taught me how to bake a cake from scratch, and not have it come out crooked."

"*You* cooked?"

"Yeah. I did okay. And then I was talking, you know, about how we cook meals around here. Like we assign them to whoever's living here, you know how we do. To tell you the truth, I don't think she heard a word I said. But what I kept thinking about the whole time I was talking, was empty arms. How she was waiting for this child of hers that she wanted to hold and love, and couldn't. And I thought, maybe she needs to bake because she needs to . . . nurture. Does this make any sense?"

"Sure."

"I see so little of that. Around here. Most of these women are so burned out, they don't have an ounce of nurture left. So I thought she might be a help. And I asked her if she would come cook for us. I told her it was dangerous, that we were being threatened. But that

191

some of the women were so upset, that the last thing they wanted was KP. And I was really surprised, but she said okay. Tell you what, she is terrific in the kitchen, Lena. I've gained three pounds."

"Valerie, you are a saint. A brilliant saint person."

Valerie paused. "She wants to talk to you, Lena. She keeps saying she's going to call you, and I keep telling her to wait."

"Just tell her that I don't know anything yet, but I'm working on it."

"Don't you think you should tell her yourself?"

"It's all I can do, Valerie, to keep my own head above water. Oh, shit. I can't believe I said that."

"What?"

"Never mind."

"Lena, is it going all right?"

"I'll make it all right. You keep Eloise cooking. Wear her out in the day, so she'll sleep at night. I'll call later, okay?"

"I hope you find her boy."

"I will, Valerie."

Lena hung up and rubbed her eyes. She took a deep breath and went to assess the damage to the front door.

42

Lena knocked on the door of Mendez's apartment, thinking she ought to have called.

"Lena?" Mendez had thrown on a pair of black sweatpants, and was shirtless, barefooted, his hair mussed.

"I know, Joel. It's early."

"Come in."

The window blinds were closed, and the great room had a dusty, unused air. The desk was cluttered with pictures, open files, and a coffee cup.

"Late night?" Lena asked.

He nodded.

She put her arms around him and laid her head in the crook of his shoulder.

"Something happened." He led her to the couch.

"Melody Hayes drowned."

"How?"

"She disappeared from Rolling Ridge after supper. She got a call around five-thirty, it was logged in. Someone saw her outside on the grounds, but she didn't come back." Lena pushed her hair out of her eyes. "Ted Moberly went down with me yesterday. We found her last night. Sally did, anyway. The dog."

"Where?"

"Upside down in a creek."

Mendez pulled away and frowned. "She definitely drowned?"

"Not without help."

"Who's in charge down there?"

"Some sheriff. It wasn't in Nashville proper, and this Sheriff Butcher is handling it."

"What's he say?"

"He thinks she just wandered off. Some coincidence, huh, Joel? Gives me the list and turns up dead." Lena frowned. "You done anything with the names she gave me?"

Mendez went to the desk. "Names matched with license numbers." He handed Lena a computer printout and leaned over the back of the couch and pointed. "That column is names and numbers from the clinic. Those are from Valetta's funeral. And that's the list you brought me. The yellow—that's where they match."

"Mendez, you got a match here from the funeral to one on Melody's list."

"Yes."

"But no match from the clinic and the funeral. But look. A match on Melody's list and the clinic list. So there is a connection."

"We've checked and rechecked the doctor. Put her under surveillance. Nothing to lead us to the boy." Mendez put a hand on Lena's shoulder. "I've thought about going to the people in LaRue County. Asking them about their association with the clinic. But to do that, I'd have to have a local cop along. And permission. And it's a small town. I'm afraid if I start asking around, whoever has Charlie—"

"Will kill him," Lena said.

"It's a hard call, Lena."

"Maybe we should of run the picture, Joel. Somebody must have seen him."

"If we alert them, they'll either kill him, or move him out of the area. Either way, we'd never find him." Mendez squeezed her shoulder. "How about coffee?"

"Yes. Think maybe you should give that Sheriff Butcher a call?"

"Maybe."

"Listen, Joel, can we get a copy of this list to Moberly? See if he gets any matches on cars parked in the recreation area?"

"Yes." He went to the kitchen and opened the freezer. "You had breakfast?"

"I had—"

"Potato chips don't count. I'm making omelets."

The phone rang.

Mendez held a sack of coffee beans in one hand and a measuring spoon in the other. "Get that."

"Where is it?"

"On the desk."

Lena picked up the phone. "Yes?"

"Is this the Mendez residence?" Woman's voice. A familiar woman's voice, Lena thought.

"Yeah, it is."

"This is Detective Casey from Louisville PD. Is Joel in?"

"He's still asleep." Mendez stopped measuring coffee and looked at her. "This is Lena, Anita. Hold on and I'll get him." Lena held the receiver out to Mendez. He cocked his head sideways, then put the coffee on the counter. "I'll start the omelets," Lena said, handing him the phone.

"Mendez. Yes, Anita. No." He glanced at Lena. "It was time I got up anyway."

Lena opened the refrigerator door. "Mendez, where are your eggs?"

". . . did you . . . Lena, they're in the door. No, sorry."

Lena opened and closed one cabinet, then another.

"I'm sorry, Anita, what was that?"

Lena saw a large metal bowl on the top shelf of the cabinet near the stove. She got a stool from the countertop bar and dragged it across the kitchen floor.

"Lena, be careful." Mendez set the phone down. He took Lena's hand, led her to the couch, and handed her a rolled-up newspaper. "Be still."

Lena waited until he was back on the phone.

"Sorry, Anita, go on. Did you get an actual face-to-face meet? What was the date?" Mendez rummaged on the top of the desk. "April thirtieth? Let me look at my calendar. This is the twenty-first. That's nine days. Tuesday night. I wonder if there's a full moon?"

Lena unrolled the newspaper. Mendez put a hand over his ear.

"Thank you, Anita. Yes, I got them. Have you picked anybody up? I see. Thank you. Yes. Yes."

Lena rattled the front section of the newspaper.

"Thanks again, Anita. Yes, we will. Good-bye."

Mendez hung up the phone. "Anita's heard from the informant. Mr. Enoch's group is meeting on April thirtieth."

Lena let the paper drop. "For sure?"

"The informant called in. Got the date from one of the higher-ups. He's sure."

"I need to call Walt Caron. You got a phone book?"

"On the desk."

The phone rang eight times before a sleepy male voice answered.

"Walt Caron? This is Lena Padgett."

"Yeah, Lena. How'd it go with Melody? Go okay?"

"You haven't heard, then."

"Heard what?"

"Walt, Melody's dead."

"What?"

"Drowned. We found her late last night. In a creek out back of the institution."

"But . . . how?"

"The sheriff thinks it was an accidental death."

"And you don't."

"No."

"Jesus. Oh, Jesus."

"I did get to talk to her first."

"How was she?"

"A little rough around the edges."

"She could have done it herself," Caron said.

"I don't think so. Listen, I need to ask you. Is there anything special about April thirtieth? You were telling me, when I talked to you, about a special holiday coming up."

"That sounds right. Hang on, let me check my notes. It may take a minute, can you hold?"

"Sure."

Lena watched Mendez slice mushrooms into thin slivers. Every few minutes he looked at her. He didn't smile, and neither did she. But they were very much together in the room.

"Lena?"

"Yeah, Walt, what did you find?"

"April thirtieth is Walpurgisnacht—one of the two biggest holidays, if you could call them that. It's supposed to be a counter to Easter Sunday, and it requires . . . a sacrifice. That's what I read, anyway."

"What kind of sacrifice?"

"There seems to be a preference for . . . a pure white male."

"Oh."

"Here's what I have. Let's see, have I got anything else? Mmmm . . . mmmm . . . okay. On April thirtieth, 1966, Anton Szandor LaVey shaved his head and proclaimed the date to be I Anno Satanas—the first year after Satan regained the earth. A lot of groups, most of them I think, date their activities from sixty-six."

"Did you say shaved his head?"

"Yes."

"Who was LaVey?"

"Is. Quite a showman, actually. The big daddy of Satan worship, starting in the trendy sixties and seventies. Publicity hound, skirting the legal, a lot of celebrity do's."

"I see. Okay. Thanks, Walt."

"Any progress on the little boy?"

"Hard to tell, at this point."

"Keep on it, Lena. Good luck."

The smell of coffee was strong. Mendez held up a cup and Lena went to it like a moth to flame.

"Walpurgisnacht," Mendez said.

"Looks like the informant was right. Did he know where?"

Mendez ate a piece of mushroom. "LaRue Lake. Somewhere in the south fork, near Croom's Landing. There'll be flashlights hanging in the trees, lighting the way."

"This is almost too easy," Lena said.

43

Benita's Shoppe of Beauty was crowded. Eight plastic chairs, aqua, were arranged in a semicircle at the front of the shop and occupied by men and women who read magazines and checked their watches. All four hairdryers were going, all three barber chairs full. People frowned when Lena walked past them to Benita's work station.

"Lena?"

"Hi. I got your message."

Benita handed a package of thin roller papers to the woman who sat in her chair. "Be right back, okay? You be okay?" Benita headed to the storeroom. "I got you what you want." She glanced over her shoulder.

"Good," Lena said. She closed the door behind them.

"In my purse." Benita opened a narrow closet and retrieved a large cloth purse. "Alexander, he got these for me." Benita glanced at Lena over her shoulder. "You not find the little boy yet?"

Lena shook her head.

"I hope this help." She dug in the purse, grimaced, and began unloading—a wallet bulging with coins and dollar bills, a wad of tissue, a comb, a blue makeup pouch, a checkbook, a granola bar, a Band-Aid box full of something that rattled, an appointment book.

"Here," Benita said, opening the appointment book. She flipped to the back, tore out a page intended for addresses, then turned the book to a calendar.

"We got seven appointments of people on the list. Five at one place; two at another, out of the city. Alexander, he is very good. And very curious. I had to tell him about the little boy, Lena. He thought I might be up to something, otherwise. Stealing clients, you believe? That okay?"

Lena nodded.

Benita crooked her finger, and Lena leaned over the book.

"See? We got one who has a weekly regular for Thursday afternoon. She come in on the eighteenth. And four of them were in last Friday and Saturday. Nineteen and twenty."

"Do they come in every week?"

"I don' know. But Alexander told me if it was a regular weekly thing, and he didn't on these. So likely not."

"Okay. What else?"

"This one here. She say Tuesday at latest, but her girl, she very busy and can't fit her in. So lady say, okay, how about Wednesday morning? Can be no later than that, she say."

Lena caught her bottom lip between her teeth. "Wednesday? That's the twenty-fourth."

"Day after tomorrow," Benita said seriously. She looked at Lena, then back to the sheet of paper. "And this other one. She say she want perm, but her lady too busy too, for perm. And she try to schedule her for Thursday, but the girl say no. Just comb out. Maybe trim. And that too, made for Wednesday morning."

"Anybody past that?"

Benita frowned. "The one wants the perm schedules it for a couple weeks later. Mid-May, I think." Benita pointed back at the calendar. "But you see the cluster. It is the twenty-fourth. They all are around and before, nobody past. That is the night you want."

Lena frowned. The informant had said the thirtieth.

"You don't see it?" Benita asked.

"Yeah, I see it." Lena shrugged. "Benita, can I have your notes? And thank you for your help."

"Alexander, he do so good. He talk to the stylists. Get them to tell what the women say. Pretty good, huh?"

"Pretty damn good, Benita." Lena patted the woman's shoulder. "Listen, I know you're booked solid out there, so I'll let you get back to work."

"You tell me, okay? When you find the little boy?"

"I'll tell you."

44

Lena went through the heavy glass doors of the central library onto the city sidewalk and into the wind. The air was lush with humidity, and a raindrop spattered on her head. She tucked the brown, mildewed library book under her shirttail, and looked up to get her bearings. She headed to the right.

It was a short walk to the police department. She barely got wet.

She went inside, almost in a daze, bypassing the front desk, heading up the stairs to the second floor. Her air of knowing what she was about kept her from being stopped.

Mendez was on the phone. His sleeves were rolled up, tucked neatly at three-quarter length. He looked up at Lena, and pointed to a chair.

As usual, his conversation was terse and to the point. It was impossible to figure what he was talking about. Lena sat very still. She kept the book on her lap, finger holding her place.

Mendez hung the phone up. "Did you come to return my handcuffs?"

Lena blushed.

"You all right, Lena?"

"Mendez. Do you know anything about this informant Anita Casey is relying on?"

Mendez cocked his head sideways.

"Look, Joel." Lena took a breath. "I'm not asking you to violate a confidence. You don't have to tell me anything. I just want to know if *you* know anything. Do you know enough about him—if it is a him—to feel confident about his information?"

"Personally?" Mendez said. "No. Anita gave me a few background details, not many. More than she should have. More than I would have given her. But she has a lot of confidence in this one. And I trust her judgment."

Lena nodded.

Mendez leaned back in his chair. "Everything is going. Getting set up."

"Meaning?"

"When the time comes, we'll be ready for these people. And if—" Mendez leaned closer and talked in low tones. "If they have Charlie, we'll catch them. In the act."

"Mendez, you have to keep this quiet, you can't have a big police to-do."

"Lena, I can't just show up one night. I have to coordinate with the locals, with Louisville. We've got, what, a little over a week? This is a bureaucratic nightmare. Everybody has budget constraints, they have to get approvals. Police departments just don't move this fast. I've called in favors and—"

"Joel." Lena gritted her teeth. "If you tell the locals what you're up to, word will get to the people involved. You don't even know if law enforcement people are in on it. This is a small town."

Mendez nodded. "It's set up as a drug bust. I've given out the wrong location. We'll change it at the last minute. In the cars, on the way."

"Oh."

"And they'll be happy to go along. Drug busts are good for careers right now. And they've got plenty of time to warn their dealer pals, if they're dirty. So they're protected, and can look good at the same time."

Lena looked at him. "This isn't going to win you any friends, is it?"

"No."

"Can I come with you?"

"Yes."

"I thought you'd give me trouble."

"I won't ace you out. If 'Sixty Minutes' can go out with the DEA, you can come with me. You'll have to sign a release. And if you get hurt and sue the department, you'll hurt my career."

"Mendez, this is going to sound really stupid, but I want you to have an open mind and listen to me."

He waited.

201

"That list of names that Melody gave me. See, from what I understand about these worshipers, this get-together is like a social thing. A bizarre social thing, but it has that importance. Melody called them family picnics. And it's like the Kentucky Derby or something. You get a new dress, you get your nails done, you go to your hairdresser. So I had these names checked. To see who was getting their hair done and when, to see if I could get a cluster of dates. This was before Anita heard from the informant. I thought maybe I could tell from the appointments when the night would be."

Mendez nodded, face unreadable.

"And I did. I got seven appointments made, and one date stands out. It's not the thirtieth, Joel. It's the twenty-fourth. Day after tomorrow."

Lena handed him the sheet of papers with the dates and notes Benita had made. He took the paper and pulled his desk calendar forward. Lena picked the cuticle on her left thumb.

Mendez looked up. He scratched his cheek.

"What do you think?"

"Lena, the informant infiltrated the group. He's been in actual contact with the people involved. The people making the decisions. And April thirtieth is Walpurgisnacht. Which fits. What you have is the twenty-fourth, a Wednesday, middle of the week. And you have no other evidence. From what I know, Thursday can be a major night for these happenings. But Wednesday has no special significance."

"Thursday?"

He studied the calendar. "The full moon is on the . . . twenty-eighth. Full quarter, the twenty-first. There's no reason for it to be Wednesday."

Lena held the book out. "I've been looking into satanic calendars. St. Mark's Eve is on April twenty-fourth."

Mendez took the book. "Judgment call, Lena. I see your point, but I think you're wrong. I think we have to go with the informant on this. I do."

Lena nodded. She did not tell him that Rick had received an invitation from Mr. Enoch. An invitation for the thirtieth of April. She didn't want him to know she was still using the boards.

"You okay?" Mendez asked.

"Yes."

"Don't be angry with me, Lena."

"I'm not."

202

45

Lena held the mouth of the canteen under the kitchen faucet. The telephone rang. She braced herself, expecting Hayes.

"Lena, it's Valerie."

"What's up?"

"Have you seen Eloise?"

"Isn't she there?"

"No. She was cleaning up breakfast dishes, and she had a coffee cake in the oven, and she suddenly just walks out. Just takes off. One of the women told me she heard her crying last night. Said she was calling out in her sleep. I'm worried she—"

"Valerie, there goes the doorbell. Hold on, maybe it's her."

Lena opened the front door. Eloise Valetta stood on the front step, her hair mussed, her one good eye red and bleary.

"Can I come in?"

"You okay?"

"Just tired. Long walk from the bus stop."

"Go sit down in the living room. I'll be right there." Lena headed for the kitchen and picked up the phone. "Valerie, she's here."

"Thank God."

"I better go talk to her. I'll call you later."

Eloise Valetta was standing at the sliding glass door. She looked at the lone rocking chair. "Your stuff get repossessed?"

Lena shook her head. "Go ahead and take the chair. Can I get you something? Something to drink?"

Eloise shook her head. She moved slowly, her steps hesitant, her back curved as if it hurt. She settled in the rocking chair, and the wood creaked gently. Lena sat on the floor, back to the wall. It was an effort not to look at her watch.

"Lena, this is going to sound nuts. You going to think I'm crazy. But I dreamed about Charlie last night."

Lena nodded.

"I dream about him a lot. Good dreams, where I don't want to wake up. Where he's home, and we're baking. Or we're going to McDonald's, and we got enough to buy whatever we want. But last night. Last night I had dreams that were bad. Dark places, scary places, like mine shafts or something. And he was trapped and he couldn't get out. And it was like I was him. Like I could hardly breathe, and I needed somebody to come and get me free." Eloise burst into heaving dry sobs. "I know it sounds crazy, but something's happening, something bad, and we just got to find him *now*."

Lena felt cold at the base of her spine. She'd been on her way to LaRue Lake anyway, thinking, in the back of her mind, she might well be wrong.

She wasn't wrong.

"Get in the car," Lena said.

"Now?"

"Let's go find him."

Eloise was rising out of the chair. "You know where he is?"

"Don't talk about it," Lena said. "Let's just do it. Go in the kitchen and get the blankets. They're on the table. And there's a canteen on the cabinet. Make sure it's full and the cap's on tight. Then put the stuff in the back of the car. I'm going upstairs to get a couple more things. Like get you a sweater. And go to the bathroom, Eloise. We got a long drive ahead."

Eloise nodded and straightened. Lena ran back upstairs, ransacking her closet for sweaters, jackets, her baseball bat. She heard the water running in the kitchen. Good. Eloise was moving. Lena hunted through the closet for the flashlight, then through the dresser drawers for extra batteries.

The front door opened and closed. Lena hesitated by the telephone. Mendez had made his decision; she'd made hers. Had he thought she would sit still on the twenty-fourth?

Mr. Enoch, she thought. What a coup it would be for you to have your nasty get-together under all our noses, one week ahead of schedule. She took a breath. She was right. The evidence was indisputable. Mama's instinct, and hairdresser's appointments. Real life, not police scams, lies, and double crosses. Not relying on the word of people who were relying on the word of somebody else.

Lena headed for the hallway, purse slung over her shoulder, arms full of jackets, sweaters, flashlights.

She checked her watch.

Plenty of time. Don't go crazy.

Her arms were too full to pull the front door closed behind her. She looked in the driveway. Eloise Valetta was sitting in the front seat of the car.

Lena squinted. The sun was bright and gentle, the sky clear, the temperature somewhere around seventy-five. The kind of day that made you want to throw off your old life, and start a new one up fresh.

Lena opened the car door and piled everything in the back seat. "Eloise? I got to lock up. Be right back."

Lena locked the front door, noted that the porch light was on. She got back in the car, started the engine, backed the car from the drive.

"You hungry?" Lena asked.

Eloise shook her head.

"Me neither. But I'm going to stop at White Castle, anyhow. Get something to have on the way."

Eloise nodded, seeming uninterested. She snapped her seat belt in place, and plucked the fur of a stuffed blue rabbit that sat in her lap.

Lena saw the bunny from the corner of her eye, did a double take, and looked again.

"What?" Eloise said.

"That rabbit. It's . . . it just looks like one my nephew had. Is it Charlie's?"

"No." Eloise stroked a fuzzy blue ear. "I found it folded up with them blankets. The ones on the table you told me to bring. I thought maybe you packed it on purpose."

"No. But you hold on to it, okay? Hold on to it, and save it for Charlie."

46

She had gotten turned around somehow, up at Old Indian Road. It was later than she liked when she drove the Cutlass across the gravel access road to Ted Moberly's fairy-tale house in the woods. Lena checked her watch. Two good hours of daylight left.

"This is Ted Moberly's place," Lena said to Eloise. "I want you to stay in the car, just till I talk to him."

"He doesn't know we're coming?"

Lena saw the twitch of a curtain. "He does now."

The front door opened and a little boy came out, followed by a teenage girl who kept a hand on the boy's shoulder. Sally pushed past them and bounded toward Lena, butting her head against Lena's thigh.

"Hey, Sally. Hey, girl."

The children watched her.

"I'm Lena Padgett." She smiled. The little boy smiled back, but the girl watched her warily. "I'm looking for Ted Moberly?"

"Lena?"

Moberly came around the side of the house. He was buttoning a cotton shirt across his bare, sweat-glistening chest. He wore blue jeans and work boots, and a bandanna tied around his forehead. He looked up at the girl on the porch.

"It's okay, hon. Lena, meet the kids. That's Shelly, my daughter. And this little fella"—the little boy leaned against Shelly—"is Shelly's little brother, Neil Junior. Y'all say hi to Lena Padgett."

"Hi," Neil said.

"Hello," Shelly said softly.

Ted looked at Eloise in the front seat of the car. She stared at him blankly.

"Eloise Valetta," Lena said. "Come on out, Eloise."

Eloise opened the car door and stood up. She held her hand up to hide the patch over her eye, and looked wistfully up at Neil.

The children tried not to stare.

"How are you?" Ted said.

Eloise nodded. "Fine," she whispered.

Lena took Ted's arm and steered him away from the porch. "We've got to talk."

"Did you say Eloise *Valetta?*" Ted frowned at her. "Is that the little boy's mother?"

"Yeah."

"What'd you bring her here for?"

"Ted, has Anita told you anything about the plans for the thirtieth?"

"Sure, she called me. I'll be there."

"So you know what's up?"

"Big devil shindig. Looks like your group. I'll be happy to have a hand in busting this one up."

"It's going to be tonight, Ted, not next week."

"Tonight?" They moved to the side of the house. It was shady and cool. Moberly stood near a forsythia that was heavy with butter yellow blossoms.

Lena nodded.

"Tonight? But it's Wednesday. Who meets in the middle of the week on Wednesday? Well, Baptists do. This is Baptist night, not devil night."

"Ted, everybody on the list, the list of people I got from Melody Hayes, the list she *died* over—they all, or some of them, anyway—they got their hair done last weekend. Or at least in the last couple of days."

Moberly looked at her.

"Don't you see?"

"Nope."

Lena sighed. "I know I'm not explaining this very well. But it's like their big social event. And they all want to get their hair done first."

"Maybe they're just getting it done for church."

"What?"

"I told you—Baptists meet on Wednesday night. Lot of Baptists around here."

"That's *every* Wednesday. This is special."

"Lena, Anita got her information from an informant. Nothing going on tonight."

"Yes, there is, Ted. I know it."

"I cannot believe this. Did you bring his mother up here on that alone?"

"Never mind her. Please come with me. I need you and Sally. It's supposed to take place in the south fork of the lake, near Croom's Landing. I don't know how to get there."

"Where'd you find that out?"

"The informant."

"I thought you didn't believe him."

"I think the information's okay, just the date is wrong."

"Lena, have you been getting much sleep lately?"

"Ted. Look, did Mendez ever give you a list of license numbers to look out for?"

"No."

"Figures. Okay, I've got one. A list of license plates from the Knoxville clinic—that's Charlie's PLS, Moberly. A list of plates from people who showed at Archie Valetta's funeral. And a list of plates of locals that Melody Hayes said were involved with the cult." Lena dug the toe of her shoe in the dirt. "Make me a deal. You and me go looking at parked cars. If we find a match, you go looking with me tonight. If we don't, I go away and leave you alone."

"Lena, I'm supposed to spend tonight with my kids." He frowned and thought it over. "If we go looking, but don't find anything by dark, I want you to go home. Promise me?"

"Promise. Thanks, Ted."

"Don't mention it. Might make me mad." He started back around the side of the house. "Come on kids, pile in the Jeep. We're going for a ride."

"Sally too?" Neil asked.

"Sally too."

It was a small Jeep, high off the ground, roll bar across the top. Eloise, Neil, and Shelly were wedged in the back. Moberly drove, and Lena shared the passenger seat with Sally. Lena pushed Sally's head away.

"What about that one?"

"That old thing? That's old lady Eggle's pickup. She's not in on this."

"Slow down. Move, Sally. Slow down and let me look." Lena checked the license number. It wasn't on the sheet.

"Daddy, I'm *hot*. This is boring. You said we were going to swim."

"I said we might swim, Neil. It's too cool. Your mama would skin me if I let you catch a cold."

"My other daddy would let me swim."

"Your other daddy's a lot of fun, Neil, I know that."

Shelly smiled. "He would not, Neil. He wouldn't let you swim if Mama said no."

"Nobody does anything when Mama says no."

Moberly grinned. "Ain't that the truth."

Lena's head began to ache.

"Getting hard to see," Moberly said. "We'll try one more place. Then I've got to get the kids back. Okay, Lena?"

She nodded.

Moberly turned onto a dirt forest road, moving uphill through water-filled ruts.

"You get a lot of rain yesterday?" Lena said.

"Our fair share."

Mud caked the tires. The road was narrow, and tree branches whacked the sides of the Jeep, making Neil squeal and duck his head.

"A little shrimp like you doesn't need to duck," Shelly said.

Neil punched her shoulder.

"Daddy, Neil's acting up."

"Hush, both of you."

The road climbed uphill, and petered out into the forest. There were no cars, no tire tracks. Moberly stopped the Jeep. He took a pair of binoculars from the glove compartment and scanned the woods.

"Nothing, Lena. Sorry." He glanced at her out of the corner of his eye. "Remember the deal."

"Sure." She would take Eloise Valetta to a hotel. She would come back alone. She would ignore the deal.

Moberly turned the Jeep around, bouncing it through deep, muddy ruts. The sun was all but gone, and it was getting cold. Neil leaned against Shelly. She put her arm around him, and he closed

209

his eyes. Lena looked into the side mirror and watched Eloise silently scanning the woods.

Moberly paused at the end of the dirt road, watching traffic. He waited for a van pulling a dirty green bass boat, then turned onto the two-lane highway.

"Maybe you should check that one," Shelly said absently.

"What one?" Ted said.

"The one we just passed."

"Shelly, there's no turnoff between here and the landing."

"It wasn't on a turnoff. It was back in the trees, behind those rocks."

Moberly looked at Lena.

"Please?"

He turned around and backtracked two miles.

"I think you passed it," Shelly said.

Moberly frowned. He turned around again, dipping into the grass on the side of the road, then pulling back onto the highway.

"There's no car along here, Shelly."

"Yes, there is. It's yellow. I think it's a Honda."

"Sing out when you see it."

"There, Daddy, see?"

"Those the rocks? I don't see anything."

"Pull up. It's behind the trees."

Moberly parked the car in the grass on the side of the road and craned his neck.

"See?"

"Yeah. Yeah, I see. Good eyes, Shelly." He looked at Lena. "Come on. Bring the list."

"I want to go," Neil said.

"I should go, I saw it," Shelly said.

"Stay in the car," Moberly told them. Something in his tone of voice kept them quiet. Shelly folded her arms, and Neil put his chin in his hands.

"Guess we're never getting any supper."

Lena glanced over her shoulder at Eloise and the children. She didn't like leaving them.

"Stay, Sally," Moberly said. He looked at Lena. "You coming?"

She got out of the Jeep.

The ground was soft, the thick grass waterlogged. The car was about a hundred feet into the woods, behind the rocks, and it had chewed up the underbrush getting there. A bird whistled, then was silent. Moberly moved quickly, a few feet ahead.

"Lena?" He glanced back over his shoulder. "Look there. Tennessee license plate."

Lena stopped behind the car. "Knox County. Knoxville." Her hands were shaking as she pulled the computer printout from her pocket. Ted looked over her shoulder. It was hard to see in the dying light, but they both found it at the same time.

"I'll be damned," Ted said.

"The clinic. Let's see. Belongs to a Delgado, Charlene Delgado." Lena chewed her lip. "Charlene. Charlene. Oh, Jesus H. Christ."

"What?"

"That's the secretary, the one at the clinic. The last one to see Charlie. Mendez and I talked to her. She said Valetta brought Charlie in and didn't act right with him, and that she was worried about him. She said he seemed hungry and she gave him suckers. She sat there . . ." Lena felt her face getting red. "She sat there and cried, that *bitch*. And promised to call if she remembered anything. Oh, God, how stupid. Mendez and Hackburton, investigating the hell out of that Dr. Whitter because she *seemed* so guilty. And all along it was that secretary and her crocodile tears. *Shit*." Lena wadded the list of license numbers and jammed it in her pocket. She looked at Ted. "That's why Charlie hasn't been seen since. She took him. She's had him all this time." Lena peered in the windows of the car, jerking the door handles. She moved away into the trees, and came back with a large rock.

Moberly caught her arm.

"Lena, what are you doing?"

"Breaking in, and don't try to stop me."

"Put that rock down and hold still. I mean it. Hold still. I'll be right back."

Ted headed back through the woods to the Jeep. Lena looked through the car windows. McDonald's bag, a folded copy of *The Knoxville News Sentinel*, an empty can of Sprite. No little boys sleeping on the seat.

"You'd make a lousy car thief," Moberly said. "You don't even watch your back."

"Shit. Don't scare me like that."

Moberly held a slender strip of metal. He pushed it down

211

between the top of the window and the rubber molding. The metal caught the door lock and pulled it up and open.

"Where'd you get that?" Lena said.

"People are always locking their keys in their car. Pretty inconvenient, way out here. Just be glad she didn't have those theft-proof locks." He opened the driver's door and reached across, unlocking the passenger's door on the other side. "I'll take the front, you take the back."

Lena went to the other side of the car. It was a two-door. She fumbled for the latch at the base of the seat, and pushed it up and out of the way.

Moberly was rummaging in the McDonald's bag. "Big Mac," he muttered. "Phew. Large fries. Ah. Happy Meal." He looked at Lena, and held up a multicolored cardboard box. "Chicken McNuggets. Didn't eat all his french fries. Barbecue sauce. Aw."

Lena looked up.

Moberly held up a plastic hamburger man on wheels, still in the cellophane bag. "He didn't get his toy." Moberly tucked the toy in his shirt pocket. "Lena, don't you cry on me now."

"I'm not."

"Sure you're not."

There were newspapers on the back seat. And wads of tissue. Lena looked down at the floor of the car. One of the newspapers had been shredded into small pieces—odd, irregular shapes torn out. She scanned the back seat, looking for the signature mosaic. She looked over the seat at the back ledge and caught her breath.

"What is it?" Ted asked.

"He was here."

"What?"

"Come look."

Moberly leaned over the front seat. Lena pointed.

"Dust," Moberly said. "And torn-up newspaper."

"You don't understand. Go get Eloise. Let her look at it. She'll know."

Moberly stared at Lena, eyes dark and worried. "He really was here, wasn't he?"

"Go get his mother. He really was here."

Eloise Valetta came quickly, stumbling through the underbrush, the patch over her eye sliding sideways. She stopped at the car door and looked at Lena.

212

"Eloise, I want you to try and clear your mind, and just answer one quick question. You say sometimes you and Charlie liked to go to McDonald's?"

Eloise nodded.

"What did he like there? What did he want you to order?"

Eloise began to breathe hard. "You found him," she said. "He's dead."

"No," Lena said. "He's not dead. But I think he was here in this car. Take deep slow breaths, Eloise. You okay? Now what did he like to order?"

"I . . . God, my mind is a blank."

"It's okay. Take your time."

"He . . . he liked. Oh. Those nugget things."

"Chicken McNuggets?"

"Yeah. He . . . that's right. He'd have a Chicken McNugget Happy Meal, with barbecue sauce, french fries, and ketchup. And he usually left two McNuggets, and about half of the french fries."

Lena looked at Moberly.

"Right on the money," he said.

"Okay, Eloise. Now I want you to look at this newspaper on the floor of the car. See that?"

"Yeah." Eloise's voice had gone high-pitched and breathy.

"Move over, Ted. Can you look over the seat okay? Look at the back ledge and tell me what you think."

Lena held her breath.

"Oh, Lena, oh, my God, he was here. Charlie done that. He was *here*." Eloise's breath came quick and hard, and tears rolled down her cheek.

Lena held her shoulders. "Keep it together, El. Don't fall apart on me now."

"Lena—"

"Come on, sweetheart." Ted Moberly put his arms around Eloise and pulled her gently from the car. "Come on, back to the Jeep."

"But he—"

"He's not in the car now, Eloise. You come on back to the Jeep with me." He looked over his shoulder at Lena. "No mud on the tires. This has been here since yesterday, anyway. You lock it up, put everything just like it was. They may check back, and we don't want anybody getting suspicious. Don't want anything to get in the way of tonight's big party, before we get there." He looked at Lena. "You and me. We'll get the boy back."

213

47

Shelly and Neil stood side by side, their eyes wide and alert. Eloise sat on the edge of the living room couch. Sometimes she looked at Lena. Sometimes at Neil.

Ted Moberly held up a shotgun. He broke it open and offered it to Shelly.

"Now, I loaded it for you, see there?"

Shelly nodded.

Moberly snapped the gun back into place and handed it to his daughter. "You know how to use it. Jordan should be here in an hour. Until then, anybody you don't know tries to come in here"—he looked at Eloise—"*you* get on the radio. Shelly"—he looked at his daughter—"you plug 'em."

"Aim for the knees?"

"No, baby. Tonight you aim at the chest or stomach. Tonight is serious business. Just don't open that door for anybody but Jordan."

Neil took hold of Shelly's hand, his eyes wide. Moberly grimaced.

"Should have sent *you* upstairs before the lecture." He bent down, balancing on his haunches. "Neil, this is all just in case. Nothing's going to happen. If I thought it would, I wouldn't leave you. And if something *does* go wrong"—he patted the dog—"Sally here is a super good watchdog. She won't let anybody bother you. Just knowing she's around will keep most folks away. And Mr. Jordan will be here before too long. You going to be all right?"

Neil nodded. "Shouldn't you call the police?"

"Son, the police we trust are a long way away. We tried, but they weren't at their office."

214

"Can I have a gun? Like Shelly?"

"No sir, not yet. You want to learn to shoot?"

"Sure do."

"I got rules for that. You don't touch that shotgun, it's loaded. You be good, and tomorrow I'll take you out and get you started. You're awful young. But if you're ready to try, I'm willing. A boy who is big enough to leave a loaded gun alone when he's told to, is big enough to start learning. We understand each other?"

Neil nodded. "Yes sir."

"Good." Moberly stroked the boy's head. "It's full dark now and we got to go. You kids take care of Ms. Valetta, you hear?"

They nodded.

"I'll be back. Now, I got three movies I rented for you, so watch the VCR all night, if you want. Make popcorn and hole up together in here."

The kids grinned. Eloise Valetta watched Neil.

"Be good," Moberly said. Sally followed him to the door. "Sally, stay."

She whimpered.

"Guard, Sally." He opened the door.

Sally yelped and barked once.

"*Sally.*"

The black Lab lay down, and sank her head between her paws.

"Stay now, girl. Guard." Moberly looked at Shelly. "Lock this door behind me."

Lena followed him out onto the porch. Moberly paused, listening to the locks click into place.

"We could wait till your friend gets here," Lena said.

"No. We're cutting it close as it is. We got a ways to go just to get there."

Lena headed for the Jeep.

"Not that way," Moberly said. "Come on."

He headed around the back of the house, past a small black barn, then into the woods. It was dark now. The ground sloped downward, and Lena followed slowly. She went left through the underbrush. Moberly grabbed her arm.

"Poison ivy," he said. He pulled her to the right-hand side of the path. "This way."

They went another fifteen feet, then they were out of the woods, angling down a slope of wet sandy soil.

"Moberly's Landing," he said.

A canoe was turned upside down in the dirt. A small flat fishing boat floated in the water, a neat black engine mounted on the back.

"Damn," Moberly said. "Forgot the gas can." He reached in his pocket and pulled out two black cotton socks. "Fill these with sand, I'll be right back."

"What for?"

"It'll come to you."

The sandy dirt was wet and clumpy. Lena dug with her hands for a while, then got a stick to gouge it up and loosen it. Grit collected under her fingernails. The wind blew her hair in her eyes. She pushed it out of the way with the back of her hands.

It took a while to fill both the socks.

" 'Bout halfway," Moberly told her. He filled the boat's engine with gasoline, then cranked it like a lawn mower with a handle and cord. The sudden buzz was loud.

Lena looked up. "They'll sure know we're coming."

"We'll cut the engine before we get close. We got to get there sometime tonight, you know. You 'bout got those socks done?"

"Yeah."

"You figured it out?"

Lena swung one in the air and Moberly ducked, though he was several feet away in the boat.

"As good as your baseball bat, and a lot less awkward. You just don't have the reach."

"I'm glad I met up with you, Moberly. It's nice to learn all this backwoods lore."

"Come on and get in."

Moberly brought the boat in close. Lena moved carefully, but the boat jiggled from side to side. The water was filmy along the shoreline.

"This won't be as much fun as the canoe," Moberly said, his voice raised to carry over the engine.

"How come you don't have one of those big motorboats? Ranger patrol and all?"

"It's being painted. And anyway, talk about advertising your presence. This is my sneak-up boat. This and that old canoe. Untie the line—not from the *boat* end, Lena, from the dock end. And watch your fingers. Get them mashed, if you don't watch out."

The rope was damp, but the knot was fat and easy to untie.

216

Moberly twisted the throttle and turned the handle of the motor. The boat turned and moved out on the lake. The wind blew Lena's hair behind her, and her sweater billowed and flapped.

The night air was cool. Lena trailed a finger in the water. The breath of the lake was warm.

They ran without lights in the darkness. As they eased into deeper water, white mist rose from the surface of the lake, shrouding the way just ahead. Lena lost her bearings. Moberly guided them across open water, around juts of peninsula, and into larger sections of lake. The water was still until they churned it, spewing white froth behind them and sending ripples to lap at the shore.

Moberly cut the engine, and the boat slowed. He pointed. Lena looked back in the trees and saw the hazy glow of a bonfire. Tiny pinpoints of light made a pathway through the trees.

"Flashlights," Lena said softly. "Flashlights in the trees, showing the way."

Moberly dredged a paddle from the bottom of the boat. He dipped it into the water with practiced, rhythmic strokes.

"You going right up there?" Lena said.

"No. We'll go around, place I know. Hush now. Voices carry over water."

They bypassed the landing closest to the bonfire. Lena counted two fishing boats, three power boats, and a ponderous pontoon boat, riding the gentle swell of their wake. Moberly paddled around the jut of the shoreline. Lena looked over her shoulder. She could just make out the fire.

They glided in. Pebbles and grit scraped the bottom of the boat. Moberly stuck his paddle in the sand, steadying them. The boat rocked from side to side as he stepped in water to his ankles. He balanced on a rock and pulled the line, dragging the boat up onto the sandy beach. He tied his rope to a marker that said Wild Geese Sanctuary.

The path was thick with dead leaves, but Moberly moved silently. Occasionally he looked back at Lena, and she wondered if he thought she was too slow or too noisy. Probably both. Now and then something rustled in the brush. Bird, Lena wondered? Rabbit? She looked over her shoulder.

Moberly stopped suddenly, and put a finger to his lips. He seemed to be listening. Lena held her breath. Gradually she became

217

aware of the crunch of dead leaves underfoot. Someone was moving their way. Lena smelled the sudden, acrid scent of cigarette smoke.

The man came within a few feet, his back to them. He was close enough for Lena to see the gun tucked into the back of his pants.

The man took a deep drag of his cigarette, then walked on. Lena breathed again, as quietly as possible. Moberly put a hand on her shoulder and squeezed. He bent down and whispered in her ear.

"Sentry," he said. "We got some pretty serious campers here. There'll probably be at least one more, maybe two, that we'll have to get by. Best if they never know we're here—they may be reporting in. Be *quieter*, Lena."

She nodded, wondering how.

The next sentry was easy to spot, swaggering noisily up and down, with an automatic rifle slung over his shoulder. Lena fingered the sock of wet sand.

The sentry froze, hefted the automatic rifle, and snapped the bolt. Lena looked at Moberly. He grimaced, and pointed.

"Tell him not to shoot," Moberly said. "Then walk on out there. Go on. Just do it."

Lena took a deep breath. "It's me," she said loudly. "Don't shoot."

"Me who?" the man said. "Come on out where I can see you."

Lena felt sweat start on her back. She crashed through a bush, and out onto the trail.

"Boy, am I glad to see you." Lena smiled. "I got turned around. How do I get back?"

The man lowered the rifle. "How'd you wander so far off? Oh, I know you, you were here last time."

"Yeah," Lena said. "Weren't you—"

The man groaned and pitched forward. Moberly stood behind him, breathing hard.

Lena bent close to the man on the ground. He looked to be in his late twenties, face round and pale, thick blond hair falling into his eyes. A radio, emitting a faint crackling noise, was wedged in his belt. Lena picked it up and turned the volume down.

"Let's go."

Lena smelled wood smoke. A ways farther in she saw pinpoint lights hanging in the trees. She and Moberly circled closer.

The fire was huge and healthy—a roaring orange inferno. Dirty white smoke swirled upward through bare skeletal branches. People milled close by, most of them dressed in jeans or slacks, and tennis shoes, all of them holding black bundles. More men than women in this group. They laughed and talked quietly. Lena smelled cigarette smoke, and a pipe. And there, just a trace, but definite. Somebody passing a joint.

A man in a black robe moved with assurance close in to the fire.

"Heeeere's Johnny," Lena said.

Moberly grimaced. "People in robes with hoods like that give me the creeps."

The man, the leader, put a wooden bowl down into the coals. Lena caught a faint, sweet odor. People began slipping behind the trees, shedding their clothes, coming back to the circle in their robes.

Moberly looked at Lena. "I don't see the boy, do you?"

She shook her head.

48

The chants rose like smoke, the words singsongy and impossible to make out. Someone—several someones, and brawny—had dragged a stone altar before the fire, and a bowl of liquid had been passed around. Lena noticed that the leader didn't drink.

Was this Mr. Enoch, this man in the dark robe, his face cowled and oddly elongated in the firelight?

Lena lay in the dirt on her stomach, inches away from Ted Moberly. The scent of wet muddy earth, sweet herbs, and wood smoke mingled oddly. The worshipers were moving like dancers, their movements dreamy and slow.

It was oddly effective—darkness, firelight, the path of light through the trees. Lena felt the hair on her arms prickle and stand up.

Ted Moberly grabbed her shoulder.

"Look. To the left of the emcee there, under the tree."

Lena saw children, three of them, sitting cross-legged. One of them pulled his hood off his head.

"Where did they come from?" Lena said.

"One of the adults slipped away a few minutes ago. Brought the kids back with . . . her, I think. Walks like a woman. You think any of the kids is Charlie?"

Lena looked at the one with the hood pulled back. His hair was thick, dark, and curly. "Not that one. I don't know about the other two. It's hard to tell with them sitting." Her voice went flat. "I think they're too big to be Charlie."

"Wonder if there's more of them. Look, see? She just slipped off again. She may be going for more kids. I'm going after her."

220

"Take the radio," Lena said. "You might want to tune in, see what's up."

"Okay. Be back."

The priest held the skull of a goat, and raised it over his head. He swayed and turned, making his way around the altar.

Must need drugs, Lena thought, to appreciate this stuff.

There was movement near the edge of the circle near the children. Two more slipped in, herded by the robed woman. She wore black tennis shoes.

The crowd hushed suddenly.

The priest held his arms high. Two robed figures moved into the firelight, tugging a rope. A naked man, bound around the wrists, neck, and waist, stumbled into the circle.

Hayes.

Lena felt the breath go out of her lungs.

She felt oddly embarrassed and more afraid, as if his vulnerability magnified her own. The urge to sneak away in the darkness warred with the urge to watch.

She knew now why Hayes hadn't met her to ransom Charlie, why there had been no more nasty reminders on the answering machine, no intruders in the house. He had lost the power struggle and become a danger to the group. They'd taken care of Archie Valetta, and it hadn't fazed him. Now they would take care of him.

Lena began to understand what it meant to come to the attention of Mr. Enoch.

Hayes sagged against the man who held his rope. His hair was growing back in dark prickles, like a five o'clock shadow on his scalp. His head lolled to one side, and he opened and closed his eyes, squinting, seeming confused.

The two robed men helped him gently onto the altar. One of the children, the one who had pulled off his hood, covered his eyes with his fingers. The black-robed woman pulled his hands away. Lena could not see, but she knew, from the way his shoulders hunched forward, that the little boy was crying.

A hand rested firmly on her shoulder, and Lena jumped.

"It's me," Moberly said, sliding in on his belly.

"What'd you find?"

"The kids were just sitting by themselves under some trees. Quiet, not making a sound. This woman comes and gets them, two

221

of them. I scouted around, see if I could find any more. Didn't, though. But something funny's going on."

"No kidding."

"I mean the sentries. They're gone."

Lena looked at Moberly. He was sweating. She was too.

"Behold," the priest said loudly.

"That's *Hayes* they've got," Lena said, looking back to the circle.

"Behold, a lost lamb." The priest rested his palm on Hayes's forehead. "Here is one who would betray *you*, betray our communion, *betray our service to the dark*. He has been brought back penitent, and ready to perform the ultimate service to the dark lord. *Redemption*, my lambs. Redemption and punishment, love and hate, pain and pleasure. All are one."

One of the men stepped forward, offering a wooden box. The priest removed a dagger, and held it high.

"They're going to kill him," Moberly said. "We better stop it."

"Nothing we can do, Moberly. There's more of them than us. I'm not going to risk my neck to save Hayes."

Moberly looked at her. "You want him dead."

Lena watched the priest. He lowered the knife in a deft, swooping motion. Hayes lifted his head, then rolled it to one side. There was a collective intake of breath from the crowd, and someone moaned. Blood welled up in a black line that swept from Hayes's groin, veered to the rib cage and stopped just under the left nipple.

"God," Lena said.

"Superficial," Moberly muttered. "But the next will be a go."

The priest smeared blood on his fingers, dabbing streaks on the right shoulder of his robe and then on Hayes's forehead.

"You want those kids to see this?" Moberly's whisper was fierce.

The watchers began to chant. The priest held the dagger over his head and swayed from side to side.

"*Everybody stay where you are.*" The voice was amplified through a bullhorn, loud and distorted. Metallic. Police officers in caps and flak jackets rushed forward, shining spotlights. People screamed and scattered and someone fired a shot.

"*This is the police, you are surrounded, stay right where you are.*"

Some of the children did not run. The boy with the dark curls pulled the hood over his head and hunkered close to the ground.

Lena heard laughter and saw a woman dance sideways, then sit down suddenly.

Enoch was bending over Hayes. Lena saw, in the flicker of firelight, that Enoch's hands were dark with blood. She stood up. Moberly grabbed her leg and pulled her to the ground. Gunfire split the air.

"Cops can be dangerous too," Moberly said.

"The woods are full of Satan worshipers. You're warning me about cops?" Lena shook his hand off and crawled forward. She heard a child crying and sensed, rather than saw, Moberly move in that direction. She looked up in time to see Enoch head into the woods, away from the flashlights, away from the path.

It was the old shell game, Lena thought, a high-stakes version. Enoch was getting away, and Jeff was bleeding to death. Which one knew where Charlie was?

She was on her feet before she'd consciously decided, tracking the dark figure moving through the trees.

She slipped past Hayes, close enough to touch. He was breathing hard, his chest heaving, rib cage slippery with red-black blood. His bare legs looked milky-white in the flicker of flame.

Lena moved through the trees, straining her eyes. Yes, that was him, right height, right build. She was as sure as she could be in the darkness, hunting a man in black.

Lena heard shouting, voices harsh. Someone was crashing through the trees behind her, and she picked up her pace. She wondered exactly what she would do when she caught up to Enoch, wondered if he still had the dagger.

There were more shots. Lena flinched but kept going. The cops were firing into the air—they wouldn't shoot into a knot of people, not with children present, not at all. Lena hoped that Mendez was out there somewhere.

Ahead, the dark-robed man turned suddenly, looking backward. Lena knew he could not see her face clearly, not in the dark. And yet she felt him looking at her, marking her, his gaze like a knife at her throat.

Lena heard the heavy crunch of footsteps and fingered the sand-filled sock in her fist. Enoch darted ahead suddenly, his robe swirling, catching a clutch of leaves. Lena broke into a panicked run.

Her side began to cramp. She put a hand to the ache, but did not slow. She was gaining on him, but she would be winded when she caught up, and whoever it was behind her was getting close. She ran faster, blindly now, hands outstretched to catch branches that whipped her face and neck. She felt the rip of thorns across her arm, felt the sting as the skin tore and bled.

Enoch must know she was close. He would hear the pound of her running feet, the heavy gasp of her breath. His pace was steady, brisk and sure, but no match for her dead run. She was closing in, the footsteps behind her getting farther away. She put on a final burst of speed, temples slick with sweat, hands flailing wildly against the branches.

Her right foot sank through soft moss into a depression. Her ankle wrenched sideways and she sprawled headlong in a belly flop, palms sliding on the leaf-covered dirt. The pain in her ankle made her sweat. She caught her breath, sobbed once, then rolled sideways, wrapping her arms around a tree, pressing tight to the scratchy bark and pulling herself up. Her ankle ached, but the soreness was fading. She put her weight on it carefully.

"Nah, you don't."

Something heavy knocked her forward and she slid to her knees, catching glimpses of a flak jacket and jeans. A rough hand grabbed her wrist, pressing hard. Her fingers went numb and she dropped the sand-filled sock.

The cop grabbed the back of her shirt and she felt a knee in her spine, the muscle-straining wrench as her arms were pinned behind her back. She was vaguely aware of the cold clasp of handcuffs, and the click as they locked her wrists.

"*He's getting away!*" She was winded, breathing hard, and she choked on the words and coughed.

"Nice try, honey."

The cop was patting her down, more enthusiastically than she liked. She turned her head sideways, trying to track Enoch. Her hair was in her eyes, her forehead thick with sweat. She couldn't see anything, much less Enoch.

"Listen, you moron, I'm one of the good guys." She was panting, and her voice sounded high-pitched and unconvincing, even to herself.

"Uh huh." The cop turned her sideways, firmly, but not rough, and pointed her downhill.

"Look, stupid, I'm cuffed, I'm not going anywhere. *He's* getting away."

"Who is, honey?"

"*Enoch*. The guy I was following. You saw him—"

"Guy in the black robe?"

"Yes!"

"Nice try, babe," he said conversationally. "But they're all in black robes, and I didn't see anybody but you."

Lena glanced sideways at the cop's broad, homely face and gave it up. Enoch was long gone.

She might never get this close to finding Charlie again.

"Move out, hon."

Lena stumbled on a tree root, but the cop kept her upright, grip firm on her elbow. They headed slowly to the bottom of the hill, the harsh lights, the knots of police. Lena spotted Mendez standing by a cluster of men in uniform, talking to Anita Casey and the sheriff.

"Joel!"

Mendez looked up. He started toward her, then looked to the sheriff and said something in a low voice, something Lena couldn't catch. The sheriff looked at Lena, then back to Mendez.

"You okay?" Mendez asked.

"Enoch got away," she said.

Anita moved toward her. "Enoch was here? You saw him?"

"I would have had him, but I got waylaid. You want to ask your pal here to take the cuffs off?"

Mendez jerked his head.

The cop fumbled with his key. "Honest mistake, folks."

Lena rubbed her wrists.

"What did—"

"Later, okay, Anita?" Mendez put an arm around Lena's shoulders and led her off from the group. He leaned close, voice low. "The informant turned up this morning. I called, but you'd already gone."

"Dead?"

Mendez nodded. "It went bad for him."

"What'd they do, cut him up?"

"Black bondage hood. Ligature strangling. Wrapped in a blanket, tossed in a car trunk, and parked in the airport parking lot. We wouldn't have found the body, but somebody went to rob the car, and called it in anonymously."

A twig snapped under Lena's foot, and she jerked, and glanced over her shoulder. "So he got fed bad information to pass along to Anita, then they killed him."

"He was sixteen. Been stringing johns since he was twelve."

"She shouldn't have been using a kid that young."

"It happens. If it gets out, she'll be reprimanded. There are no parents to complain, so she may skate through."

"Mendez, those kids—"

"No. No sign of Charlie. He's not here, Lena."

She sagged against him. "He *is* here. He was here. We found Charlene Delgado's car and I got inside. The signs were unmistakable. Charlie'd been in it."

"What signs?"

"I was right about the hair appointments, wasn't I? Trust me, Mendez, he's here somewhere, I know it."

"Our best bet is to take these people in and question them. If they know where Charlie is, we'll get it out of them."

"Fine. You question them. Meanwhile, let Moberly get his dog and do a search. Is Ted okay? You got him handcuffed somewhere too?"

"No. He was rounding up the children. He's got them gathered up in one spot."

One kid short, Lena thought.

"Moberly's dog can't track with the woods full of people," she said. "How fast can you get everybody out of here?"

Mendez looked over his shoulder and grimaced. He squeezed Lena's hand, then walked away.

Lena watched him and chewed her bottom lip. He had a quiet word with Anita and the sheriff, then stood talking for a long moment with Moberly. Ted nodded his head, looked at Lena and raised a hand, then handed a curly-headed toddler to Mendez. Joel took the child absently, unsmiling, moving his hand automatically to pat the child's back. She nestled into his shoulder and closed her eyes.

"You getting Sally?" Lena asked as Moberly passed close. "You're not taking the fishing boat?"

"I'm taking him in the power boat." The voice came directly behind her, and Lena turned and faced the cop who had cuffed her. "Want to come?" he asked pleasantly.

"Not with you, hon."

Lena paced back and forth in the moonlight, weaving her way

in and out of the trees. Mendez moved through the harsh glare of spotlights, giving quiet orders, managing not to wake the child who slept on his shoulder.

It took well over an hour for Moberly to make it back and for Mendez to clear the woods.

Lena was chewing the back of her knuckles when she heard a yelp and a whimper, and Moberly and Sally came up from the landing. Sally whined and strained toward her, but Moberly kept her close.

"Kids okay?" Lena asked.

He nodded. "Eating popcorn like there's no tomorrow. We about clear?"

"I think so."

Lena looked to Mendez, who was handing the sleeping toddler over to the sheriff. The child woke up and began to cry. Lena chewed her lip, listening to the little girl sob as the sheriff carried her down to the landing.

Moberly nodded at Mendez. "Everybody gone?"

"You're clear."

Moberly unsnapped Sally's leash. "Find," he said. "Go find, Sally."

The dog sniffed around the dying embers of the fire, then whimpered and looked back to Moberly.

"Go on, Sally. Sally find."

The dog hesitated, then bounded into the woods.

Lena stayed behind Moberly, Mendez at her heels. The flashlights still hung in the trees, some of them dark, batteries burned out. It was getting familiar, following this dog through the woods. Sally veered left, moving uphill, leading them onto a path that widened as it went.

Mendez moved close and touched the back of her hand.

"If we don't find Charlie tonight," Lena said, "chances are we won't." She glanced sideways at Mendez. "That's why you're here, with me, instead of questioning all those fruitcakes."

"If you and Moberly find something, I want it official. You understand, don't you? We've got next to nothing to hold these people on. Looked at in a certain light, we're interfering with their religious freedom."

"Their freedom to human sacrifice?"

"They'll deny it."

"Hayes was hurt."

"He'll deny it too. Loudest and longest, in the hopes they'll let him live. Our best bet is to cut a deal, get him to testify against the others. If he doesn't go into some kind of protective custody, he's a dead man."

Sally began to speed up, weaving left and right on the trail. Moberly moved quickly, and Lena and Mendez hurried to catch up. The trail widened, intersecting with a gravel service road. Sally padded down the road, scattering gravel, and they crested a hill. Moberly flashed his light.

Sally had found the cemetery.

She squeezed under the splintering wood fence and meandered across the graves, head down, tail stiff.

"*Sssshit.*" Moberly lurched backward. "Be careful. This one's been dug up."

Mendez turned his flashlight on the grave.

Sod and dirt were piled next to a gray headstone. Hattie Burgess. 1941–1962. Beloved Daughter of Robert and Gaye Burgess. Hattie's coffin was open, her bones a heaped rubble at the foot of the box. Her skull was missing. A black satin pillow rested at the head of the coffin, and the cushion that lined the lid of the coffin had been covered with black cloth.

"Jesus," Moberly said.

Mendez squatted beside the grave and ran his fingers through the grass. He picked up a piece of rubber tubing and held it up. "Someone spent the night in the coffin." He played his light along the open lid. "There. See where the hole's been drilled through?"

Sally whined, nose to the ground, and zigzagged out of the cemetery. Mendez wrapped the tube in a plastic bag, and followed. The woods were thinning now.

The sound of a panel door sliding shut caught them by surprise. They rounded the ridge and stopped. A few yards away in the darkness was a van, passenger door gaping open, four men standing close.

One of the men held an automatic rifle and he snapped it up, aiming for the dog.

"*Sally!*" Moberly yelled.

Mendez had his gun out. He fired. The man with the rifle went down without getting off a shot.

The van's engine caught. Moberly headed for the open door and flung himself into the front seat. Mendez collared one man, and the other ran past, colliding with Lena and knocking her backward.

Sally snarled and leapt. Lena hit the ground sideways, going down hard under the weight of the man and the dog.

The man screamed, arms and legs flailing. Lena saw Sally's lips pulled back in a snarl, the white of her teeth.

"Sally." Moberly's voice, breathless. "*Release*. Good girl. Let him up. Release."

Lena felt the weight come off her, felt rather than saw the dog move back. Mendez shoved the man face down in the dirt. Lena heard the click of handcuffs.

Moberly gave her a hand up. "Okay down there?"

"Yeah," she said, breathless. "Yeah."

Sally was panting, growling deep in her throat.

"Good girl," Moberly said. "No, Lena, don't touch her. Give her time to cool off."

Lena nodded. Her ankle ached and it was hell just to straighten up.

Mendez bent over the wounded man, unbuttoning his shirt. He wadded his jacket into a ball and pressed it to the man's chest, staunching the ready gush of blood. He took a radio from his belt and handed it to Moberly. "You'll have to tell them where we are. Can they get an ambulance back here?"

"Main worry is how long it'll take. He's losing blood fast."

"We have a unit on standby."

Lena looked at Sally, sitting at attention, too wired to be still. What a good dog she was, bringing good news and bad with the same sloppy, doggy smile.

Sally was still winded, sides heaving.

"She's not going to be in any shape to keep looking tonight, is she?" Lena said.

Moberly hesitated. "We'll start fresh in the morning."

Lena leaned against the van and shut her eyes, picturing Moberly and the dog ranging through the underbrush, the air cold and sharp. Tomorrow would be the first morning of many.

Charlie's picture on milk cartons. Leads from Nashville or Knoxville—leads that always petered out. Herself, avoiding phone calls from Eloise, who would be swallowed by the dark, festering loss.

Melody Hayes had said to hurry.

I'll find him. How many times had she said that?

She heard the demanding bleat of a siren. Her ankle was hurting and she was cold. She got in the van and sat down, pulling the door shut behind her. It was warmer inside, without the small but constant chill of the breeze. The van was almost new, upholstered in silvery blue velvet. The windows were smoky dark, private.

Lena leaned her head against the seat, frowning, conscious of the deep mumble of male voices, movements outside the van. She opened her eyes. She felt it all at once—awareness—the inaudible heartbeat, the working synapses of another brain, the smell of another human being. She wasn't alone in the van.

Lena raised up on her knees. She grabbed hold of the headrest and looked into the back. Something—someone?—huddled under plastic, not moving. And there, at the edge, could it be a small finger?

It could.

Lena scrambled over the back of the seat, leaving muddy footprints, snagging the lush velvet with the eyelets on her tennis shoes.

Things in the van—boxes she did not want to look into, shovels with mud clumped in the middle, black candles, lengths of rope, enamel bowls. Things she barely noticed. Details that would come up later, at night, in her dreams.

Crouching beside the plastic, she almost lost her nerve.

It was a garbage bag, the big size, for garden work and grass clippings. The plastic crackled when she peeled it away.

Lena's stomach muscles clenched. She had looked so long, and wanted so bad—how odd to find little Charlie at last.

And no doubt it was him—straight blond hair, finger stuck in his mouth. The eyes, shut tight, would be blue if they were open. And, best of all, the rise and fall of his chest, letting her know that, yes, he was alive—drugged, deeply asleep, but alive.

She held him in her lap and rocked him, just as she had little Kevin, the night she found him dead but still warm in his bed.

49

Eloise Valetta had an inner glow; she moved in a haze of happiness. Charlie peeped out from behind her legs, finger in his mouth. He wore a pair of beige overalls, and the blue bunny was tucked down in the front.

"We're *almost* ready." Eloise sounded breathless. "Just one more . . . come on in, Lena. Here, let me help you with that. How'd you get it up the stairs by yourself?"

Lena shoved the box into the living room.

Eloise shut the door and locked it. "That door's gotten warped or something. It won't close right anymore."

Charlie stayed in her orbit—or she in his—neither of them letting more than a foot of space come between them. It seemed unconscious, their dance.

"What's in the box?" Eloise asked.

"Umm . . . Nothing much," Lena said. She had spent all night sorting, packing carefully. "You may not even want it."

"What?" Eloise moved close to the box, Charlie close close close beside her.

"You may not really, Eloise." Lena clasped her hands behind her back. "Some people might feel funny about it. It's my nephew's things. Some clothes and toys he had. They're hardly used, some of them. I thought you might . . ."

Eloise nodded, gracious now, almost shy. "I think Charlie and I would be pleased to have them."

"Would you, then?" Lena let out a deep breath. "Good. These are toys, in here. The clothes are down in the car. Two boxes. Can I bring them up?"

231

"I'll help you."

"No, you and Charlie go on and get ready. It's about four hours to Nashville. Long ride for counseling."

"It's pretty nice of her to do it." Eloise's voice went low and thick. "We don't even know what-all Charlie been through."

"You and Charlie will like her, I think. Walt thought she'd be the best one to talk to. It's kind of a speciality of hers."

But Eloise wasn't listening. She was watching Charlie, who peeped cautiously into the box of toys.

Lena and Delores Criswold stood in the hallway and watched through the glass partition. No two-way nonsense here. If you were observed, you knew it.

The playroom was bright—so many windows. The carpet was thick and yellow. The shelves were stacked with toys and books. There were child-sized tables and chairs, big pillows on the floor, giant stuffed animals in one corner. Eloise sat quietly, safe security in the corner.

"Usually, we have the moms go somewhere else," Delores said. "But I think, in this case, we'll hold off on that. For now, I just want him to think of this as a happy, safe place. And it's interesting, seeing them together."

Charlie had spent a long time on his mother's lap, and Eloise had rocked him and waited, letting him decide when to move. He had ventured out finally, and worked in the clay, building a stick figure, which he was now burying under a pile of blocks.

"She knows enough to let him be," Delores said, looking at Eloise. "I don't want to sound like Mary Poppins, but I think she and I can bring him through this in one piece. It makes such a difference—dealing with it now, instead of years later, when the scars have worn groove after groove." She looked at Lena. "How's the legal end? Will Charlie have to testify in court?"

Lena shrugged. "No telling. The DA is iffy on it, but he doesn't like a four-year-old witness. I'm not even sure we'll make the grand jury. Hayes won't testify, and there may be trouble with the kidnapping charges. But everybody is blaming everybody else, so Mendez is hoping they'll turn on each other. Hayes is coming on like a victim." Lena looked at Delores. "Walt Caron says Hayes *is* a victim."

"Walt Caron is a nice boy," Delores said dryly.

"Most of the people they hauled in aren't going to be charged."

Lena grimaced. "The four in the van are up on kidnapping, and some of the others on minor drug charges and child endangerment. And Enoch got away." Lena glanced at Delores. "You don't seem surprised."

"I'm not. What will happen to Hayes?"

"No telling. LaRue County still has him. He's under a full-cash bond for one hundred thousand dollars. They're holding him on some kind of trumped-up drug charge. They're going to try and stick him with kidnapping, but Mendez doesn't think it'll go. And Louisville PD wants Hayes as a witness—they're gunning for Enoch. They've got a file full of crimes they'd like to snag Enoch on. So far, Hayes isn't cooperating, but they figure he'll break. Mendez thinks Hayes will be dead twenty-four hours out of custody, or back in the general prison population. So they're hoping he'll see it their way."

"It might be worth it," Delores said. "To get Enoch. Melody mentioned him now and then."

"Not if Jeff comes out to the good. He's got special solitary protection. If you can believe it."

"I believe it."

Lena looked back through the glass. Charlie had found a box of construction paper and was tearing purple paper into bits.

"I can pay for some of this," Lena said.

"No. This is for me and Melody. Making something right."

"You always get that close with your patients?"

Delores snorted. "Not and survive. Some of them, I don't want to know better. Bad thing to admit, isn't it?" Delores glanced at Lena. "How about you? How do you feel about things?"

Lena looked back in the playroom, watching Charlie. She thought of Kevin and how he would have loved the giant stuffed animals. She felt a dull throb of regret.

"I feel good," Lena said. "I'm done with it now. This is all over for me."

Delores looked at her sharply, but said nothing.

50

Lena was tired when she pulled into her driveway. The trip back from Nashville had been tedious, with numerous stops for Charlie, who was restless in the car, too exhausted to sleep. He had finally nodded off a few miles out of town—he and Eloise both.

The porch light was on, just like she'd left it. Lena noticed, even in the darkness, how high the grass had grown. The house looked neglected.

The relief that had come with finding Charlie had somehow ebbed away and she felt a flat depression. Lena reached into the back seat for the cake Eloise had insisted on giving her. She could be nasty, and give the cake to Rick. A gift, she would tell him, for keeping the cat—then he'd never get his shirt tucked in. She would give him all of Eloise's cakes. He would get fat, and she would be skinny.

The house seemed empty; she was missing her cat. Tomorrow she would go and get Maynard. She locked the front door. Her home was her own again finally, no midnight visitors slipping in and out.

Lena dropped the cake off in the kitchen and went upstairs to change her clothes. She would take a shower, put on the old football jersey, have a glass of wine, and curl up for a while with a book. Tomorrow she would sleep as long as she wanted. Charlie was home; no worries at last.

She went through the bedroom doorway and stopped. It was funny, in a way, because before, she had always had a sense, some prickly feeling, whenever someone had been in the house. This time, she hadn't had a clue. Lena crossed to the bed that she never bothered to make, and stared at the tangle of blankets and sheets.

Scattered in the middle were seashells—seashells by the dozen—gritty with sand and unpolished, smelling of the sea and the sun. She picked up a shell that had slipped to the floor. She felt a cold stillness inside her, like a disease that would never be cured.

Lena stood by the bed for a long while, too many thoughts in her head. She reached for the phone to call Mendez, then pulled her hand away. She thought of Melody, of herself standing in the hallway and telling Delores Criswold that everything was over. She thought of Maynard and Rick and Judith, then of Whitney and Kevin, and her unborn niece. Then she thought of Jeff. That thought drove out all the others.

Lena went back to the kitchen and ate the cake.

51

The bank had unlocked its doors only minutes before, and the employees were slow moving, sleepy. Lena got in line for the same teller she'd used the last time she'd withdrawn all her money. F. Breeding. That time had been for Jeff, too.

The man ahead of her made his deposit, then slowly tucked the receipt in a worn plastic wallet. Lena stepped closer.

The teller recognized her and smiled warily. "Good morning."

"Morning," Lena said. "I'm closing out both my accounts, checking and savings, and I want everything in cash."

"Again?" The word was out of his mouth before he could stop it. He blushed.

"Again."

"I see. May I have your—"

Lena slid a piece of paper across the counter. "Account numbers."

"Yes ma'am." He bent over his terminal. "Let's see . . . the balance of your savings account is eighty-nine thousand, nine hundred thirty-two dollars. The checking account . . ." He cleared his throat. "Seems to have a negative balance. Twenty-seven dollars and forty-nine cents."

Lena frowned. "Take what you need to from savings. The rest I want in cash."

"You wouldn't prefer a cashier's check? Or—"

"No," Lena said. "But feel free to let Mr. Franklin in on this. That's the procedure, right?"

"He'll just want to ask you a couple of questions; shouldn't take more than a minute. I'll just go let him know, and then we'll get your money together."

The teller smiled again and passed through a swing door to a corridor lined with offices. Lena dug in her purse for her checkbook, then studied the register, wondering how she'd come up short. She flipped the thin pages backward, but could not concentrate on the figures. The only thing she was sure of was that the checkbook had not been balanced for three months.

The teller walked softly. Lena didn't hear him till he was back behind the counter.

"Ms. Padgett? Mr. Franklin's office is this way." He led her through the swing doors, across thick beige carpet, to a mahogany door sporting a brass plate that said Franklin, Asst. Mgr. He knocked, then opened the door.

Franklin and his desk were both large, both decked out with a great deal of expense. Franklin was stuffed into an economy-sized pinstripe suit and wore a gold ring shaped like a horseshoe and glinting with diamonds. His smile was huge, like the rest of him, a ray of sunshine in a dark room. Behind him, wooden miniblinds were clamped tightly against the morning sun. Lena smelled the thick odor of cigars.

"Please." Franklin fluttered chunky fingers toward a maroon leather chair. "Just a few points to cover, Ms. Padgett." He glanced at the teller. "While we talk, Mr. Breeding will be getting your withdrawal ready. Can we convince you to take a cashier's check?"

Lena shook her head.

Franklin nodded and Breeding closed the door softly.

"Let's see, now," Franklin said. "You redeposited this money several days ago, and now you want to take it out again and close out all your accounts."

"That's right."

Franklin smiled again. His teeth had a yellowish cast. "Ms. Padgett, it's not my job to pry into your personal business. But when one of our customers makes a substantial withdrawal—we just like to make sure you're not being coerced in any way. Or being victimized by some kind of scam, say someone who offers to—"

"Mr. Franklin, let's make this easy. I need the money to post a full-cash bond for my brother-in-law, Jeff Hayes. He's in the LaRue County jail, and I should have him out by this afternoon."

"I see."

"I doubt it. But give my regards to Enoch, Mr. Franklin."

His smile never faltered. "I beg your pardon?"

"I doubt that too."

Lena sat on a crumbling concrete retaining wall next to the LaRue County Courthouse, an old red brick building that also housed the ancient jail Jeff would soon be leaving. The American flag hung limp on its pole in the still, sun-bright afternoon. Lena checked her watch. Surely by now the circuit court clerk's office had let the jail know that bond had been posted. Jeff should be cut loose anytime.

Lena swallowed thickly, feeling lightheaded. She had been in the same spot over three hours. She had not taken the time to eat lunch, because she didn't want to risk missing Jeff on his way out of jail.

She wasn't hungry anyway.

The lightheadedness wasn't caused by too much sun or too little food, but by handing over one hundred thousand dollars to the LaRue County Circuit Court clerk. The money included every cent Lena had left from Whitney's insurance policy, minus a few hundred for future expenses. She'd had to put her house up as collateral for the other eleven thousand. Lena wished the judge had set bond lower, but she saw his point. A man who had killed his pregnant wife and child and was being held on a drug charge was not a very good risk.

A navy blue LTD with dark-tinted windows moved slowly down the street in front of the courthouse. Lena had not been alone in her afternoon vigil. The Ford had been making shark passes all afternoon.

Lena heard footsteps on the concrete stairs and the tap of a ring clicking against the iron railing. She looked up for the fiftieth time that afternoon.

Jeff stood at the top of the staircase, blinking in the harsh glare of the sun. Lena felt a flutter of nerves in the pit of her stomach, but not a single regret. She folded her arms, waiting, smiling just a little. Jeff's steps were slow and hesitant, and he passed her without looking up.

"Hello, Jeff."

He turned on the staircase. "*Lena?*"

He didn't look as bad as she'd hoped, but he didn't look good.

He was pale and unshaven. His hair had grown but was still short, giving him a raw, unfinished look.

He took a quick glance over his shoulder, then faced her again, smiling. "Come to see me off?"

Lena folded her arms and cocked her head sideways. "Yeah, I did."

"Great criminal justice system we got, don't you think?"

Lena nodded and smiled. "Let me ask you something, Jeff. Is it just me, or . . . the sky is *really* blue today, isn't it? I mean, I'm actually tingling. Somehow . . . I don't know. The colors. Everything is very intense. Does it seem that way to you, coming out of jail and all? Because I thought it might strike you the same way."

Jeff gave her a puzzled look, then shook his head and smiled. He glanced over his shoulder again.

"Looking for anybody special?" Lena asked.

"Just my friends."

"I don't think you have any friends, Jeff."

"I got one who just posted a hundred-thousand-dollar full-cash bond. If I'm not mistaken, that's him there." The Ford had reappeared. Jeff raised a hand at the car and headed down the steps. "Be seeing you, Lena."

"You *are* mistaken, Jeff. I posted your bond."

He stopped moving, then circled slowly till he faced her again. For once, there was no trace of a smirk on his face.

"And why would you do that, Lena?"

"For Whitney. And for Kevin. And my niece who never got born." Lena smiled gently and inclined her head toward the jail. "In there, Jeff, you were in protective custody. But out here on the street, you're not."

She knew she'd remember the look on his face—it would come to her later, in dreams.

He swallowed, then managed his familiar smile. "You wasted your money, Lena, they're not going to find me. I'm just going to disappear."

"I think they already did find you, Jeff."

The Ford passed again, not stopping.

Lena brushed past Jeff, her shoulder nudging his. The sun-baked Cutlass was parked right out front, leaking oil onto the angled parking space. Lena noticed that the oversized gray parking meter was in the red violation zone. She noticed everything.

The inside of the car was hot, and Lena had to crank the Cutlass two or three times before the engine caught. It *would* act up, now that she had no padding whatsoever in the bank, no more insurance money, and a brand-new lien on the house.

She fumbled in the glove compartment for her sunglasses. Jeff stood on the courthouse stairs, watching. She pulled the car up alongside the curb and leaned out the open window.

"You watch your back now, Jeff," Lena said gently. "I hear Enoch is hard on lambs."